MW01615826

GUARDED BLAZE

MOON LAKE PROTECTORS

KAT BAMMER

KILO BRAVO SIERRA PRESS

ISBN: 978-3-903379-21-3

This book has been previously published under the title: Meant to Be

A KiloBravoSierra Press Book

Guarded Blaze - Moon Lake Protectors

I'm grateful for you lovely readers, who make writing these books both a joy and an honor.

1

"No. No. No."

The car sputtered, "Come on. Just a couple of miles until Moon Lake. Don't give out on me now."

But the engine stuttered one last time before it stopped, with steam coming out of the front.

Claire steered the car off the road while there was still enough momentum to keep it moving.

Great, just freaking great.

She looked outside, but it was already dark.

She'd been to Whitebrook to run some errands, then found this beautiful little café/bookshop where she spent hours perusing an antique copy of Persuasion—her favorite Austen novel—enjoying the best latte since moving to this part of the world and sitting in the most comfortable chair ever.

And to top it all off, the owner, Grace, had been super friendly.

She'd found a gem and couldn't wait to show it to her best friend, Lisa, the next time they visited the city.

City, how funny calling Whitebrook that. But it truly was

the only city near Moon Lake—her new home as of a couple of months ago.

She grabbed her phone.

The bad news—she'd wasted hours, and now she had no one to call. Peter and Lisa were on a date. Lisa's mother Jo had been invited to the neighbor's for dinner, and the new mechanic in town—she had yet to meet and make sure he was trustworthy.

That left Blake, her friend—with benefits—as the obvious choice, even though he was undoubtedly busy with his bar, and she really didn't want to call him.

But there was no question in her mind he would stop at nothing to help a friend.

Because that's the standup guy he was.

Claire sighed, locked the doors—nothing like being stranded at night on the side of the road to conjure up all the traumatic memories of Lisa being kidnapped by a serial killer just a couple of months ago—then called Blake and settled in for the wait.

A wait filled with deep breathing paired with obsessively searching social media for information on Moon Lake's new mechanic—deeply ingrained trust issues—rearing their ugly head.

It took only ten minutes until he knocked on her car window and ripped her out of her not-freaking-out routine.

She looked up, and their eyes met through the window. And even in the barely-there illumination of his headlights, his arctic blue eyes kept her rooted to the spot and caused her heart to do a double flip, just like every damn time he really, truly looked at her.

Not good.

Only friends.

Nothing more.

Nothing more to give.

His unruly hair fell into his face—he needed a haircut—but it wasn't enough to lessen his edge.

An edge that physically manifested in his chiseled square jaw, and as if that wasn't evidence enough of his absolute badassery—he was a former Navy SEAL, badass was part of their job description, right?—his height and Adonis-like steeled body did the rest of the convincing.

That's the guy he was.

The whole damn package.

He had the looks, the brains, and the I-will-fix-it attitude.

He was too perfect.

Too perfect for her.

Thank God, since nothing else lined up—not their looks or their attitude towards tackling life's problems.

Insert badass Navy SEAL vs. newly small-town owner of an Inn here.

At least what they wanted out of their relationship did—friends with benefits.

No strings, no drama, and no feelings besides friendship.

Right?

He motioned for her to unlock the door, then held it open. "Come on. I'll give you a ride home. I already called Bailey; he's on a job, but we don't have to wait. He will grab the keys from the bar and tow the car later. "

Bailey—the new mechanic she hadn't met but should've called.

Claire grabbed her purse and the pastries she'd bought and transferred both into his SUV.

"Anything else?"

"No." Everything else she didn't need immediately, and she had the distinct feeling Blake was in a hurry.

Even though he didn't show it.

But he must be. His bar was probably bustling, and he was on a rescue mission for her.

"Those for me?" His sideways grin melted her panties away.

Damn.

She'd never met someone quite like him.

Charming.

A pro-flirt, but at the same time, so damn chivalrous and protective it hurt in your teeth.

A commitment-phobic player. Who—for whatever reason—liked to play with her.

"Maybe." She smiled back. Two could play that game. And she was getting better at it. Maybe his flirting abilities were rubbing off on her.

As soon as they'd buckled in, he steered them back on the road. His chuckle pleasantly rolling down her spine.

Hot damn.

When his phone rang, he accepted the call. "What now? I've been gone five fucking minutes."

Claire shrank in her seat, which earned her a concerned sideways glance from him. He rarely snapped at anyone.

"Boss, we had a little mishap." Milan's voice drowned over the speaker.

He was Blake's cook and all-around sweetheart, and he sounded freaked out.

"Mishap?"

"Kitchen fire."

"Fire?"

"I managed to get it under control. Guests are evacuated. Firefighters are on their way."

"Everybody okay?"

"Yep."

"You okay?"

"I'm good, boss."

4

Blake sighed, then dragged his hand through his hair. Most likely not for the first time today, and probably why it looked so unruly.

"I'll be there in a sec." He looked at her sideways. "I'm sorry, I need to—"

"Of course."

When they arrived, guests crowded the parking lot, their drinks still in their hands.

Blake jumped out of the SUV and ran straight into the bar.

Toward danger.

She followed slowly, then hovered around the entrance, unsure if she should go in or wait with the other guests.

But just as she decided to go inside, two firefighters, Blake and Milan, stepped outside.

"You got lucky," one of the firefighters said.

Blake nodded. "Thank you, boys."

They said their goodbyes with a handshake, and off they went.

"Everything good," Blake announced to the crowd, "the next round is on the house," he said, which was met with an enthusiastic reaction by the guests who streamed back inside.

Blake stayed back, grabbed her arm, and led her to the side. "I'm sorry."

Claire scoffed. "You don't need to be sorry for anything." She shook her head. "Go in there and do whatever you need to do. I can walk back to the Inn from here."

His features tightened. He crossed his arms and crowded her.

It was the wrong thing to say. It had been a stupid suggestion, and she knew it as soon as the words had left her mouth.

But before she could backtrack, her back hit the wall,

5

and Blake stepped even closer. "You are not walking anywhere in the darkness." He worked his jaw. "Do you copy?"

A shiver ran down her spine.

She loved him taking charge—in bed. But she'd never experienced his dominance directed at her outside the bedroom.

Not that she didn't understand.

Lisa had been taken right here, right outside the bar. And every single male in Moon Lake had been overprotective ever since, and nobody more than Blake.

"You can have a drink, or make yourself comfortable at the apartment until things settle down, then I'll drive you home." He leaned back slightly, and breathing suddenly became much easier.

"I could help."

He smiled. Then kissed her forehead. "Thanks, Claire, but I got this."

It felt like a dismissal, even though he probably didn't mean it like that.

But she decided waiting in his apartment was the better option, given the circumstances—and his tenseness.

He didn't need one more person in his hair right now.

So she settled down for the wait on his sofa—and immediately fell asleep.

Until someone grabbed her.

Him.

He was there. His face a contorted mask of cruelty.

A scream, shrill and desperate—her own—pounded through her skull, evoking horrors and that familiar choking sensation...

No way out.

His face hunkered over her. His arms around her like a vise.

6

She struggled—no escape.

Pain.

Begging.

Making herself as small as possible.

To no avail.

No amount of begging or cowering ever stopped his violent outbursts.

The violence that obliterated every breath, hope, and joy... sucking into its blackness the picture-perfect family—that never was.

Claire tore her eyes open. Sweat trickled from her neck. The thrashing of her heartbeat drowned out any sound.

Blake.

She could see his face, his lips moving above her, before she could hear his voice.

"Shhh. Claire, please wake up. It's me. Everything is okay. You're fine. Everything is fine."

Safe.

She was safe.

It was just a memory.

So long ago.

Not real.

She inhaled and then looked around.

She was in his bedroom. In his arms. Had he been carrying her?

Why?

Then she could feel nausea—a familiar aftereffect of her nightmares—settle into her stomach.

Bile rose in her throat. "Let me go. Now."

He let her down immediately.

She wobbled, and he grabbed her side and stabilized her until she gained her bearings.

Then she darted to the bathroom.

Fuck.

She hadn't had a nightmare in a while, and she never had them with Blake as a witness.

One of her rules was never to spend the night.

That's how they were working. That's why they were working.

She threw up and could hear Blake come into the bathroom behind her.

She whimpered.

Please go away.

But instead, he gathered her hair and held it back while she emptied her stomach.

She never wanted him to witness her like this.

This was too much, too close.

She needed to get her distance back.

Maybe even end this whole thing.

"What can I do?" Blake's voice was soothing, and his hand caressed her back while holding her hair with the other one.

Tears gathered in her eyes. She never wanted him to see her like this.

Didn't want him to know.

Nobody needed to know.

It was in her past.

She'd trusted Lisa with some of it—because of the nightmares. But not all of it.

Once the urge was over, she sat down on the floor, spent.

He handed her a glass of water.

She could feel his eyes on her.

Knew he probably had a million questions he wanted to ask.

Not that she would give him any answers.

This was not in their agreement.

Friends with benefits. Nothing more, nothing less.

And this, him witnessing her throwing up after a nightmare.

This was too much.

"Can you drive me home?"

He nodded, but his eyes were stormy.

He had questions.

But she had no answers to give.

2

"Great view up here, Blaze."

"Yeah." Sebastian Blake handed the two coffee cups, he had somehow successfully maneuvered up the ladder, to his best friend, Peter, who sat above him on a beam of the soon-to-be roof of Blake's soon-to-be new home.

It wasn't often Peter used his old call sign. But their days fighting side by side as Navy SEALs were over, so why would he?

"You should build a second floor up here. You would even have a lake view if you cut the trees down there."

Blake scoffed. "Nah, got better things to do when I'm up here than looking out the window."

He didn't need a lake view; he just needed a place where he would have some damn peace and privacy.

Living in the small apartment behind the bar had been okay for a while when he took over the bar and moved to Moon Lake.

But it was getting old.

He surveyed the place. There had been a hunting cabin up here, but it had been old, the wooden beams broken, and it had a hole in the floor the size of a bathtub.

So logically, the fixer in him instantly fell in love with the place.

The clearing around the old cabin hadn't been huge, just big enough not to feel too confined by the trees surrounding the meadow, and it had nearly doubled in size with the felled trees he used to build the new cabin.

After mulling over his plans, he'd decided just to start fresh and build exactly the kind of home he'd always dreamed of when he was young.

Well, it wouldn't be exactly like that.

He'd dreamed of a big house for a big family.

But dreams change.

It would be big enough for him to feel comfortable.

Glass and wood and open space.

He stepped from the ladder onto the beam and sat next to Peter on what would soon be the roof construction.

They silently sipped their coffee.

"Winter'll be here in no time. You need to have the roof up by then," Peter said.

Blake's face tightened.

Not only the roof but windows, as well. It was already October. He had to increase his hours up here, or he wouldn't make it before the snow came.

"I should hire some people to help with shit up here." His tight face turned into a frown. Blake didn't like to ask for help.

Ever.

Not even paid help.

"Maybe you should. Everybody in Moon Lake would be happy to help. The boys will be back in a few weeks too. Just turn our hunting plans into house-building plans. Would be fun, and we'd get a shitload done."

"Fun. Or agony." The teasing would be relentless.

But Peter was right.

With the boys—their former teammates—here, they would have the roof up in no time.

Peter's stomach rumbled loud enough that even Blake could hear it. "Hey, what happened to those cookies you promised me for breakfast?"

Blake winced. "I'm sorry. I could've sworn I didn't even open the packet. But it was empty. If I didn't know better, I'd say someone's eating my stuff."

Blake's eyes scanned the area, but there was nothing out of order.

First, he'd thought it was animals that helped themselves to his food. But he had it stored away in a metal chest for weeks now, and there were still things missing, things he could swear he'd left in there.

"Don't sweat it. You can make it up to me by buying breakfast at the café."

Blake's stomach rumbled, as well. "Deal. I just have to skip by the bar first. Beverage delivery arrives in"—he looked at his G-Shock watch—"shit—fifteen minutes."

They both moved down the ladder in a choreographed maneuver.

Blake rinsed out their coffee cups by the well hand pump and stored them back in the chest.

Water would be another issue. He needed to get the plumbing in order. He would start with that later today. After fixing the stove and getting the kitchen at the bar up and running again.

But first things first.

Bar, then breakfast, then bar, then plumbing.

He checked one last time if the gas of the camping stove was off—once bitten—and left the cottage by the front door.

Peter stood by his truck, one foot already inside. "See you at the cafe, or do you need help with the delivery?"

Blake shook his head before he gave Peter a two-fingered

salute. "No need. I'll just put it inside and leave it for Milan to store the stuff.

Shouldn't take more than ten minutes, max.

Meet you at the cafe."

Peter was always eager to help, and Blake couldn't have wished for a better team leader and friend.

He tipped his head back and closed his eyes for a second.

Peter had been like that in the Teams.

He'd always been there for every one of them.

Had listened, had been a wingman, and had helped wherever he could.

Now he'd found a job that suited his personality as well. Being a deputy sheriff allowed him to still serve, protect, help, and assist wherever possible.

Could he say the same about himself?

Sure, he liked the bar. Loved to be his own boss.

He listened to his patrons. Was in the loop.

And Claire?

He sighed.

Claire was something else.

The images of her waking up from that nightmare, or her throwing up afterward..he was still not over that.

Though she wouldn't confide in him. Had made that abundantly clear when he drove her home.

They'd started hooking up soon after she arrived in Moon Lake.

They'd just felt drawn to each other, and they both wanted the same.

But boy, if it didn't sting.

For the first time in his life, he found a woman who meant more to him than an easy hookup.

And she?

Well, she didn't want more.

And she was vocal about it.

And even though that fit perfectly into his life plans. No family, no commitment. It didn't sit right to be on the other side of the no-commitment speech.

On the other side of her secrets.

He watched Peter hop in and accelerate down the gravel driveway.

Before getting in his SUV, he took one last sweeping look across the clearing.

He really loved the silence and nature out here. Claire would probably like it too.

He shook his head—no time to enjoy his surroundings. He got in, turned the key in the ignition, closed his door, and sped down the driveway.

At the end of the clearing, he looked back through the mirror and caught a glimpse of movement.

He stepped on the brake and turned around in his seat. Waited.

Nothing moved, but he could've sworn there had been a small kid running across the meadow.

Unless he was seeing ghosts.

Should he go back? He sat still for a moment, his eyes sweeping his surroundings, but there was nothing.

He looked at his watch again.

He really had to get going. And whatever he'd thought he saw, why would a kid be running around in the woods alone?

There wouldn't.

Maybe it had been a deer, and his eyes had played a trick on him.

Blake's stomach growled again, and he lifted his foot from the brake and sped up again.

He needed to hurry to get to the bar in time for the delivery, and Peter was waiting for him at the cafe.

He would go on a lookout another time. He also could spend the night up here tomorrow and check things out then.

The empty package of cookies came to his mind.

Maybe there was something or "someone" going on that was worth investigating further.

3

Moon Lake really was Claire's home now.

And she felt like a fully accepted citizen.

She inhaled deeply and enjoyed the fresh air after having spent the whole day in bed—a forced time-out—after burning her hand on a hot baking sheet this morning. All thanks to still being shaky after her nightmare and all that came after.

She was still horrified Blake had witnessed it. The nightmare and the state it left her. She'd thought about it all night. And she didn't know what to do—after that torturous ride home when she could practically feel his struggle to restrain himself from demanding answers.

Answers that would transgress the friend code.

Answers that would lead them into uncharted territory.

Not somewhere she was willing to go.

Not somewhere he would want to go—not with her.

She shook her head, clearing it of all those negative thoughts.

She'd taken the bike out for a quick afternoon ride to Blake's Bar to see how they were doing after the kitchen fire and if she could help somehow, or grab dinner—if possible.

But the ride over took already longer than anticipated. She'd been stopped three times to chat, and right now, their neighbor Mrs. Brooks told her about her son Paul who was doing pretty well this season with his new NHL franchise team, the Hamilton Mohawks.

Claire nodded and smiled.

Not that she had anything to contribute.

She didn't follow hockey at all, but Paul was Julie Brooks' brother, and she'd met him and some of his teammates when they visited back in June.

So between Julie's updates about him and Lisa, Peter, and Blake watching the games, Claire already knew more about hockey than she cared for.

Hence, whenever she had the choice between a cooking show and some sports hoopla on TV, cooking would always win—hands down.

So she smiled at Mrs. Brooks and nodded and congratulated her and tuned the rest out.

The people of Moon Lake always made time for a quick chat, and even though Claire still felt a little under the weather, it would be rude not to take a few minutes to chat with the neighbors.

"Did he find you at the Inn?" Mrs. Brooks looked at her expectantly.

Claire pulled herself out of her own thoughts. "Did who find me at the Inn?"

"The man who tried to find you." Mrs. Brooks looked at her as if she was a little slow on the uptick.

A man was trying to find her?

Her pulse quickened, and alarm bells immediately rang in her mind.

Nobody had ever been trying to find her. Nobody had a reason to find her.

And the only one who might've ever had any reason

to...she shivered just thinking about it.

Thinking about him.

She remembered the nightmare from last night. Was this a sign?

But it couldn't be.

It had been too long without contact. Without anything.

Why the hell would he show up here?

Now?

She took a deep breath to calm herself down. "No, he hasn't. I didn't know someone was trying to find me?"

She forced a smile at Mrs. Brooks. "You didn't, by any chance, catch his name, did you?"

She was surprised at how calm she sounded when everything inside her screamed at her to run.

Was she overreacting?

Probably.

"No, sorry, my dear. But if I meet him again, I'll make sure to get his card."

His card.

What a joke.

Claire nodded and said goodbye.

Should she turn back? She could hide in her room. Or maybe she should tell Lisa. Or contact the police?

Was her protective order still valid?

She took another deep breath.

She was overreacting. Why would her ex come here? Why would he try to find her now, after so many years?

Nothing had changed, and there was no reason for him to come for her after all those years.

She really needed to get a grip.

It was probably one someone who wanted to book a room or something like that.

Totally unrelated to her past.

She continued on, and by the time she arrived at the

parking lot of the bar, she'd calmed herself down again.

Crazy that her first reaction was still to go back there. But it was in the past.

Almost a lifetime ago.

And it was time she got over it once and for all.

Get rid of those stupid nightmares too.

She looked around. Not a lot of cars.

Maybe Blake wouldn't be too busy, and they could have a nice, friendly chat… which might end up in a quick make-out session, which might lead to leaving last night's mess in the rearview mirror.

Business as usual.

Friendship as usual.

It had been quite some time since they'd spent time together—aside from hooking up, which happened fairly regularly—or quick meetings, like last night.

She remembered Peter and Lisa, home at the Inn.

All cozied up on the couch, ready for their movie night, and Claire hadn't wanted to impose on them.

She rounded the corner and leaned her bike on the side wall of the building.

Trying hard not to look at the spot Blake had pushed her against yesterday.

Instead, she looked around.

The lake's surface resembled a mirror in the fading sunlight, reflecting the mountains and trees surrounding it.

She watched Blake's boat on the dock behind the bar, swaying gently on the waves. Maybe they could go out on the lake this weekend.

She always loved spending time on the lake with him.

Claire turned around to the heavy wooden door of the bar, and when she stepped inside, the smell of great Mexican food assaulted her.

She stood for a minute and sniffed the air.

Cilantro, chili con carne, and oregano.

Her stomach growled. So the kitchen fire hadn't been a big thing after all.

Claire's gaze swiped across the room. Blake was not behind the bar, and there were only three tables populated. Maybe he was behind back and would come out any minute.

She took a seat on a bar stool and nodded to Mr. Brown, a fisherman, and Mr. Patterson, the owner of the only grocery store in Moon Lake, who sat on the other end of the bar.

Then she heard Blake.

Rolling laughter accompanied by a cacophony of female giggling.

Claire's stomach clenched.

She turned on the stool and could see him in one of the booths with his back toward her. The three young women were literally hanging on his every word, smiling and nodding while Blake spoke.

Claire clenched her teeth and turned back to the bar.

A womanizer.

She knew that. It was part of his appeal.

But she also knew how those women felt.

He was good at making you feel special.

The night they'd first been together, he had made her feel cherished, safe, and as if she was the center of the universe.

She had been new to Moon Lake and had been a little overwhelmed and lonely. Lisa had made out with Peter, and she'd been sitting there by the fire, reflecting on her choice to up her life and take over the Inn with Lisa.

Blake had been kind and charming. Funny and caring at the same time.

He'd swept her off her feet and into his bed that very

same evening.

She didn't regret it.

But she knew from day one it would go nowhere.

They'd have fun and keep it simple. That was the deal.

Friends with benefits. More just wasn't in his cards, he'd said.

Well, lucky for him, it wasn't in hers either.

Not anymore.

It had been once.

But the reality of being in a relationship, being a wife, hadn't resembled how she'd envisioned it to be.

And being a mother... Claire's stomach tightened, and she shook her head.

No use thinking of it.

It'd been a long time, and she had closed that chapter of her life, had left all of it behind.

Even though it still hurt like hell thinking about Anna, her Anna, who was never allowed to live.

And she was still scared of him.

She shook her head.

What was it about today that the memories were so much closer?

Threatening close.

Enough.

Another bout of laughter and jealousy speared through her.

Shit.

Maybe it was time to create some distance.

Make the boundaries crystal clear again.

Claire stood up, and her eyes darted to the exit, but she stiffened her spine, and with a fake smile to the old men sitting at the bar, circled back to the kitchen.

She wouldn't leave without a taste of the deliciously smelling concoction.

4

"Hey, girl, long time no speak. How're you doing?" Milan, Blake's gorgeous cook, embraced her in a bear hug against his rock-solid chest and abs.

Blake wasn't the only handsome guy in town.

He smiled and leaned back. "I didn't get to say hello yesterday, and Blake didn't say you were coming in today. I would have made tamales de pollo if I'd known."

Gorgeous and beyond nice.

Warmth radiated through Claire's body, and with a smile on her face, she said, "You know I like everything you whip up, and that chili smells off the charts. I'm surprised everything's fixed already."

She took a seat at the small table and looked around. The kitchen looked—unharmed—she relaxed.

"Oh, it was just a minor incident. And my cooking is nothing compared to yours. If you ever want to take over the kitchen here, I'm game. I'm still craving that risotto of yours and the blueberry pie. I don't think I've ever tasted something quite like it." He smiled at her, and she chuckled.

She had cooked for Blake once, and Milan had devoured

the leftovers the next day, begging her ever since to cook for him or take over the kitchen of the bar and grill one day.

Maybe she should.

Or not.

Then Milan's eyes fell to her bandaged hand, and his face turned serious. "So, how are you doing? You look kinda pale—everything all right?"

"I'm fine. Just plenty hungry and a little tired, that's all." Wasn't it strange that someone like Milan was so perceptive to catch even a mild unease, while the man she hooked up with hadn't even recognized her presence at all?

That meant something.

And was kinda depressing—thinking of it.

Or as it should be.

Claire nibbled on her lip, and when Milan still looked at her with his head cocked to the side, she perked up on the chair and smiled again.

Time to change the subject. "If you want to get your hands on truly delicious baked goods, Holly, from the Black Cat, is the pastry and pie queen around here. Compared to her stuff, mine doesn't even compete. And I found this adorable little café in Whitebrook yesterday. The prettiest and nicest owner you can think of. And she has baked goods." Claire waggled her eyebrows. "By the way, what about your love life? Caught one already?"

He laughed, and Claire smiled.

She always asked him this question, ever since one evening, when he'd complained about his latest love-related disaster to Lisa and her.

"I'm still waiting for you to get rid of that scoundrel"— he pointed with his thumb to the door—"and ride with me into the sunset."

They both laughed about that, and Claire relaxed.

He was the real deal.

Even though his mean-looking biker exterior could fool you at first.

But he was a bad guy with a heart of gold.

He always made her feel good.

It was a wonder nobody had snatched him up. Although most likely, finding a mate in a small town like Moon Lake would be a challenge for anyone.

"Well, well, well. You can't even leave your girl a minute alone before the competition starts closing in," Blake said when he swaggered into the kitchen.

He smiled and kissed Claire on the top of her head before he punched Milan's shoulder and leaned against the counter.

When he looked at Claire again, his brows lifted. "Didn't see you coming in. Why didn't you wait for me out there?"

Claire's stomach tightened, and she crossed her arms in front of her but kept her emotions in check.

"You were...occupied." She loosened her muscles not to show the jealousy she was feeling.

On a rational level, she knew it was his job to accommodate his guests.

And didn't she just decide it would be better to cool things off between them?

She had no right to demand anything, want anything.

But hell.

It was still hard for her to watch him flirting with other women. Especially ones that were that interested in him, and young and beautiful.

Claire had come to accept her body. She would never be as thin or lean as other women. She didn't like to exercise and was a chef, for God's sake. She loved cooking and baking and eating too much to starve herself.

She'd put on weight excessively after Anna, but time,

change, and the emotional healing she'd been doing, had regulated her weight back to her normal, curvy self again.

She'd never once felt less than beautiful with Blake.

On the contrary.

He worshiped her curves, every time they were together. "Occupied?"

Blake watched her for a minute without saying anything else.

His eyes scanning her felt like a caress and inquiry at the same time.

Heat crept up her neck.

Damn.

What this man could do to her by just looking at her.

Then he straightened and turned to the counter. He filled a bowl with steaming chili con carne, grabbed a spoon and a basket of bread, and placed it in front of Claire.

He grabbed her chin. Caged her gaze with his mesmerizing arctic blue eyes.

His eyes had been her downfall from day one. Alert, a cold fire burning in them.

Dangerously attentive beyond anything she'd ever experienced.

Seconds ticked by.

His easy smile was absent. Instead, she saw heat, lust, and something else.

He was still trying to figure her out after last night.

After a lifetime, he loosened his grip but didn't let go.

"Eat. You get testy when you're hungry, babe."

Her mouth watered.

Not only for the food.

He pressed his lips against hers, then let go.

"But I understand." His devilish grin caused a squeeze deep in her core. "I get testy when I'm starving too."

His mouth said one thing, but his eyes told a different story.

One of lust, hunger, and passion.

He was not referring to food.

A delicious shiver ran down her spine.

Holy shit.

He let go of her, turned back around, and leaned against the counter again.

Watching her in intense silence.

He wasn't interested in anyone else but her.

And she was being petty, wasn't she?

"Thank you, Blake." She gave him a seductive smile.

A promise of what he could expect later.

Maybe him witnessing her nightmare hadn't changed anything between them.

Maybe they could just go on like before.

He had taken the same position as before, relaxed, except for his face. His eyes were still hungry, untamed, and he looked at her as if she was his next meal, and he was indeed starving.

She dug in, and the spices exploded on her tongue.

She moaned.

This was exactly what she needed. Great food always made everything better.

Suddenly he narrowed his eyes. "What happened to your hand?"

She looked at her hand, tried to cover it up with the other one.

Then shrugged her shoulders. "Burned me this morning —nothing serious."

"Let me take a look." He stepped toward her and grabbed her hand, but Claire pulled back.

"I said nothing serious, okay."

Her face flushed red. What was wrong with her? He was

just trying to take care of her.

Like a friend would do.

And she?

She had a hard time not wanting more.

And when his caring side came out. That's when it was hardest to remember.

They were in this for the sex. Sure, they were friends, kind of.

But they were treading a fine line. And she needed to reinforce that line and protect her heart.

Blake immediately let her go and raised his hands. "Okay, got it."

She settled again and began eating her delicious meal when Blake cleared his throat.

"You don't need to be jealous, you know."

Her spine stiffened.

He was circling back around to her initial feelings.

She swallowed, but the last bite nearly got stuck in her throat.

And there she thought he didn't notice.

Or didn't care.

Or both.

She should've known that beneath all his flirting and hot masculine energy, he was way more observant than she gave him credit for.

"Are you starting to get all possessive on me, babe?" He waited for her answer.

Could she give him one?

Was she?

And didn't she just decide she didn't want more?

"We have fun together, remember—keeping it simple, that was the deal."

Claire's chest tightened; she loosened her death grip on the spoon and looked at Milan, who looked back at her with compassion.

Great, just what she needed. A witness to her humiliation.

She nodded. "That is the deal." The moment she said it, she could feel her heart miss a beat.

Damn heart.

But he was right. They both didn't want a serious relationship. They'd talked about it, and they'd agreed on it. They'd also agreed on being exclusive, and she trusted him.

So why was she even worried about those other women?

He wasn't the kind of man to break this promise.

Ever.

Of that, she was certain.

She took the next bite. She'd sworn she would never fall in love again.

She wasn't a naïve eighteen-year-old girl anymore, giving everything for a little attention and love.

So what the hell had gotten into her?

Blake apparently could feel the dropping tension, because his easy smile, the one that reached his eyes and made him look even sexier, was back. "What are you up to this weekend? Care to join me? We can take out the boat tomorrow."

Claire's belly felt like a knot.

She really wanted to say yes.

Wasn't that what she wished for when she came here this evening? But maybe she should take a step back.

Cool their relationship down a little.

She had to get her feelings under control. Because falling in love with him would destroy everything, and Blake clearly didn't have the same attachment problems she had.

She put down the spoon and pushed away the bowl.

Then shook her head and took a sip of water to clear her throat.

"Sorry, I can't—got a lot to do at the Inn. No time for fun and play."

Blake's face stayed emotionless when he shrugged, straightened, and turned to the door. "Right, I should get going on the cabin's roof, anyway. Winter will be here soon."

He pushed through the door, and the silence after the door closed with a click was deafening.

5

"Hey, Claire, can you come in today? I got your test results back and want to discuss them." That was all Dr. Alan Radley had said on the telephone earlier.

Now she was sitting on the porch in front of the doctor's office, waiting for him.

Since he'd called her five minutes ago to tell her, he was running late.

Claire's stomach churned, and she clutched her purse while waiting for him to arrive.

She remembered her first visit three days ago. It had been her first medical appointment with Alan Radley, the resident physician in Moon Lake.

When he'd shaken her hand and welcomed her to his office, he had been very professional, and it had been completely weird after she'd gotten to know him over the course of the summer.

During his weekly visits to check in on Lisa's father and, after his death, to check on Lisa and her mother, he'd always made time for a cup of coffee, a chat, and a treat.

Now, seeing him in his professional capacity.

It was just plain weird.

During her first visit, he'd asked her what he could do for her, and after she had described her tiredness and dizzy spells to him, he'd suggested running some blood work.

Just to make sure, he'd reassured her.

The noise of a car, driving up the gravel road, disrupted Claire's musings.

When the suburban of Alan came into view, Claire stood up.

His reassuring smile through the windshield quieted her somewhat queasy stomach.

"Hello, Claire. Thank you for making time on such short notice. I'm sorry it took me longer than expected, but I ran into Lisa at the store, and she needed some advice."

Claire steeled herself. She hadn't told Lisa she was having a doctor's appointment, but he didn't say anything further.

"Hey, Alan, no problem. I enjoyed the sunshine out here."

The test results couldn't be that bad, could they? Because he wouldn't be in such a good mood if something were seriously wrong with her.

They entered his small office, and Alan took a seat behind his desk and, with a hand gesture, invited her to take a seat on the other side of the desk. He booted up his computer with surprising speed.

"So, how're you feeling today?"

Claire quivered inside. There was just something about a doctor's office that made her uncomfortable.

Bad memories.

"I'm okay—still tired a lot but much better."

Alan nodded and took his time to read through her medical file on his computer.

Then he turned his gaze toward her.

"So, you have a little iron deficiency which would

explain your tiredness. But that is not exceptional given your current situation."

He looked at her, and a grin lightened his whole face up. "Congratulations, Claire, you're pregnant."

Claire jerked back. A sudden coldness hit her at the core, and a shiver ran down her spine. "I am what? That can't be...they told me... I can't, I don't...not since..."

She was stammering, she knew it, but her thoughts were fuzzy except for the clear picture of her dead Anna in her mind, which drowned everything else out.

Alan watched her for a moment without saying a word.

He folded his hands and said with a sympathetic voice, "I take it this is a surprise."

Claire's chest hurt, and her lips trembled. "I'm not, I just don't know what to say. This is unexpected."

He nodded his head in understanding. "So, our next course of action. Get an ultrasound to determine how far along you are. Your hCG levels are not that high. Do you know when you had your last period?"

Claire's body stiffened, and she shook her head.

Aside from this being a topic she felt strange discussing with Alan, she had no clue when her last period had been.

There had been so many other things occupying her mind lately: Lisa's recovery, the guests at the Inn, and finding her footing in a new town. She hadn't even realized she'd skipped her period.

Could it really be?

Alan obviously thought so.

"They told me I couldn't get pregnant anymore."

"Who did?" Dr. Alan asked.

"The doctors did. I-I lost a child before."

"What happened?"

Claire had difficulty breathing. Her eyes welled up, as they did every time she talked about what had happened.

"I was married." Her voice choked with tears, and she had to take a deep breath before she continued with a monotone voice. "My husband lost his job, and when he couldn't find a new one, he spent his days in some dive bar. It went downhill from there. Somehow, every time he came home, he'd find something I did wrong.

"Even though I was holding down two jobs to keep us off the street. Sometimes my just looking at him infuriated him... He got abusive, and one night...."

Tears were spilling down her cheeks now—too many to hold them back. "I'd already decided to leave him, but he came home early. Saw the bags... He knocked me around and got furious when I refused to kiss him. I don't know what happened then, but my unborn child...Anna...she died that night."

There was a long pause after that.

Alan's hands clenched and unclenched, but he remained silent until she gathered her bearings again.

"How far along were you?"

"Six months." Her voice cracked.

"They told me something ruptured, she didn't have a chance, and that I wouldn't be able to ever carry a child again. I really don't remember the details; everything after is pretty hazy.

"But I'm okay with it. Got over it. I don't want another child. I couldn't live through something like this a second time."

Alan clasped her hand on the desk. "I'm really sorry for your loss, Claire."

His voice was raspy, and his face sincere. "And you have options, you know.

But we need the ultrasound first.

I have a friend who is an OB/GYN in Whitebrook. I could call him; maybe he could slip you in today."

Claire nodded and let her gaze slide over his office while he called his colleague.

Apparently, his colleague had an open spot an hour later, and Alan confirmed they were leaving right now and should be able to make the appointment in time.

"I'll drive you—I needed to go to Whitebrook anyhow."

Claire just nodded.

Somehow she was numb when she preceded him outside the office, and they both settled into his suburban.

After a while of driving in silence, Alan looked at her and said, "You left him, right?"

Claire nodded.

But Alan was still alternating his eyes between her and the street as if he wanted her to say it.

"Anna, her death gave me the strength to leave—so I divorced him. I left him, my old life, and everything else behind."

"How long ago did that happen?"

"It will be fourteen years next March."

Alan nodded his head. "You know, our bodies have powerful healing powers, more than even medicine understands right now. Maybe this is a second chance for you."

Claire couldn't think about this now; she would just get the ultrasound over with, and afterward, she would think about everything else.

"What about the father?"

Claire inhaled sharply.

Crap, Blake.

She would have to tell him.

He didn't want kids, had even told her that.

Claire shook her head.

She wouldn't think about this now.

One step after the other.

First, the ultrasound, then everything else.

6

"Hey, Mom, please call me back as soon as you hear this."
Blake ended the call.

His stomach tightened, and he frowned.

This was the third time he'd called in the last two days.

He couldn't reach her, and she hadn't called back.

Which was out of the ordinary.

"Everything okay?" Peter was standing right next to him
on the construction site of his new home.

Blake looked up at him. The tight feeling in his stomach
loosened.

"Mom hasn't picked up the phone or called back since
yesterday. I'm getting worried."

Peter laid his hand on his shoulder. "Maybe she's just
busy. How are things with Paula?"

Blake scratched his pecs, right where he felt that pang
whenever he thought about his little sister.

"They are well. Mom has some woman come help three
times a week, but the bulk of care depends solely on her."
Blake didn't know how his mom did it.

She cared for his sister 24/7 since Paula's failed suicide
attempt left her unable to care for herself.

His kid sister had been the sunshine of the family until that day when their father changed their entire universe.

He'd killed himself, and four years later, Paula did the same damn thing.

Just she, unlike their father, survived, severely damaged.

"What about Jessie?"

"She's working as a horse trainer somewhere up north. I lost track of where she is right now. Haven't heard from her in months."

"Blaze."

Blake looked at Peter, alarmed by his sharp but toneless voice.

He hadn't heard it since they left the Teams.

Peter signed that they were being watched, and Blake concentrated on his surroundings.

He could hear a twig crack to his right, and focused his eyes there, but couldn't see beyond the first line of trees.

Then he heard the noises of a vehicle making its way up the gravel road.

He stared at the tree line, but whoever or whatever had been there was gone.

But this time, Peter had sensed it too.

"Human or animal?" Blake whispered.

Peter shook his head. "Don't know. Just got that sense of eyes on us."

They didn't have time to discuss it more because a pickup truck emerged from the trees and drove toward them.

"Oh shit. I totally forgot to tell you." Peter slapped his forehead. "I met Tara Patterson yesterday and told her about your house and the unfinished roof. She has a construction company over in Stone Valley and offered to take a look, and I told her today would be perfect."

Blake's eyebrows lowered.

He didn't like it when someone overstepped their boundaries. Even if it was his best friend.

Peter watched him.

Years as teammates gave him the ability to read Blake intuitively.

"I'm sorry—shouldn't have meddled. Look, the decision is yours; just talk to her for a second."

Blake relaxed and clapped Peter on the shoulder.

"It's okay. I can be civil."

They both watched the petite young woman jump off the truck and close the door with a forceful push.

He looked at his buddy with a single raised eyebrow. Peter shrugged, then grinned.

Then she came toward them with a wide grin on her face, her hand stretched forward eagerly.

"Hey,"—she shook Blake's hand with a surprisingly firm handshake—"I'm Tara Patterson."

"Seb Blake."

"Call him Blake. Everybody around here does." Peter and Tara embraced with a degree of comfort that proved they had a longstanding friendship.

Peter turned to Blake again.

"Tara and I go way back. I've known her forever."

Tara nodded. "Peter said you could do with some help with your new home. Why don't you show me?"

Blake hesitated before he turned on the spot and presented it with a sweeping gesture. "There's not much to it."

Tara stared at the cabin and then at Blake, making him feel more and more uncomfortable.

"You did this?" Tara inquired. "Alone?"

Blake felt a hot flush rising up his body, but years of practice helped him cool down immediately. "I had a little help from friends"—he nodded to Peter—"but yeah, planned it and built it so far. Now the roof's a little tricky."

Tara nodded and said, "Okay, here's what I think. I can get you two men with a crane up here within the week. You would have the roof up in a day, is my estimate. Why don't you make the roof a little steeper? You would have an A-frame and a little wiggle room upstairs," Tara said.

"Great plan," Peter chimed in.

Blake said nothing for a moment.

His first instinct to dismiss her suggestions washed through him, but after he handled his inner resistance, he could see how the changes Tara suggested would be great.

"How much would that be?"

Tara looked at him and then back at the house.

A smile spread across her face.

"How about free meals for me at the bar for a year? And you pay for the wood, the roofing materials, and the crane."

She turned to Blake with an inviting smile.

Blake crossed his arms, looked down, and shuffled his feet on the ground for a moment.

Was she hitting on him?

Didn't matter.

"How about you bill me the material, the crane, and the work on an hourly basis, and I invite you for dinner at the bar one time? Peter can come too."

Blake saw her smile slip for a second before she looked him firmly in the eyes again with a bemused grin.

She stretched her arm toward him to shake on the deal. "Can't blame a girl for trying."

Blake shook her hand and grinned.

No, he wouldn't blame her for trying.

But he was not interested.

He got all he wanted and needed in Claire. Superb

female companionship, great conversations, sexy times, and no expectations.

The images of her nightmare appeared, but he shoved them out of his mind.

She didn't want to talk about it.

Made that abundantly clear. And he had no right to demand more.

Not with their current arrangement.

The phone in his pocket vibrated, so he took it out and, after a look at the display, excused himself and turned away from Peter and Tara. "Hey, Mom, I was worried. I've been trying to reach you since yesterday."

"I'm sorry. Paula had an episode yesterday morning. We've been in the hospital since then, and I left my phone at home."

Blake inhaled sharply. "Is she all right?"

"Yes, she is. Don't worry. We're home again, and I called as soon as I could."

Blake exhaled slowly. His mother was hands down the strongest person Blake knew.

The way she handled everything life threw at her was awe-inspiring.

"Have you talked to Jessie lately?" Blake's mother pushed him out of his thoughts.

"No, haven't talked to her in ages. Why?"

"I don't know, just a feeling. She hasn't visited in months. Said she was busy, but she sounded different, as well. A little down, maybe. Distant. Even though she insists everything's all right."

Blake's chest squeezed. "I'll call her ASAP. Don't you worry, Mom."

Blake turned and watched Peter and Tara talking and laughing.

"Hey, I'm in the middle of something right now. I'll call you back as soon as I've spoken to Jessie, okay?"

He ended the call and returned to the others.

They stopped talking, and Tara turned toward him. "I gotta get going. I'll get back to you with what day works, and an estimate. We'll be in contact, okay?"

Blake nodded, shook her hand again, and watched her hop into her truck.

"That was fun," Peter said. "You know, she built up her company all on her own. Tough business for a woman too. She's amazing."

"Are you trying to sell me on her? You know I'm with Claire."

Peter raised both hands. "I just got the feeling you were cooling things off a little. What with you both spending her free weekend separate from each other?"

His friend paused and studied him. "I guess I got the wrong impression, hah."

Free weekend?

Blake knew nothing about a free weekend.

She'd been busy working nonstop since they last saw each other.

At least, that was what she told him every time they talked on the phone.

Maybe it was time for a little face-to-face talk.

7

Blake opened the driver-side door of his truck, wiped the sweat from his forehead, and looked back at the house.

Tara Patterson came through with her offer.

Insanely cheap too, which Blake had called her on.

But she just laughed and told him about her good friendship with Peter and how they grew up in Moon Lake together, and Blake let it go.

This was the way it worked in Moon Lake.

So tomorrow, they would do the roof, and after that, it was doors and windows.

He slipped behind the wheel, turned the ignition, and drove down the driveway.

Blake loved how the house was smack dab in the middle of the clearing, so enough light from all directions reached the house even though the trees surrounding it were so dense it preserved the scents of dampness and moss.

He reached the end of the clearing when his phone rang. Blake took a cursory glance at the display and slowed down to a stop just after entering the wood.

Peter—what did he need now? "Hey, bud, what's wrong? You left, like, ten minutes ago. You already miss me?"

"Not at all—hey, you still at the house?"

"Yes, I am, but I'm leaving right this second. Gotta hurry too."

"Cool, hey. I left my tool belt in your kitchen. Can you please grab it for me? I'll swing by the bar later to get it."

Blake grimaced and looked at his watch.

"Why do you need your tool belt? Just come by tomorrow and grab it then."

"Ahem, I really need it tonight, and no, you don't want to know why."

Peter's voice had changed. He wasn't sure he was willing to go down that path, but he just couldn't resist roasting his friend. "Yeah, if you want it, I really wanna know."

Peter cleared his throat. "Lisa and I," he hesitated, "we kinda have this date tonight and decided to try something new."

"Heh?" Blake asked. "You need your tool belt for a date. Are you shittin' me?"

Peter sighed. "Role-playing, you dumb ass."

Blake inhaled sharply.

"Don't start. You wanted to know."

Blake squeezed his eyes shut and pinched the bridge of his nose before he chuckled, which soon led to roaring laughter.

"You're an ass." Peter sounded pissed about Blake's reaction, so Blake reigned in the laughter.

"I'm sorry. Not what I expected," Blake said and shook his head slowly.

This conversation was all kinds of awkward, so he needed to shut it down, and fast. "Good for you two. Really. I'll go grab it and bring it with me to the bar."

He ended the call and chuckled again.

Role-playing, goddamn, but then again, why not?

He could envision Claire and him doing some fun stuff like that.

Maybe he should bring it up next time they were together.

He shook his head again and forced the disturbing picture of Peter in nothing but his tool belt out of his mind.

Then put the car in reverse and looked through the rear-view mirror.

In a split-second decision, he shut down the car, applied the handbrake, and opened the door. Climbed out of his truck and jogged back to the house, enjoying the view.

He remembered his first visit to the hunting cabin when it was for sale.

It had been old, and the right half of it had collapsed.

The cabin he didn't care for a lot, but the land and the secluded location had spoken to him immediately.

When he came up to the entry, he envisioned the covered porch he planned to build soon with some chairs.

He entered the house and came to an abrupt halt.

Frozen, inside the empty frame of the back door, stood a dirty, young boy.

His eyes were huge, and he stared at Blake.

Blake's body tightened up, and adrenaline flushed through his body.

He crouched and grasped at his side for a weapon, just to come up empty.

The boy darted around and fled through the door he came in before Blake could even say a word or make another move.

Not that he was about to say anything.

He'd been caught completely off guard, which didn't sit very well with him, considering his training and past occupation. He was getting soft.

But the boy must've entered the house at the exact same moment, through the opposite door.

"Hey," Blake yelled after the boy, while he chased him, out the back door.

The boy was already at the edge of the trees, disappearing in the shadows.

Blake sped up but lost sight of him.

His head was spinning.

What was a kid doing out here?

He couldn't be older than—Blake came up empty—somewhere between five and ten.

The boy's face and hair were filthy, and he looked like he was living out there, in the woods.

Blake entered the tree line, stopped for a minute, and closed his eyes.

There was silence, a bird's call, then the crack of a branch to his right.

He immediately turned toward the direction of the cracked branch and settled into a slow trot.

Why was the boy in his house?

Was he searching for food?

The missing groceries came to mind.

So he'd been right.

And it hadn't been some animal.

Blake found the cracked twig and, after looking down, could identify a trace.

He followed the tracks the boy had left.

He wasn't heavy enough to leave any marks on the ground, and Blake lost sight of the tracks multiple times.

Each time he had to retract until he found them again. He followed the boy until he came up short at a small creek.

He sighed and went completely still.

There were no unusual sounds.

Just the natural background noise of the forest: the

chirping of birds and some rustling in the brush caused by a bird searching for bugs, the wind blowing through the tree-tops, and the hissing and gurgling of the creek.

Not a single misplaced sound.

Nothing to disturb the silence.

He couldn't find any traces of where the boy had crossed the creek, but neither did he find any more signs on this side. The boy had just vanished into thin air or followed the creek. Though it must be cold as ice.

Blake looked up, and down the small stream then he looked at his watch.

He'd been chasing the boy for ten minutes already.

He turned on the spot to orientate himself. Then he made his way back to the house and his car he'd left sitting at the end of the driveway.

At the last minute, he changed his direction as he remembered Peter's tool belt, the only reason he returned to the house in the first place.

Blake scratched his head and looked back when he arrived at the clearing.

What the hell was that kid up to?

Calculating the speed of his movement, he knew his way around here.

And by the way, his clothes had looked, he most likely wasn't part of civilization.

He had to talk to Peter about it.

Maybe some families were living up here that he didn't know about.

But then again, why would the kid need to steal his food?

Didn't they have enough?

Was the boy in some kind of trouble?

He needed to talk to Peter, maybe the sheriff too. Somebody had to know why this kid was up here and what exactly he was doing here.

He also had to speed up the order for the door and back door. He didn't like the notion of his house being open to all kinds of people and animals.

Until then, he could set up a photo trap, and if he could get a clear shot of the kid—maybe it would help with identification.

He again entered the house through the back door and searched for the tool belt.

He passed the chest with his food and opened it. The boy seemed to like cookies, so he grabbed a pack and laid it out on the table.

Blake's eyebrows drew together.

Hopefully, he would come back, not starve out there.

He grabbed Peter's tool belt and took a long look out the back door.

There was definitely something going on out there.

And with winter coming, the situation for the boy wouldn't get any easier.

Blake took a deep breath and left the house.

His truck was still sitting where he'd left it. The scene looked unchanged. Even the background noises were the same, but in his mind, nothing was the same.

He didn't like unknowns.

Didn't like it at all.

8

"We need to talk." Claire walked into their shared office, and Lisa looked up from the computer.

They had adapted the small office, so both Claire and Lisa had a small desk facing each other with their laptops on top.

Cookbooks and recipes printed off the internet cluttered Claire's desk while Lisa's desk overflowed with business books and folders filled with everything from invoices to the blueprints of the Inn on one side and wedding stuff on the other side.

They even matched in their tidying habits.

Lisa and Peter's wedding was about to happen in three weeks, the last weekend of October.

Hopefully still a fall wedding.

At least, that's what Lisa was aiming for.

But anyway. Whatever the weather, they'd finished most of the preparations, and the last-minute organizing frenzy hadn't yet begun.

Claire went to the window and looked outside.

The office had a calming view of the rose garden. The

rose nearest to the house still had some rosebuds, but most likely, they wouldn't open before it became too cold.

Kinda like she felt about being pregnant. A rosebud, a possibility. But the circumstances for blooming were less than ideal.

"Okay, I'm all ears. What's wrong?"

She turned her back to the rose.

Lisa's stared at her and her bouncing foot—one of her friend's habits that didn't usually faze her—increased the tension in her.

Her stomach knotted, and her hands turned cold and clammy.

To say it out loud would make it real.

Not that there was any kind of doubt left.

Doctor Larson—the OB/GYN she'd visited with Alan—made that clear.

She was already thirteen weeks along, and how she had missed it was beyond her.

Stress.

She'd been stressed out a lot, but it shocked Claire how disconnected she'd been from her body.

"I'm pregnant."

A sharp inhale. Lisa's gaping mouth resembled that of a fish out of water.

Then there was silence in the room.

Seconds ticked by, and they just looked at each other.

"You are what?"

Claire returned to her desk and immediately sat down because standing with her knees feeling like jello seemed a little risky.

"I am pregnant." A sob escaped her, but Claire steeled her spine and took a deep calming breath.

Crying wouldn't help. Nothing helped.

"Okay…I mean…you told me you couldn't…you know… after Anna." Lisa rambled, and Claire's heart sped up.

"I know. I thought so too, but apparently, those doctors were wrong, because I most definitely am."

Claire fumbled around in her purse and pushed the ultrasound pictures toward her.

Lisa looked at them and then back at Claire, who sat with her shoulders hunched.

"Are we happy about it? Please tell me we're happy about it."

Claire would have laughed if it wasn't for the sick feeling in her stomach that overpowered all the other emotions she had.

She shrugged her shoulders.

Was she happy?

Kind of, but disbelief, uncertainty, and sorrow were also there along with it.

"Okay, we're happy. It's decided." Lisa grinned and stood up, doing a silly happy dance. "This calls for a celebration. Ice cream is in order."

She came around their desks, kneeled in front of Claire, and took her hands. "This is a miracle, Claire. Your miracle. Maybe you can't feel it yet, but you will soon. Stop worrying for now. This will be okay." And in a sing-songy voice, she stood up. "We're going to be a family."

There was a huge something logged in Claire's throat, making it impossible for her to speak, so she just nodded. That was good enough for Lisa, who then dragged her up from her chair, into a huge hug, and a while later into the kitchen for their ice cream celebration.

They sat at the kitchen table, both with their own container and a large spoon.

Lisa licked her spoon, savored the taste, and swallowed. "So, how long till we know if it's a girl?"

Claire's lungs constricted, making it hard to breathe for a moment.

A girl.

The baby could be a girl.

She shivered and shook her head. She wasn't ready to talk or even think about that possibility just yet.

The outside door to the kitchen opened, and Lisa's mother entered with a cake in her hands. She took one look at Lisa and Claire, put the cake on the counter, and grabbed herself a spoon.

"Perfect timing. Are we celebrating or drowning our sorrows in ice cream?" Josephine sat down next to her daughter and dipped into Lisa's container.

"Celebrating," Lisa replied.

Claire wasn't so sure and would have gone with both at the same time.

She looked at mother and daughter sitting next to each other.

Those two had come a long way. Lisa had changed a lot since they arrived back in Moon Lake, and her mother had softened and opened up since the death of Lisa's dad.

"What are we celebrating?" Josephine asked.

"Claire's pregnant."

Claire gasped and looked at Lisa in indignation. "Lisa."

Lisa sighed. "Sorry, Mom, forget what I said."

Josephine looked at Claire. "What? Why? Aren't you happy?"

Claire shrugged her shoulder and dipped her spoon into the rapidly melting ice cream.

"What's the deal, Claire? You're not thinking about abortion, are you?"

There was silence in the room.

All three of them sat there with their spoons in their hands.

The way she said it, and the dramatic pause right afterward, you'd think she had just said something about mass murder. And well, okay. Some people would say it was just that, well, murder. But either way, it would've been her decision, and hers alone, had she not been too far along for that option.

"Are you really considering that?" It was Lisa who broke the deafening silence. "Please don't—there's always another way—it will all work out. Not like with Anna. I promise. You're a different person now, and your life and your circumstances are totally different."

Claire swallowed hard at the mentioning of her little baby. A huge lump in her throat blocked her breathing, and her vision got blurry when tears crept into her eyes.

Josephine grabbed her hand and squeezed it gently. "I can help. I can take over cooking or babysitting. Whatever you need. I'm ready for a challenge."

She grabbed Lisa's hand, too, and held onto them both. "I needed some time to get over the loss of Carl, but I'm getting antsy alone in the cottage. I need something to do. I considered traveling, but I don't want to do that alone. So, you would do me a favor if I could help out here."

"Oh, Mom." Lisa's eyes were brimming with tears. "Of course, you can help."

Claire looked at mother and daughter.

It was still mind-boggling to her how much their relationship had changed these last short months.

Josephine had been the leading cause for Lisa staying away from home for over ten years, but now...they had really turned their relationship around.

Claire thought about her own mother.

Not that she would ever call Miriam Gunterson a mother. She'd been an addict and had never really cared about anything other than her next fix.

Luckily, her grandpa did take her in, but Claire knew her mother-issues were one of the main reasons why she married Jeff in the first place.

And why she had tolerated his treating her badly for as long as she did.

"So, Claire."

Claire looked at both their faces, looking at her expectantly, then at their hands that were still connected.

"No, abortion is not an option. But I was scared about juggling being a mother and my job here. So yeah, I would love your help, Josephine."

The three of them started eating again.

But the ice cream didn't relieve the tension inside Claire.

"When are you due?" Lisa asked and licked her spoon clean before she stood up and walked to the dishwasher.

"April 10th." Claire felt a hot flash creeping up her ears.

They hadn't asked yet, but it was really the only question left, and she really didn't want to talk about him.

"So, who's the father?" Jo looked at her expectantly.

Claire knew her ears were turning red, and her face started to feel hot too.

She stared at her spoon, where the little scoop of ice cream melted before her eyes.

Gross.

She popped it in her mouth anyway, just to avoid the question a little longer.

She couldn't tell them, not without talking to Blake first.

She swallowed down the sweet mush but immediately regretted it. A pressure formed in her stomach.

Shit, she was going to be sick.

Claire stood up and went to the dishwasher, and put her spoon there.

"Blake," Lisa said, looking out the window.

"Hey." Claire gasped and turned toward Lisa to give her a "death stare."

Why did she do that?

It wasn't her place to tell, and Lisa's mom could have gone without this piece of information until she had time to talk to Blake.

"No, I mean—"

"Blake, really? Such a fine young man. He'll make a great dad. Have you told him? Will you get married?" Josephine stood up, too, and turned with her spoon toward the dishwasher.

Could this situation get any worse?

Claire felt her head exploding and the ice cream demanding its way back up.

"Mom." Lisa's voice got desperate.

"What?" Josephine looked at her. "What did I say?"

"Nothing. Just stop talking. All I wanted to say was that Blake's here."

All three of them looked at the back door, which opened at that exact moment.

Blake looked breathtaking.

At least Claire stopped breathing for a second before the onset of nausea threw her into action.

She made a mad dash for the bathroom, nearly bumping into Blake without saying a word to him or looking at him.

She hadn't been sick at all while pregnant with Anna.

Not at the beginning and not after the first few months like now.

Claire lamented the fact while the ice cream made its way back up.

Later, when she rinsed her mouth and looked at herself in the mirror, she prayed that the two other women would have covered for her somehow.

9

There was silence in the kitchen after Claire left the room. What the hell just happened? Blake looked at Lisa and Josephine, then at the door, through which Claire just ran as if a swarm of bees was after her.

"Too much ice cream." Lisa broke the silence and gave him a peck on the cheek.

"She always has a hard time stopping when it comes to ice cream."

Lisa picked up the container from the table and threw it in the trash.

"Hello, Blake. Do you want a cup of coffee?" Josephine asked, but his phone chimed at the same time.

He took it out of his pocket and looked at the display, then back at Josephine, who had a cup still raised in question.

Something was not right.

He couldn't pinpoint what it was exactly, but he could still feel the tension in the room.

"I'm sorry. I have to take this call, but I would love some coffee."

He stepped outside the door again to have some privacy for the dreaded call ahead.

He'd played catchup with his sister Jessica all day long.

"Jessie."

"Seb, good to hear from you. What are you up to?"

"I'm good. Nothing unusual. Same boring small-town life, I guess. How about you? What are you up to these days?"

Blake passed the house to the waterfront and turned around to look at the Inn.

It was an exceptionally beautiful place.

Before Peter started having a romantic interest in Lisa, Blake had only ever seen the Inn from the boat out on the lake, glimpses between the trees which populated the shore. The flowers on every window and balcony gave the Inn a colorful skin—a beautiful sight even from out there on the water.

Now that he had gotten to know Lisa and Claire, the Inn appeared homier than ever.

"I'm okay, actually. How is Moon Lake? Do you still love it? Mom told me something about a cabin in the wood you bought."

Blake looked out at the lake.

The mountains surrounding it were already snow-capped. Winter wasn't far.

Today was probably one of the last warm days. He really had to wrap this up and get Claire on the boat.

He watched it bobble up and down on the small pier that belonged to the Inn.

"Yeah, I still love it. I got the roof ready this week. Needed a little outside help, but that's okay. So, stop deflecting. What's wrong? Why is mom worried about you? And are you driving right now? You better be on speakerphone."

Blake heard a sharp inhale from Jessie. Then there was silence.

Was she counting to ten under her breath?

Blake tapped his foot.

He hated when his little sister did that.

So what if he was protective of her?

It was his right and his duty as her big brother.

"I'm waiting, Jess. Give me some answers."

Jessie growled, and Blake knew he got her riled up.

"You are such an ass. It's amazing how we are even related."

"Yeah, I know, so, answers. Mom's worried, and I'm worried too." He was hard on her, but they pushed each other's buttons.

"Mom is always worried about all of us—you should know that better than anyone. What with you going to war and stuff."

"We are not talking about me, Jessie. At least you don't sound depressed, which is a relief."

There was a pause in the conversation.

They both thought about their dad and Paula.

Depression often ran in the family—that was what the doctor told them after Paula's suicide attempt.

They both were very much aware of the fact.

Jessie groaned. "So that's what this whole thing is about. It's not that at all. I just had some tough times these last couple of months, but it's all resolved now."

She sighed. "I just didn't want Mom to worry more than she already does. You know she has her plate full with Paula. And yes, I'm in the car, because I'm moving, and of course, both my hands have a very good grip on my steering wheel. Ten and two, like you told me when you taught me how to drive."

Blake could hear the sass in her voice. She was mocking

him, but he knew he had it coming.

She'd always done that.

But at the same time, had clung to him after their father died.

Leaving their mother and his sisters behind had been challenging but a frequent part of his life as a Navy SEAL.

But Jessie came through okay.

She grew up to be a terrific horse trainer.

The last time he'd watched her handle a particularly fearful horse, he'd been awed.

When Jessie had started the session, the horse had tensed up and thrown its head up every time somebody had tried to touch it. He'd watched from outside the fence and feared the horse might attack her any second.

But it turned out to be a beautiful dance.

Jessie didn't try to come near the horse but moved with it in a choreography he couldn't understand.

No words, no soothing tones, just some kind of weird body language to gain the trust of the black gelding.

Ten minutes later, the horse followed her around like a puppy, relaxed and relaxing even more when she started to touch and caress it, with no sign of the fear and mistrust it had started out with.

Blake shook the memory off.

Then realized what she had said.

"What tough times? What happened, and why the hell didn't you call me?"

"It's fine now. Don't worry. Hey, do you know if there's a horse trainer in Moon Lake? Maybe a horse ranch or something?"

"Huh, no, I don't think so; at least I haven't seen any horses around here. The old doctor had some because the paddocks are still there, but no."

"What about a school? Do you have a school in Moon Lake, or do the kids have to go to school somewhere else?"

"Yes, there's a school. What the fuck, Jess? Why do you want to know? You are deflecting again. Tell me what's wrong."

"Nothing much. I just, um, Justin and I broke up. Well, actually, it turned out he'd been married and didn't tell me. So, I was the other woman, and that was not something I preferred to be. So. End of story."

Blake's muscles quivered, and he kicked a pebble.

What the fuck?

But he immediately reigned in his anger. Losing his shit wouldn't help Jessie one bit.

And if he learned something from growing up in a house full of women, they sometimes just needed to be heard.

But damn.

He took a deep breath. That shit wasn't something he would let go of. "Wow, when did he get married? Weren't you, like, together for years? What the hell? I can catch a flight tomorrow, come down there, and whip his ass."

Jessie chuckled. "That would be nice, big brother, but unnecessary. I whipped his ass myself. And I'm not in Springdale anymore. I'm moving."

"You said so. Where are you going?"

"Erm, I'm heading east. I will visit a friend for a few days. After that, I haven't decided yet."

"Hey, why don't you visit me here in Moon Lake? Now that the roof is up, I will sleep up at the cabin, anyway. You can have the apartment at the bar for yourself."

"Well, thanks, Seb. I will think about it, okay? Let's talk in a few days."

"Fine with me. But if you don't check in every day, I'm

gonna come find you. And call Mom. She's really worried about you."

"I already did. But I'll tell her I talked to you. Bye, big brother."

"Bye, sis'."

After the call ended, he looked at the display for a solid minute. Should he call his mother right away? Nah, give Jessie a chance to make things right herself.

He crammed his phone back into the pocket of his jeans.

He had to go visit his mother real soon. Maybe he could coordinate with Jessie so they could have a big family get-together.

He turned and straightened his shoulders.

Ready to tackle the next woman in his life, who had been quite elusive the last couple of days. Hopefully, she was feeling better after her bout of sickness.

He really wanted to take her out on the boat.

Get her relaxed and talking to him.

Because there were too many things left unspoken these last couple of weeks.

And openness was one of the things he valued most in their relationship.

10

Claire kept herself busy and away from the window by furiously cleaning the Inn's kitchen, instead of checking on Blake every five seconds—which she truly wanted.

She felt the breeze on her neck and his eyes on her as the door opened even before she heard him step in.

She turned, leaned against the counter, and looked at him.

There it was.

The familiar flutter in her chest whenever he was near.

But below it, her stomach knotted.

She watched him close the distance.

The way he moved, like a predator advancing on his target. All this self-confidence was sexy as hell.

He knew what he wanted and went for it without compromising or backing down from a fight.

He reached her and took her hand softly. "Hey, baby, are you okay?" Blake leaned in for a kiss, and everything felt right in Claire's world for a moment—until she realized she'd just thrown up.

Gross.

She laid a hand on Blake's cheek, gave him a closed-mouth peck, and leaned away.

He looked at her. His eyes narrowed for a split second. Studying her.

Assessing her.

Why did it seem like he could look right through her protective walls and into her soul?

That was why he was so good at anticipating her moods and needs.

That was probably what made him the lady's man he was.

But this time, he seemed okay to go with the flow.

"Feel better?"

She nodded.

And he smiled as if he had no care in the world. "I'm here with the boat to sweep you away for an hour. What do you say? Ready for some fun and relaxation? It's likely the last day it's warm enough to go out with the boat."

Claire swallowed excessively. Her mind was racing.

This was her chance to tell him.

"Okay, I just have to check with Lisa first."

Blake grinned, which made his face more handsome than ever.

"Way ahead of you—already asked her—said it's okay."

Claire forced a smile and curled her toes.

This was it.

Time to come clean.

Being on edge didn't sit well with her anyway. "Well then, I'll just go grab my coat."

Claire walked out of the kitchen and clenched her jaw.

When she entered the office to get her coat from the small coat rack they had there, Lisa looked up from her computer. "Hey, I'm sorry. Should have checked with you first."

Claire took a deep breath and grimaced. "I'm not ready to tell him," Claire whispered. "I know. I gotta, but, I'm just not ready."

Lisa frowned. "Claire, look, I know it's hard, but it's not getting easier the longer you wait. You will never be ready, so just tackle it head-on. You will feel better afterward."

Claire fiddled with her coat and looked out the window into the rose garden.

She knew she had to tell him eventually, but she was just coming to terms with the fact that she was pregnant herself, and her decision to embrace this pregnancy was too shaky and new.

What if his reaction was bad?

They'd talked about this—as in no commitment in their future.

Kids were the ultimate commitment.

She sighed and looked again at Lisa, who was still frowning, and without another word, she turned and went back to the kitchen.

Time to face the music.

When she entered, he was still standing where she'd left him, bathed in sunlight that came in from the open door that made his hair sparkle.

He smiled at her and held his arm out to her.

Claire's chest tightened.

Yes, he was cocky and a flirt, but he was honest and authentic about it. It was part of his charm.

And in reality, under that surface, he was such a great man, always willing to help and support everyone around him and insanely loyal to his friends.

She knew their thing was just a fling, but she felt so cared for when she was with him.

Safe and protected.

He had the ability to make her feel beautiful and whole.

She wasn't ready to lose that, not yet, even though it was a real possibility.

Claire went to him, and he took her in his arms.

"You look beautiful," he said and nuzzled her hair.

And her insides melted.

This man.

This bulky, hard man, with a tender core, that only made him more attractive.

She leaned back and smiled up at him.

And his grin was the most beautiful thing ever. They hugged again briefly before he took her hand, led her out into the sunlight, and they made their way toward the pier where his boat was waiting.

Halfway there, Blake intertwined their fingers before he pulled her hand to his mouth and gave her a small kiss.

The queasy feeling in Claire's stomach increased.

Maybe, just maybe, it would be all right.

Don't all men say they didn't want kids until the right woman at the right time came along?

Maybe this was the right time.

For both of them.

Blake winked at her and cleared his throat.

"Hey, you know who just called? Did I ever tell you about my sister Jessie? She's making some huge changes in her life, moving and all. I have the feeling that family will always be trouble, no matter how old I get."

Family meant trouble to him.

Just great.

"Isn't she the horse trainer? Where's she moving?"

"Yes, that's Jessie. Apparently, her boyfriend led some kind of double life, so she just upped hers and is on the move. She doesn't know where she's headed just yet. Irresponsible. But maybe she'll come visit, and then you can meet her."

Claire nodded. "How long were they together?"

They stopped at the boat, and Blake pulled it near and entered it with a graceful jump. "Oh, it was quite some time, three or four years, I think. At least they didn't have kids—that would have been the worst."

Claire swallowed more than usual and crossed her arms over her belly.

Yeah, kids—that would really be the worst.

Her hope for some kind of positive reaction to her news plummeted.

Who was she kidding?

Blake would not be happy.

He offered her his hand, but even with his help, her step onto the boat wasn't very graceful.

Blake unfastened the boat and steered it toward the imposing cliff on the other side of the lake.

The wind and the noise made talking nearly impossible, so Claire closed her eyes and enjoyed the little reprieve she got. She snuggled deeper into her coat and the front seat of the boat. The wind already had a sharp bite to it, and the snow-topped mountains were a constant reminder of winter just around the corner.

Lisa had told her they had had an exceptionally warm October so far. Most years, Moon Lake was already six inches deep in snow at this time of year.

She wasn't fond of snow.

As in not looking forward to winter.

But it came with the territory, and maybe winter in the mountains differed from her past experiences with frozen rain and dirty slush.

Blake throttled the boat and, after a minute, stopped the motor entirely.

The sudden silence was deafening.

And the heaviness in Claire's stomach returned.

"Blake"—Claire turned her seat in his direction—"I, actually, I got something I need to tell you."

He nodded and turned his seat, so he was facing her.

"So, shoot. I had the feeling there's been something bothering you for quite a while. Let's hear it."

Claire's heartbeat quickened, and she started to sweat despite the clamminess of her skin.

Her gaze bounced behind Blake, where she could still see the Inn and the edges of town in the distance. A sailing boat crossed behind her, and Blake greeted whoever was on there.

"I'm, um, actually..." She straightened her spine and inhaled deeply before exhaling and swallowing the excessive amount of saliva, that made talking difficult.

Then she focused on his face again.

"I'm pregnant."

Blake jerked his head back as if she had slapped him. His eyes grew huge, and his brows nearly touched his hairline.

"You are what?"

The disbelief in his voice made Claire's stomach roil, and a sick feeling closed up her throat.

She rubbed her stomach.

"I'm..." She cleared her throat. Did he really need to hear it again? But he just sat there, with no inclination to help her out. Now she could really use him touching her. Now she could really use his soothing qualities.

"Pregnant, I'm pregnant, Blake."

His look changed.

She could see it in his eyes and in the way his mouth tightened before it distorted into a snarl.

"We had a deal. You knew very well I didn't want kids."

Claire's throat went dry, and flushes of heat rolled over her body. He looked at her as if she was a traitor. "I know. I didn't do it on purpose. It was an accident. I don't even know how it happened."

His look didn't change.

No warmth. Not an inch of understanding.

Just a stony mask.

She nodded, then shrugged. She knew what their deal was. But she couldn't change the situation. "It is what it is." Claire looked at the bulging vein at the side of Blake's throat.

"There are options." He stared her down, his face grim, but the redness of his neck that slowly flushed over his whole face, and the tightly clenched fists evoked in Claire the image of a lion getting ready to attack.

Claire braced herself for it.

The now familiar waves of nausea got worse. Slowly, she shook her head. "No, not really. At least not the option you're thinking of. I don't want that." Claire's shoulder slumped.

She'd prepared herself for his reaction. But it felt worse than she'd expected.

He crossed his arms.

"If I'm the father, I have a say in this."

Claire ground her teeth. "If, did you really just say if?"

Blake didn't budge.

"Oh, so now I'm a slut." Claire's nostrils flared.

Enough was enough.

Yes, neither of them planned this. But like hell would she let him treat her like this.

"Fuck you, Blake. Really, fuck you."

She crossed her arms. "You know, you have a say—you can choose between being part of this kid's life or not. Your choice, your decision." Then she turned her seat away from him.

He grabbed her seat and turned her back to him.

"It's not whether or not I want to be a part of. I don't want any kid of mine living on this earth. Period."

Claire's body tensed, and her heartbeat pounded. Just a week ago, her first reaction was to get an abortion. Just a few hours ago, she had been conflicted about this baby.

But now.

After this.

After talking to Lisa and Josephine, after making plans about how this could all work out.

She couldn't even imagine losing this child.

But she also couldn't fault him for having the same damn reaction.

She looked at Blake; she could see the turmoil in his eyes and the barely contained anger in the tension of his body.

Claire's heartbeat slowed.

He was really struggling.

This strong man. She'd never seen him lose control.

But he was struggling to hold on.

She would have touched him but didn't dare. "Listen, Blake." Claire's tone was gentle. "It must have happened early on, and I'm really sorry that it happened. I didn't plan it. I thought it couldn't. But I truly want this. And if you can't accept that, I understand. But I won't change my mind."

He snapped his jaw closed and turned away from her. Nothing more to say.

What's more, it was probably better if they didn't talk at all before one of them said something they couldn't take back.

She felt empty and drained. "Can we please go back? I think I'm getting sick again."

Blake moved, pushed the button, and the motor roared back to life.

His movements were mechanical.

And he didn't look at her again. "I still feel betrayed."

The boat sped up, and the wind took away her ability to answer loudly enough. She watched Blake, who seemed withdrawn and even a little despaired.

Betrayed.

By her.

The pain in Claire's chest deepened when she looked at him. She raised her hand in a fluttery movement, almost touched him, but chickened out at the last moment.

Why was he so devastated?

She figured he would be angry at her. Maybe even blame her entirely. But this devastation she hadn't accounted for that.

They reached the pier, and Blake held the boat steady with his hand on it.

"I really didn't plan for this to happen. I would never betray you like this. Honestly, I didn't even think it was a possibility. But this child is a reality, Blake. With or without you in its life."

He didn't react to what she'd just said, didn't even look at her. He also didn't help her disembark, which she managed just fine, but left her feeling empty.

Usually, he was the first to help.

A true gentleman.

But not now.

He just stared straight ahead and steered the boat away from the pier as soon as she stepped off it.

Claire's eyelids felt hot, and her chin was trembling as she watched him retreat. She waited desperately for him to turn around, but he didn't look back, not once.

Claire rubbed her chest to ease the hurt that centered

there, then she laid her hand on her belly and turned back to the Inn.

She had to think about the future.

She would be a single mom.

But she would be one hell of a mother.

11

He watched from behind the trees.

She looked older than in the pictures. Not as fragile as she had at eighteen.

He gritted his teeth. It didn't matter how the bitch looked.

She didn't deserve it.

Didn't deserve any of it.

He just had to find a way.

At first, he just wanted to see her. But the anger deep inside had increased.

She was behaving as if nothing had happened. Led her stupid little small-town life as if nothing had changed.

As if she wasn't the reason, all his hopes and dreams were being squashed. He spat on the ground.

The bitch wouldn't know what hit her. But he would get what was his.

One way or the other.

12

Claire entered the Inn through the kitchen door.

Luckily there was no one around.

She grabbed a glass of water and made her way straight up to her room. When she passed the office, she could hear Lisa talking on the phone. But she'd had enough talking for the day.

Claire just wanted to die, or at least hide under her comforter.

Stupid tears were running down her cheeks, and closing her eyes and shutting out the world sounded like heaven.

She entered the room and locked the door before she went to bed, clothes and all.

She really didn't care.

After she lay there in silence for quite some time, staring at the ceiling.

There was a knock on the door.

But when she didn't react—she just couldn't deal with anyone—whoever was at the door gave up, and she shut her eyes.

She prayed for sleep to come.

Her arms and legs were heavy enough—just her mind couldn't stop replaying the conversation with Blake over and over, in her head.

Successfully hindering her from sleeping.

So she just laid there and stared and cried.

A while later, there was another knock.

Claire sniffed.

She just needed to be left alone. She turned and rummaged through the drawer on the nightstand for more tissues.

"I can hear you in there—let me in," Lisa shouted through the door.

"Go away."

"I know you're hurting. Open up, or I'm coming back with a key."

Claire found a tissue and blew her nose.

She turned back, facing the wall, and clutched a small, white sheep against her chest. It was soft and a mixture of a cuddly toy and a small blanket.

She'd bought it for Anna, and ever since, it had been the only thing she always kept near.

The only thing she kept.

Period.

Tears welled up again, and Claire sobbed.

Anna, she would have been fourteen this year.

A teenager.

She probably wouldn't have been very enthusiastic about getting a sibling. Or maybe she would.

Claire heard some scraping at the door, and the key on the inside fell, cluttering to the floor.

Then the lock clicked, and Lisa opened the door.

Claire didn't turn around when she heard Lisa crossing the room.

Then there was some movement on the mattress, and she felt her best friend lying in bed with her and hugging her from behind.

Warmth permeated her cold body.

"He'll come around. I'm sure it was a shock for him, just as it was for you. You needed some time to come to terms with it. So give him the same. Once he deals with his shock, it will be okay. Blake's a good man. He'll come around."

Claire sighed. She remembered his devastation. It hadn't been just shock about an unplanned pregnancy, or even anger.

There had been more to it.

Deeper feelings, reasons she didn't understand. The strange way he worded it.

"I don't want any kid of mine living on this earth," was what he said.

It still gave her goosebumps.

"And what if he doesn't?"

She bit her lip, unsure if she even wanted the answer.

But Lisa hugged her close.

"Then this baby will have the best family ever. We'll make sure of it. Screw Blake. We don't need him to give this baby all it needs."

Claire could feel something vibrating at her back, and Lisa squirmed to get her cell phone out of the pocket of her jeans.

"Hey, Lizzy, I'm down in the kitchen as promised. Where are you?"

Claire could hear Peter's voice through the phone, and Lisa sighed. "We'll be right down. Give me a minute. Get yourself something to drink." She disconnected.

"There is some last-minute wedding stuff Peter is here to discuss. I need you in on this. Are you up to it?"

Claire turned around and sighed. No, she clearly wasn't up to it. But sleep wasn't about to come, and lying here, thinking about Anna, Blake, and the new child, growing in her, didn't make her feel any better.

Plus, she was the maid of honor, and Lisa's wedding was only two weeks away.

"Please help. You are so much better at that stuff than Peter and me. This wedding would be a hot mess without you." Lisa got up from the bed and stood there, begging like a puppy.

Claire bit her lip, took a deep breath, and moved into a sitting position.

"I'm coming. Just give me a minute to get a grip on myself."

Lisa left the room, and after a short glance in the mirror, Claire decided there was really nothing she could do to fix her swollen eyes and blotchy face.

So she followed Lisa downstairs.

Peter leaned against the kitchen counter in jeans and a plaid shirt.

Traditional mountain-man cool.

He was kissing Lisa, which soon transformed into a serious make-out session. At least in her friend's life, everything was running smoothly.

"Hey, guys, please get a room."

They both ended the kiss, and Peter looked at Claire.

"Holy shit, what happened to you? Are you sick or something? Maybe you should go lay down, or see a doctor or something."

Claire grinned, turned around, and was about to leave the kitchen when Lisa grabbed her by the shoulders and hindered her departure.

"Not so fast; you are not sick," she turned and threw a

74

dirty look at Peter, "I just got her out of bed, so don't sabotage me, dear future husband of mine."

Peter raised his hands in defense.

"I'm sorry. I just think she looks sick."

"And I say she isn't, so drop it."

"Hey, guys, I'm still in the room. Peter, thank you for your concern. Lisa's right. I'm not sick, just pregnant."

Peter's eyes bulged, and he gasped at the news.

"Did you tell Blake?" He rubbed the back of his neck. His gaze settled on Claire, and he drew his brows together.

Lisa scoffed. "Why do you think she looks like that?"

Peter sighed. "So, I guess he didn't take the news very well?"

Claire just nodded and swallowed through the tightness in her throat.

"Shit, I'm sorry, girl." He swooped Claire into his arms.

The warmth and the feeling of safeness reminded her of the bear hugs Blake was so generous to give.

Or had been—as in, not anymore.

She squeezed her eyes shut but then took a step back.

She was done being weak.

She didn't need a man to make her feel safe.

Or raise a child.

She went to the counter to prepare tea for them.

"Okay, now what is this wedding stuff, that needs our attention, Lisa?"

When Lisa didn't answer, Claire looked up and witnessed one of these weird nonverbal communication moments between Peter and Lisa. They didn't talk, but it looked like a whole conversation took place between them.

"I'll talk to him. I promise he'll come around."

Lisa grinned and kissed Peter on the chin.

Claire swallowed. "Whatever, I don't care."

And she wouldn't care.

She could do this alone.

She didn't need him.

And she had Lisa and Josephine, so she really wasn't alone at all.

13

Blake looked up from wiping down the bar when the door opened again.

The bar was packed solid.

As was usually the case on Friday evenings.

But today was total madness. At the back, they had a bachelor party for a groom from out of town, where a solid amount of drinking, shouting, and laughing was happening.

By the door, the respective bride-to-be partied with her friends, with lots of giggling and laughter involved.

Blake never understood the need for something stupid like that, but even more so didn't understand why they would both party at the same bar, at the same time.

He shrugged.

Who was he to judge?

His lips curled when he remembered Claire. They'd met hours ago, but he was still all over the place. Could barely get control over his thoughts and feelings.

Pregnant.

His body tensed, and water from the rag in his hand trickled onto the bar.

He hurled it into the sink and forced himself to take a deep breath.

Peter and Richard Travers—both out of uniform—entered the bar and looked around before they made their way toward him and took a seat right in front of him.

"Hello, boys. What can I get you today?" He placed a bowl of chips in front of them and looked at them expectantly.

"Hey, Blake, full house today, eh?" Travers nodded to the back of the bar, and Blake nodded.

"Since we're off duty, I'll take a beer," Peter said and clunked his keys and cell phone on the bar while Travers signed he wanted the same by holding up two fingers.

Blake nodded and looked at Peter while he tapped the first beer.

His buddy looked pissed.

His eyes were cold and staring him down.

"Hey, Sheriff." Blake directed his eyes to Travers. "I gotta ask you something. I had a run-in with a little boy in my house a few days ago. Is there anyone living up there in these parts of the forest?"

Sheriff Travers tilted his head to the side and furrowed his eyebrows. "You bought the old hunting cabin, right?"

Blake nodded.

"Don't think there are any houses or inhabited cabins up there. At least, that I know of, but I'll check that and get back to you."

Blake scratched the back of his neck and tilted his head to the left until there was a crack.

"Is there a missing-child report somewhere around Moon Lake?"

Sheriff Travers and Peter both raised their eyebrows.

"Why would you ask something like that? Maybe the

78

boy was just hiking with his parents and was nosy enough to stop by your house."

Blake shook his head and sighed. "Don't think so. The kid looked like he was living in these woods. Filthy, torn clothes. He ran away as soon as he saw me. Knew his way around there too. I chased him but lost his tracks at a creek.

"I don't think he was just hiking with his parents. I think he was looking for food. There's been food missing ever since I left some up there—thought it was animals at first, but now I'm not so sure anymore."

Richard nodded.

"We'll look into it. If a child is living somewhere in these woods, we'll find out."

Blake nodded, too, and avoided Peter's gaze.

There was a crash, and Blake looked up at the minor upheaval at the back of the bar.

His nostrils flared, and he felt a pounding in his ears. "Fuck." He really didn't need any more shit today. Blake ground his teeth.

The new waitress, Sharon, returned with an empty tray and looked at him apologetically.

It was her second day working for him, and today she was really grating on his nerves. "God, you are clumsy. I don't think this will work out."

The minute he said it, he immediately felt like the biggest asshole ever.

It was her second, goddamn day, for Christ's sake. Of course, she wasn't a pro at this.

Fuck.

Her eyes filled with tears, and she bowed her head in defeat.

"I'm sorry, Blake. I'll just clean up the mess, and then I'm outta here."

She turned around with the broom, and Blake stomped into the kitchen.

He wanted to kick something.

Preferably himself.

Heat flushed through his body, and at the same time, he felt like the worst piece of shit ever.

Sharon hadn't done anything wrong.

She didn't deserve his wrath.

He squeezed his eyes closed and took a deep breath and a second one.

He needed to get his shit together.

The door opened and closed behind him, and Peter cleared his throat. "What the hell, Blake? That was fucking mean."

Blake ground his teeth and snorted. He crossed his arms in front of his chest and leaned against the counter. "Oh, come on, nothing I said was wrong. And what makes you the expert?"

Peter shook his head. "You don't need to be an expert to realize you were mean to the poor girl when you didn't need to be... when you didn't want to be. You and I know that your mood has nothing to do with her. But you behaved like an ass. That's what I'm calling you on."

Blake snarled. "You know shit."

Peter shook his head and sighed. "Claire's pregnant. She told you today, you lost your mind, and you're still out of control. That's what I know. So, tell me if I'm wrong,"

His matter-of-fact tone grained on Blake's nerves, and he wanted to punch the smug look off his friend's face.

Even if his best friend was right.

But Peter continued. "What I don't know is why you're behaving like an ass. Okay, I get it. You never wanted to have kids. But it isn't like you and Claire hate each other. Or that she'd try to trap you. She's cool—she doesn't seem like the girl who expects a marriage proposal. I know it's a shock and everything, but your reaction is way out of bounds."

Blake opened his mouth, but Peter raised his hand to stop him.

"As far as I know, it was a shock for her too. Lisa told me she thought she couldn't get pregnant. So, it surely wasn't some kind of scheme of hers that made you so mad. So what exactly is your fucking problem?"

Peter stared at him in silence for a couple of seconds. "It's your dad, isn't it?"

Blake could see and hear the compassion in his friend's face and words and felt lightheaded.

His ears turned impossibly hot.

Fuck.

He hadn't, not for one second, been thinking about Claire. Just what it meant to him, or what could possibly happen to any child of his.

Blake swallowed excessively before he started to speak. "Depression runs in families. Look at Paula. I don't want that for anyone. I can't be responsible for that."

Peter exhaled and positioned himself next to Blake, leaning against the kitchen countertop.

"It can run in families. But look at you, you don't battle with it. Jessie doesn't either. And there is never a guarantee for anything in life. You should know that better than most, given what we've seen on missions. Life is not fair. But it's precious."

Blake shoved his hands in his pocket.

They'd seen unbelievable suffering. Injustices that had happened to good people. Drone strikes that killed whole villages.

Savages that killed everyone in their wake, even children.

Watching teammates die or get maimed had been one of the hardest things they'd gone through.

Steel was right.

They'd experienced grief and misery. And unbelievable agony.

And life was precious.

"I just didn't think it was worth the risk."

Peter snorted but laid his hand on Blake's shoulder. "Well, I'm sorry, buddy, but that ship has sailed. Now you have to decide how you want to handle the situation. What kind of dad you want to be."

Compassion entered his gaze. "You don't know what the future holds, and it doesn't have to be the same way it was with your dad and Paula. You get a chance to change your life story. Make it a better one. So, pull your head out of your ass and handle it like the honorable human being I know you are."

Blake took a deep breath. "What if the kid's better off without me?" His chest tightened as soon as the words left his mouth. He couldn't imagine leaving his child to wonder, just as he'd wondered after his father's death.

Peter grabbed him by the shoulder. "You are a good man, Blake. The best I know. No kid would ever be better off without you. You will figure it out. Just get a grip on your emotions and do nothing you have to regret later."

Blake groaned and doubled over. "I was so cold and mean. I need to apologize to Claire."

"Hell yeah, you do. And better make it a good one. And to, what's her name—the new waitress—better apologize to her too."

Blake exhaled deeply and nodded.

He'd been such an ass to Sharon. He would apologize to her right away. She was new to the job. She told him that when she applied for the job.

Today she'd been on the receiving end of his shitty mood, and she didn't deserve his harshness.

Claire was a whole other story. He not only handled the situation badly but also made some comments he was truly ashamed of.

He needed to make things right. But before he apologized to her, he had some serious soul-searching to do.

He was going to be a father.

Claire was going to be the mother of his child.

Holy Fuck.

Peter straightened and patted him on the shoulder once again.

"Do you love Claire— Wait, let me rephrase, do you like Claire enough to envision a family with her?"

Blake shrugged his shoulders. He had no clue about his feelings right now.

Claire was great.

Easy to be around, kind, and caring.

He was infatuated with her. But he never intended their relationship to be that deep.

To be that much more.

They had fun. They had great sex. He loved spending time with her.

But family?

That would imply marriage.

And he didn't know if he was ready for a commitment like that.

Well, he better get ready.

They would be parents.

Together.

His chest tightened.

And that would be one hell of a commitment.

But first things first.

He followed Peter back out to the bar.

14

Blake stood up from his chair and went across his small office to open the window.

The office was part of the built-in flat, which was situated at the back of the bar.

He still lived in here, but now that the roof was done and the doors and windows would be delivered within the week, it was only a matter of days until he packed his meager belongings and moved up to his new cabin.

A stiff breeze from the lake blew inside, and Blake inhaled deeply. He hated being trapped inside.

Strangely enough, this never happened to him when he was standing behind the bar.

Maybe the action and the constant ebb and flow of people and noise made it better out there.

But in here, especially going over the books, always made him feel stifled.

Blake inhaled once more and returned to his big mahogany desk. He wouldn't have chosen this desk, but it came with the bar, and Blake liked to imagine the old guy, whose heirs sold him the bar, sitting at the same desk doing the books.

Blake was deep in concentration, so he at first didn't react to the quiet knock on his door.

When the knocking didn't stop, he narrowed his eyes, and his "come in" was sharper than he intended.

The door opened just a crack, and Sharon, his waitress, peeked inside.

Ever since the day Claire had told him about the baby, and he'd yelled at her, Sharon was tiptoeing around him, overly cautious in doing her job and trying not to provoke him in any way.

This had to stop.

"Come in," Blake said, his voice as gentle as he could make it.

Sharon stepped inside the office and looked around, avoiding eye contact with him.

Blake clenched his jaw before he deliberately loosened his posture and smiled at her. "Stop being afraid of me. You know I'm sorry about me going mental on you. It will not happen again. It was just me, being a dick that day— nothing you'd done wrong."

A quick smile changed her face completely.

According to her application, Sharon was only twenty-one, and this was her first job as a waitress. Sometimes she looked younger than twenty-one and sometimes much older, but she was a quick learner, and the patrons loved her.

Whatever brought her here to Moon Lake was none of his business, but it was his lucky day she stumbled into his bar.

"I know." Sharon sighed, then shrugged. "I'm trying. You apologized every day since then, and it's okay, Blake. I got it. Everybody has a bad day once in a while."

She smiled, and he could see mischief dancing in her eyes. "Let's make a deal. You stop apologizing, I stop

85

tiptoeing around, and you will give me a free pass, for someday when I'm having a bad day."

Blake grinned. "Deal. And by the way, you are doing good. Getting better and better each day."

Sharon grinned back and was about to turn toward the door but spun back on her heels. "Oh, the reason I'm here. There's a pregnant lady out there, who needs to talk to you."

Blake's pulse quickened.

Claire was here?

He leaned forward, ready to get up. He hadn't had the chance to apologize to her, even though he was eager to do so.

He'd taken the last few days to really think things through, and even though he still had mixed feelings about the baby thing, he was sure he wanted to support Claire in every way he could.

Starting with an apology and reassurance, he was in for the ride.

Maybe even make a relationship work.

"Yeah, she's, like, really huge." Sharon depicted a huge belly, and Blake frowned. Claire wasn't even showing last week. Either Sharon was exaggerating, or this was someone else pregnant.

How was it that now he knew Claire and he were having a baby, he suddenly saw pregnant women and babies everywhere around?

He closed the office door behind him and followed Sharon back to the bar.

It was late afternoon—silence, right before the crowd would come in.

The same old fishermen sat at the bar, like on every other day, and the noises of a news broadcast running on the TV in the background completed the scene.

The familiar scents of wood, smoke, and fish and chips, Milan's special of the day, permeated the air.

Blake did a double-take at the lady who leaned against the bar with her back to him.

He knew that hair. A huge smile split his face. "Jessie."

His sister turned toward him, and her pregnant belly was threatening to burst the buttons on her plaid shirt.

He came to an abrupt halt.

The happiness he felt just seconds ago vanished, and the smile slipped from his face. "Holy shit."

He couldn't believe it.

His sister was pregnant. And not just a little-baby-bump pregnant, but full-on, ready-to-pop pregnant.

Unbelievable.

Didn't she just tell him she got rid of her boyfriend and upped her life to move to somewhere she didn't know just yet?

Blake recovered slowly from his shock and started to move again.

"What the hell, Jessie," he said, with a look of reproach.

Jessie ignored his behavior. She laughed and closed the distance. "Hello to you too, big brother. Good to see you."

She pressed her belly against him in a sorry attempt at an embrace.

Blake suppressed his discomfort and hugged her back, but after a second, he took a step back, effectively ending the contact.

"What the hell, Jessie? Why didn't you tell me you were pregnant? Does Mom know? Why didn't she tell me?"

Jessie shook her head and smiled.

"I visited her after our phone call and told her. I wasn't sure how she would react, but she seemed happy to become a grandmother. I told her not to say anything, so I could shock the socks off of you. Mission accomplished, wouldn't you say? So, how about you, happy to be Uncle Sebastian?"

Blake rubbed the back of his neck. His instinct was to turn around, go back to his office, and start this thing over. Preferably, with Jessie not being pregnant and him not becoming an uncle.

Uncle Seb.

He shook his head. No, he really wasn't ready to be an uncle. Then he focused his attention back on his sister. He'd always taken care of his sister...as much as she'd let him.

But this time, he'd failed miserably.

"How, when, why, Jessie? And what the hell are you doing on the road when you're that—pregnant? Shouldn't you, I don't know, be in the hospital, or in bed, or something like that?"

Somewhere safe and cared for, at least. Not driving around completely alone.

Jessie flattened her lips in irritation. "Actually, I'm not sick, Seb. I'm pregnant. Women have been bearing children since the beginning of humankind. Not that you understand anyhow."

His eyes narrowed.

He hated it when she talked to him like he was an idiot.

She had some major man-hating vibes going there.

"Okay, okay." Blake lifted both hands. Time to take a step back. "But you are, like...huge, and, as far as I can tell, driving alone across two states, heavily pregnant—kinda risky."

Jessie squinted at him, and her frown deepened.

"Stop being an ass, big brother. I am a responsible adult. I can take care of myself. But I can just leave again if it's too much for you." She sighed. "I'm done with things that aren't good for me and my baby. And you talking shit. That is something I definitely don't need."

88

She turned on her heels, and Blake caught her arm just in time to stop her.

"I'm sorry, Jess. Didn't mean to harass you. It was just. Unexpected. But for real, when are you due?"

She slowly turned back to him. Her eyes were brimming with tears.

Seeing his strong sister like this almost broke his heart.

"A month. I got a month to sort out the mess, that is my life." She inhaled deeply. "I know nothing about this is perfect. But I'll figure it out. I always do. And now it's not me alone anymore."

Blake swallowed down the knot that had formed in his throat and took her in his arms. "It's okay, we will figure this out together."

He let go again. "What do you need? Something to eat, drink? Do you want to lie down?"

And there it was. The look of adoration he sometimes, not very often, got from his sister, which made all the hassles that came with having two little sisters worthwhile. There was nothing just like the feeling of making the world better for someone else.

Jessie sniffed. Her blue eyes huge. "I would love to lie down a little. A cup of tea would be great too."

Blake leaped into action. He went behind the bar and prepared her tea, relieved to temporarily have something to do. He would think about this shitty situation later. With the tea in hand, Blake led Jessie to the back, and into his flat.

"Couch or bed?" He looked at Jessie, who looked around. She'd never visited him in Moon Lake. Knew nothing about the life he'd made for himself here.

"Couch is fine. A toilet would be even better." She chuckled. "You have no idea how tedious it is to stop every five miles with the need to pee."

Blake pressed his eyes closed and pointed toward the bathroom.

He shook his head. He had no idea, and if he had the chance, he would leave it at that.

Then Claire popped into his mind.

In a few months, she would be huge like Jessie and would need to pee all the time, as well.

He rubbed away the tightness in his chest.

He hadn't talked to her since that dreadful afternoon on the boat.

He cringed every time he thought about the wounded look in her eyes when he left her standing at the pier.

He was the reason for her pain.

He had to fix this—and fast.

Tomorrow.

Tomorrow he would apologize.

15

"Hey Claire, we're leaving." Lisa peeked into the kitchen, where Claire was angry-baking up a storm.

"Are you sure you don't want to come with us?"

Claire shook her head and forced a smile. "Nope, I'm good. Have a fun evening."

Was her friend insane? She would rather clean toilets with a toothbrush than hang out at Blake's bar.

Not after the way he'd treated her. Not after what he'd said and how he said it. And especially not since she hadn't heard a peep from him in the days since.

"He talked to Peter and told him to invite you specifically." Lisa said.

Invite her, her ass. He probably had a guilty conscience or was delusional if he thought they could just go on as if nothing had happened.

Not when everything had changed. And the one time she needed him to really step up.

He'd let her down.

"Okay then, we won't be long. Are you as excited for tomorrow as I am?"

Claire sighed, shook her head, and grinned.

After an impromptu dance session earlier today in the big dining room of the Inn, Lisa had decided she and Peter needed professional help before the wedding to avoid public humiliation.

So she booked a dance lesson for tomorrow and demanded Claire come with them.

She didn't want to come at first, but Lisa had nagged her to go until she relented.

Maybe being the maid of honor wasn't worth all the hassle.

"Okay, gotta go. Call if you change your mind, and we'll come to get you." Her best friend said and slipped out the door.

They had a strict no-one-drives-alone-in-the-dark policy since Lisa's kidnapping by a serial killer/taxi driver.

Claire watched through the window. Her friend practically bounced toward Peter, and they kissed once inside his truck.

She sighed, and a heavy weight shifted over her chest.

Her friend deserved all the happiness she could get, especially after what had happened with her stalker and after the years Peter and she were separated.

But watching them didn't make things easier for her.

Blake and her relationship had been so easy. Uncomplicated and drama free.

And look at her now.

She was hurting and moping. And all because of one little accident.

Fuck this.

She sat down at the kitchen table and started eating. The still-warm treats tasted heavenly.

She should take care of office work and handle the mail

since both Lisa and her had been slacking off for the last couple of days.

She sighed.

Nope, she'd deal with that tomorrow.

Tonight she would veg on the sofa and watch a movie to kill time and take her mind off things.

16

Hours later, the bar was brimming with people.

Blake had gotten a live band to test if it would attract more customers on a weeknight.

Today was the debut event, and the bar was crammed with people.

Apparently, his plan worked.

Sharon navigated the crowds like a pro, and he had his hands full manning the bar.

Blake served another beer to Alan, the resident physician, and his friend, who devoured Milan's version of fish and chips. "You are not on duty, are you, doc?"

Alan laughed. "It feels like I'm always on duty, but no. Not officially, anyhow. Hey, Blake, do you know my friend Caspar?"

Blake shook his head and exchanged a handshake with Caspar.

"Caspar just moved to Stone Valley. We went to the same university back in the day."

Blake leaned against the back of the bar and took a sip from his beer. He grimaced and poured it down the sink. It'd gone stale. "So, you're a doctor as well?" He looked at Caspar.

"No." He shook his head and grinned. "Geologist."

Blake nodded and turned to Sharon to fill her new order.

The door opened again, and Blake looked up from the tap. A couple entered.

He'd soon have to turn people away.

Behind the couple, Peter and Lisa entered, and Blake's heart leaped.

Would Claire come too?

Peter had promised to talk to her and extend the invitation after they'd finalized his plan for his apology tomorrow.

The door behind Lisa fell closed, and Blake lowered his head. His heart felt like it was shrinking a little.

She didn't come.

He looked up again, when Peter and Lisa arrived at the bar. Lisa threw him a dirty look. Looked like Claire wasn't the only female pissed at him.

Blake put the last beer on the tray and turned toward Lisa. "I'm sorry. I really am."

She looked at him with cold eyes, and her lips curled. "You better be, asshole. But I'm not the one you need to apologize to. She's the one you crushed with your asshole behavior. So, you better apologize to her. And make it a good one."

Blake nodded. "Roger that. And thanks for playing along."

She narrowed her eyes. "And Blake"—he watched her face go pensive—"tomorrow—you'd better mean it, or else…"

Blake wrinkled his nose. "Or else you'll sic your fiancée on me?"

Lisa smiled diabolically. "No, this is personal. You know, women are so much more creative at revenge."

Blake's eyebrows rose, and he looked at Peter, who chuckled before he kissed Lisa's forehead. "You heard the woman. Better do as she tells you."

Blake nodded again and looked after Lisa, who went to sit with Julie and Holly at one of the booths.

His shoulders dropped—Claire should be with them. He missed her, more than he thought he would.

She deserved something special.

Which was exactly what he planned to give her. Tomorrow. With the help of his friends.

He'd set the plan in motion shortly after Jessie arrived.

When he realized that Claire was the first one, he wanted to call to talk about the whole Jessie disaster.

But she deserved better, than him just showing up and dumping more of his shit on her.

The thought of Jessie made his pulse leap.

She was still sound asleep on his couch, drained from the long drive. Blake still didn't know how to proceed.

Sure, he could start camping at the house and leave the flat to her, but other than that... Claire would know what to do. She was good with people. Compassionate and kind. And, most of the time, she had a gift of calming him down and making him see pathways that he hadn't been able to see before.

Peter looked at him funny.

"What?"

He just shook his head. "We'd like a beer and a virgin margarita, and by the way...you look miserable. I can see you miss her, so why wait until tomorrow? Just get on with it. Woo her, apologize, grovel if necessary—just do it already so that everything can go back to normal. Well, new normal, that is."

Blake clenched his jaw. Peter had always read him well. The years together in the Teams created that kind of bond. He scoffed and flipped him off but secretly agreed with him. Shit, he really was done for.

"Hey, by the way, there's a massive horse trailer outside on your lot. There's a horse in it, too—I checked, you know. What's the story with that? You offer pony rides now?"

Blake sighed and ran his hand through his hair. "I know there's a fucking horse trailer outside my bar." He knew there was a horse in it, too—Jessie's horse. Blake had led it out of the trailer in the afternoon, watered and fed it, and even took it for a goddamn walk. He'd had no clue if that was what you did, but, since Jessie was out cold, he didn't get a chance to ask.

He pressed his eyes closed and pinched the bridge of his nose. "Jessie's here."

"She is? Where is she?" Peter turned and searched for her in the bar.

"She is out back. Fast asleep."

"Oh, guess we'll meet her tomorrow then. I think the last time I saw her was when the whole team visited your mom. Must be going on five years now. God, she had the energy levels of a live wire back then."

Blake remembered it. Those were good times.

Easier times.

"Actually, Jessie is pregnant."

Peter's eyes grew wide. "Are you shittin' me?" Then he chuckled. "Looks like babies are in your future a lot, Uncle/Daddy Blake."

Blake grimaced.

"Apparently, not so far future, too. She's like, huge, due in a month." Blake could feel a slight headache coming on.

He wasn't ready. He would never be ready.

"For real? Why is she visiting now? Shouldn't she stay home or something?"

"Yeah, well. Seems that Moon Lake is her new home, at least for now. At least until the baby is born and stuff. She broke up with her boyfriend and doesn't have a plan where she's going now. So, I just need a place for her fucking horse, and everything is settled. Any ideas?"

Peter shook his head with a thoughtful look. "Not at the top of my head. Let me think about it. You could build a shed behind your cabin, you know."

Blake shook his head. "I thought about that, but the horse can't stay in the trailer until then. I need a place right now to bridge the time."

Peter agreed, and there was silence while each man collected their thoughts.

Alan, who was still sitting at the bar, right next to Peter, cleared his throat. "Ahem, sorry for eavesdropping, boys, but I might have."

Blake looked at him, confused. "You might have what?"

"An idea." Alan chuckled. "See, there's this barn attached to my house. My predecessor had held some horses there, and the pastures are still fenced. I don't know if the fencing is any good anymore, but at least it's a start, right?"

The tension in Blake's stomach released as he scratched his jaw and then grinned at Alan.

He hadn't thought about the doc's home with its barn and pastures.

"That's a great start—thanks for the offer, Alan. Can I come by with Jessie tomorrow and check the place out?"

Alan nodded.

They agreed upon a time the next morning, and Blake sagged against the back of the bar with a shaky laugh.

That's why he settled here in Moon Lake.

That's what made this place so special.

Not the lake, or the mountains, or the forest.

It was the people. People who knew each other.

People who cared.

Lisa came back from the booth and slipped in front of Peter, who instantly wrapped his arm around her from behind.

Blake watched them. He remembered the night when Peter had nearly lost Lisa. Those were some hard and scary hours, but they made it through, together and were now happy.

"Do I get something to drink in this joint, or do I have to go elsewhere?" Lisa slapped her hands at the bar, and Blake jerked upright, effectively ending his musings.

He prepared her drink, and after drawing a beer for Peter, he checked the rest of the bar.

Nobody made eye contact, and it looked like Sharon had everything under control. He really had to get his head back into his work.

But he also knew he wouldn't be able to fully do so until he had cleaned up the mess his personal life had become.

He would get Jessie and her horse settled, and as soon as that was done, he would head over to Claire and beg for forgiveness.

Blake's stomach clenched when he thought about the baby, but it was months until then, so surely he would learn to deal with it.

Maybe even make peace with the situation.

Having Claire by his side would help.

He would be a dad and an uncle, and he couldn't hide or undo this, so he had to find a way to be okay with it.

Blake thought about his father's funeral. His mother hadn't talked to any of them for weeks after.

Nobody could understand why he did it, or how he did what he did.

At least he and Jessie had dealt with it okay.

He envisioned Paula, sitting in her chair, not able to move or talk or eat.

She hadn't dealt with it, okay, and that was a real risk.

He had to talk to someone.

Blake's eyes caught Alan in an animated discussion with his friend Caspar.

Maybe he should talk to him.

Alan would surely have the professional background to know the odds and get him some information and clarity about the issue. Maybe steer him to get professional help too.

Depression runs in families.

He remembered the day in the hospital vividly when the doctor who treated Paula said it.

Depression runs in families.

That was what Blake feared. That's what had made him determined not to have kids.

Too late now.

He would be a dad. And he would be the best fucking dad he could be.

17

She was half asleep watching the rom-com she'd chosen when she suddenly startled awake.

She thought she'd heard a noise. Maybe Lisa and Peter were back already.

She paused the movie, got up, and opened the door. "Hello?"

A cluttering sound from the office made her turn there. Why would Lisa be in the office at this time of night and without saying hello?

She crossed the corridor and stopped outside the door.

They usually locked the door so no guest could accidentally get in there.

Was it now?

What if it wasn't Lisa?

Claire's heart rate increased. She stopped breathing and listened.

There was someone in there.

She turned around as silently as possible, sneaked into the kitchen, and grabbed the biggest kitchen knife she could find.

She was pretty sure she wasn't alone in the house, even

though she should be.

Her pulse was pounding as if she'd just run a four-minute-mile.

But she needed to be sure.

It wasn't that long ago that Lisa had been kidnapped by a serial killer right outside in the parking lot.

Had she locked the doors?

She thought she did, but couldn't remember. How stupid!

But she wouldn't be stupid enough to become a victim ever again.

Her phone. She needed her phone.

Damn. It was still in the living room.

She tiptoed back to the living room, not once letting the door to the office out of her sight, and sighed when she reached her target. She locked the door, grabbed her phone, and called Lisa.

"Hey,"

She could hear the music in the background of her friend's voice.

"Lisa, I think there's someone in the office."

"My mom?"

"I don't think so."

"Fuck. Peter—"

Claire could hear the alarm in Lisa's voice.

"There's someone at the Inn. Claire's scared."

Lisa handed the phone to Peter because his voice came on next. "Where are you?"

"The living room."

"Make sure the door and windows are locked and don't move," he said.

Then nothing.

He'd kept the call connected, but all she could hear was background noise, mumbled voices, and footsteps.

18

Peter's alarmed eyes met Blake's across the room.

No words needed.

Immediately on high alert, he jumped over the bar and met him at the exit.

"Claire," Peter said.

Blake froze, then his mind went into overdrive.

Had something happened to her? What the hell? Was she having a miscarriage?

His eyes flipped over the people, then landed on Alan.

"Doc. We need you. And Caspar, can you take over the bar?"

He didn't even wait for an answer. Didn't give a fuck what happened to the bar. Instead, he followed Peter outside and jumped into his truck.

They waited until Alan was inside as well; Peter handed his phone to Lisa and floored it.

Blake held on, then breathed through his constricted throat. "What happened?"

"There's someone at the Inn."

"Inside?"

"Positive."

"Is Claire alone?"

"Yes."

"Where?"

"Locked inside the living room. Safe."

"You'll stay in the car," Peter told Lisa, who nodded.

"I can stay with her," Alan said.

Of course, he would. Even though Peter had mentioned a while ago how Alan had done a stint in the service. They'd never gotten the chance to talk about the doc's past.

But military trained, was military trained.

Peter called it in to the sheriff.

But if his friend thought he would wait, he was mistaken.

It took them about five minutes to get to the Inn. And another five for Peter and him to survey the outside while Lisa and Alan stayed in the truck.

All doors had been locked, but the window to the office had been open, which had his spidery senses lightened up.

"Possible entry point."

Peter nodded.

They peeked inside but couldn't make out any movement.

Was whoever had been there gone, or was he somewhere in the building?

Blake's breath quickened when he thought about Claire in danger, but his training took over immediately.

They entered through the kitchen door using Peter's key.

Next, they methodically cleared the ground floor. Thanks to their years of CQB—close quarter-battle—training, they moved from one room to the next like a well-oiled machine.

When they stopped outside the door to the locked office, Blake breathed a little easier.

Whoever broke into the office didn't get farther into the building.

They breached the door and cleared the room. The open window was causing the curtains to sway in the wind, and documents and papers were strewn everywhere.

As if someone had been searching for something and left in a hurry.

Fuck.

What the hell? He'd thought, after that serial killer went after Lisa, they were done with shit like this.

And now a break-in?

What the hell was going on?

Crime was not something that happened regularly here in Moon Lake.

They both cleared the upstairs before they gave the all-clear.

Peter went outside to fetch Lisa and Alan.

While Blake knocked on the living room.

"Claire, it's me. You can unlock the door now."

He heard the lock turn, and before he could prepare himself, the door crashed open, and Claire flew into his arms.

With a knife the size of a machete in her hand.

He grabbed her wrist and stopped her in midair.

"Wow, Claire. I know you hate me right now. But I don't deserve to die."

She hesitated for a split-second, looked at her hand as if she hadn't realized what she was holding, then let go of the knife, which cluttered to the floor.

He loosened his grip and pulled her against his chest and into his arms.

He sighed and breathed in her sweet scent, realizing how tense he'd been.

How tense he'd been ever since he left her standing at that pier.

Holy hell, what an asshole he'd been. And how he'd missed her.

He could feel her shudder against him and nuzzled her hair. "I got you, babe. And I'll never let anything happen to you. Promise."

"Claire." Lisa rushed toward them, and Claire immediately stepped back and embraced Lisa instead.

"It's okay. Everything's okay." Lisa murmured, probably trying to calm herself as much as her friend.

He instantly missed the physical contact, missed holding her in his arms.

A cold emptiness.

And it hammered home, even more, the one thing he already knew.

He'd messed up big time, but he would move heaven and earth to make things right between them.

To make her his again.

For real, this time.

19

Holy shit.

He giggled. Enjoyed the adrenaline flushing through his body.

That was a close one.

But it felt fucking fantastic.

Almost as good as when he was on a roll at the poker table.

Almost.

When he'd heard the car stop, he'd immediately got out.

What a rush.

He laughed again.

He'd jumped out the window and escaped.

Like a superhero.

His laugh subsided.

The stupid bitch had probably called the cops on him as she did on his dumb-ass brother.

And he'd learned nothing from the papers he'd shuffled through until he found the letter.

It had been unopened.

She didn't even know.

This would buy him time.

But he was running out of time.

He made his way through the wood and to his parked car.

If he'd had more time, he could get to her. Get her to give him what he deserved.

It would be a dangerous move, but the people he owed were far worse.

He started the car, eased it onto the highway, and then floored it—time for him to get as far away, as fast as he could.

But when he saw the flashing lights in his mirror, his breath hitched.

Shit.

The cops.

20

Blake looked at Jessie out of the corner of his eye before he glanced farther up the street through the windshield.

"The turn is up there, left-hand side. There's a sign too—you can't miss it."

He hummed and drummed with his fingers against his leg to the rhythm of the song that played in Jessie's top-notch car stereo.

Jessie looked well-rested. She'd slept on the couch the whole night, because he didn't want to wake her up.

And it didn't matter anyway since he hadn't slept a wink last night.

Once the sheriff had arrived at the Inn, they'd processed the scene. But nothing appeared stolen or missing.

And besides the brief moment, he'd had Claire in his arms. She ignored him completely for the rest of the time he'd been there.

Treated him as if he wasn't even there.

And he let her.

He sighed.

Nothing he didn't deserve.

At least coming back to the bar was a pleasant surprise.

Caspar, with the help of Julie, Holly, and Sharon, had managed just fine without him.

He stared outside and tilted his head until his neck cracked.

Tonight, he would sleep on the couch, and tomorrow he would set up camp at the cabin.

Jessie slowed down and took a wide turn at an open gate that displayed "Doc's Peak View Ranch" overhead. He looked back at the trailer, which rocked a little when they entered the gravel.

"The house is around that turn." Blake pointed forward as they passed the wooden gate that marked the beginning of the property. On both sides, wooden log fences hemmed in the gravel road, and it had a very ranch-like feeling.

"Is this a ranch?" Jessie asked, and Blake chuckled.

"As far as I know, it has been the doctor's office/hospital of Moon Lake for a long time, but the wife of the last one did a little ranching on the side. Mostly horses. She died of cancer a few years back, and the doc left town to go live with his daughter. This all happened before I came to Moon Lake, but the place and position stayed empty for a while before Alan finally came here."

Blake looked around. "Apparently, he was some hotshot doctor somewhere, before he decided to settle here. Nobody knows exactly what happened, for him to relocate but, we're lucky to have him. The next hospital is in Whitebrook—it's a half-hour drive there. So, make sure you tell us soon enough when the birth starts."

Jessie looked at him with a frown.

"What?" Blake's thoughts scrambled. What had he done now to deserve a frown? "We just need enough time to get there."

"Nothing, just"—Jessie swallowed—"I don't have a clue

how it feels when it starts. Now I'm afraid to not recognize it soon enough."

Great.

Blake wrinkled his brows. Now he was worried on top of being worried.

He had to talk to Alan about all of this delivery crap. Maybe he should find a room in Whitebrook for Jessie, preferably right next to the hospital.

Soon the house and, to the left of it, the barn came into view, and the pop and crunch of the gravel stopped when Jessie parked the car in front of the house next to a beat-blue suburban.

They both got out, and Jessie turned full circle before she grinned and bounced on her toes. Surprisingly nimble despite her belly.

"Wow, this place is huge—look at the barn and the pastures." She giggled.

Blake smiled at her but turned when the door opened.

Alan, dressed in a white coat, stepped out with one of the fishermen, who had his finger in a white bandage. They said goodbye on the doorstep, and Alan came toward them with a smile on his face.

Then he signed that he needed a second, turned on his heel, and peeled off his coat while climbing the stairs.

He disappeared for a second and reappeared without the coat.

"I'm Alan, and you must be Jessie." He extended his hand, and Jessie shook it and smiled at Alan.

Alan didn't pay any attention to her pregnant belly before he turned to Blake and shook his hand, as well.

"So, what do you think, Jessie?" He turned with a sweeping gesture. "Good enough for your horse?"

Jessie giggled, and Blake looked at her with narrowed eyes.

Giggling? Really?

"You got enough space for a small herd, Alan." Her flirty tone grated on Blake's nerves.

"Would you like a tour?" Alan asked, and Jessie immediately took him up on his offer.

They chatted animatedly with each other, and Blake slipped his hands in his pockets before he followed them at a distance.

He listened to the birdsong.

Soon it would stop when the first snow arrived.

He thought about the kid, up by his cabin. He had heard nothing from the sheriff, and Peter didn't mention it either when they last talked.

Of course, they had other, more significant problems then. Whatever was going on at the Inn, he didn't like it at all.

He just hoped his plans and apology later would get him out of the doghouse, so he could actually do something.

Like forcing her to live with him or move in with her.

He shook his head. Yeah, right. As if either Claire or Lisa would ever let him.

At least Peter stayed with them last night.

And they would find a way to ensure they were protected from now on.

Jessie and Alan entered the barn, and Blake experienced a moment of panic, adrenaline flushing his body, before he took a deep, calming breath and entered the darkness. He had entered too many buildings in his former career, not knowing what to expect on the inside, unable to not still feel the spike of adrenaline. Even though here, back home, it was completely unfounded.

Most of the time.

Blake's eyes adjusted slowly, and he watched Jessie enter a stall on the right side of the barn.

"The structure is sound—I had it checked when I moved in. The lady, that owns the construction company in Stone Valley, said it was still in good condition," Alan told Jessie.

"There's even a small room up there. Nothing fancy, just a bed, a desk, and a small oven." Alan pointed to a small stairway when Jessie reappeared at the stall's opening.

"You can get to the pastures through the back door. Shall we?" Alan led Jessie through the back door, and Blake huffed when Jessie looked at Alan with a smile.

They were mighty friendly for people who hadn't known each other five minutes ago.

Blake shuffled with his feet and followed them out back.

Outside, Blake touched one of the fence logs—the surface was hot and rough under his hand.

"There are some rotten logs, some loose nails too. But I'm sure Blake and I could replace them. Don't you think?" Alan turned toward Blake. "I haven't seen your new house yet, but I hear you are pretty proficient with wood and building and stuff."

Blake nodded and folded his arms across his chest. "Yeah, that shouldn't be a problem."

Jessie smiled at him, making him feel better.

"So, how much is the rent?" Jessie asked.

Alan blew out a long breath and then smiled at her. "Well, the situation is that I don't use the barn and the pastures at all, so I don't think I will actually charge you anything."

Jessie hesitated and bit her lip. "Well, that's nice of you, but I don't think it's fair. Horses cost money, so I'm okay to pay you."

Alan shook his head and laughed. "No, really, I don't want your money. It all sits here unused, so I'm glad if someone used it and kept it all in shape."

Blake pressed his lips together and started to disagree when Alan's phone rang.

Alan immediately took it out of his pocket and checked the display. "I'm sorry, I need to take this. You just continue to check things out." He turned and moved away from them before he answered the phone.

"You know, I can build you a small barn up at the house; there's even a meadow out back that we can fence. It would just take a week or two." Blake looked at Jessie. He could see the tension around her eyes, while she rubbed her forearm.

"Thanks, Blake, that's a sweet offer, but this all sits here empty; there is even a round pen back there." She pointed to the side of the barn. "It's too good to say no. I'll figure out the paying issue. I'm sure I can talk Alan into taking some rent money."

"But it's pretty isolated. And Alan's on the road a lot. If the horse was at the house, you wouldn't be alone. And you are in no condition to muck the stalls anymore. I can support you much better at the house." Blake wondered why he thought this was a good idea in the first place.

Yesterday the idea of having Jessie and the baby up at his house was daunting at best. Now the thought of her being here all alone didn't sit well with him either.

Jessie crossed her arms across her chest and passed by Blake. "I am not sick. I can take care of myself, Seb." She entered the barn again, and Blake followed her up the staircase to the small room. It wasn't more than what Alan had said. A bed, a desk, and a wood oven up here, but Jessie gasped as if it was covered in pure gold. "This is actually perfect."

Blake frowned, and his muscles went rigid. "No way in hell."

But Jessie had already turned and was on her way down the stairs, where Alan was smiling up at her. "Sorry to cut this short, but I gotta get going. So, what do you say? Are you taking me up on the offer?"

Jessie made her way down the stairs and extended her hand.

"I take you up on the offer, plus, I want to rent the room up there as well. And I mean rent as in money, and I won't take a freebie on this one."

Alan chuckled and shook her hand, while Blake stood at the top of the stairs, his jaw clenched, and his hands curled in tight fists.

She was being flirty. Always had been, always would be.

And Blake didn't like it at all. Never had.

Never would.

"Okay, I need to leave, but you just get comfortable. There are some hay bales in the last stall, but you have to check if it's safe to feed a horse."

Jessie nodded, and Alan waved them goodbye before leaving the barn.

"Let's move Tempo in here. Come on, Blake, I'll even let you lead him out of the trailer."

Blake descended the stairs slowly and shook his head, not too happy about how this all had transpired. Old impulsive Jessie. Never thinking anything through.

21

Claire's chest tightened as soon as Blake's jeep turned onto the Inn's parking lot.

She pushed the head of Cookie, Lisa's old Chinook mix, from her lap and slowly stood up from the steps leading to the Inn's kitchen.

What the hell was Blake doing here? When she was waiting for Lisa and Peter to pick her up for their dance lesson.

The silence that followed the stop of Blake's car jangled Claire's nerves.

She clenched her fists and had to make an effort to release them again when she stepped toward the jeep.

He'd been there for her last night.

She appreciated that.

Appreciated the brief moment he took her in his arms and made her feel safe.

But it didn't change a thing.

"What are you doing here?" She looked into Blake's face through the driver's side window. He offered her a smile, that faded as soon as he recognized her stormy mood.

"Lisa told me to pick you up. Didn't she tell you?" Blake's

eyes narrowed. "She said you agreed...to drive to White-brook together."

When realization dawned on Claire, she shook her head. Lisa had set her up. She fished her phone out of her handbag and dialed her number.

"Would you please come and pick me up?" Claire didn't hide the anger and hurt in her voice, and Lisa picked up on it instantly.

"I can't. We're already halfway to Whitebrook. We would never make it back in time for our dance lesson. And you two need time to talk, anyway."

"No, definitely not."

"Yes, you do."

"What a good friend you are, throwing me under the bus like that. Well then, I'll stay here. You don't need me there, anyway." Claire removed the phone from her ear a little to escape the whining.

"You promised you'd be my maid of honor, and I need my maid of honor, right here with me. So, please, suck it up and go with Blake. Don't talk to him, shout at him, I don't care. Just don't leave me alone in this; you know I can't dance for shit. I need your moral support, especially if Peter starts laughing at me."

Claire had a sinking feeling in her stomach.

Why she was such a sucker for her best friend, she had absolutely no clue. Maybe she should see a shrink about that.

Couldn't be very healthy behavior. She sighed and looked at Blake, who was staring at her the whole time.

She hadn't seen him for nearly a week—before yester-day. Had tried not to think of him and had failed miserably for every minute of every hour of those days.

She had mentally replayed their conversation over and

over in her head, but she wasn't able to figure out what she could have done differently to change the outcome.

Yes, their situation wasn't ideal, but accidents happened.

His reaction, though, wasn't rational.

And the man she thought she knew, the man she thought she'd been falling in love with, had always been rational in his opinions.

He might've been the least irrational man she'd ever known. But his reaction had been completely out there.

Claire considered any alternatives. She and Lisa didn't have a car. Moon Lake was a small town, and they took their bikes everywhere they needed to go. They could also always borrow Josephine's car, because she almost never needed it.

Never, just today.

Today, Josephine was out shopping for dresses for the wedding with Peter's mom, Mary.

Claire knew there was a bus to Whitebrook every hour, but she would never make it in time.

"Okay, but this was your last stunt like this. One more time, and you're in need of a new maid of honor." She ended the phone call and rounded the jeep, and hopped in.

In a few months, this wouldn't be so easy anymore.

"Thank you." Blake waited until she had fastened her seat belt before he turned the key in the ignition and made his way to the highway to Whitebrook.

Claire replied with a humming sound and looked out her window for the first couple of miles. She wouldn't talk to him.

But being this close to him was almost too much for her.

Her heart still hurt, and having him this near made breathing hard.

His clean scent, herbs, wood, and slightly lemony, enveloped her, and the drumming of his fingers, along with the music... it was so typically Blake.

It was all too much.

She thought about yesterday. Whoever had been inside the Inn, whatever he'd been searching for, they had no clue. They didn't found any fingerprints or other evidence. And Claire wasn't sure if she hadn't imagined it all.

But Blake had been there for her. Had taken her in his arms and calmed her down. Had stayed a while, even though she didn't acknowledge his presence.

"I owe you an apology." He paused slightly as if to make sure to find the right words. "I know I behaved like an ass. It wasn't fair to you, and I'm sorry." Blake looked at her, alternating his gaze between her and the road.

Claire's spine tensed, and her mind raced. She wasn't ready to forgive him. Maybe if she just ignored him, he would stop talking.

"I know I hurt you, and for that, I'm truly sorry. You deserve so much better. And I know that. What I said…I didn't mean to say those things. At least I didn't mean what I said. We're good together. Friends, a good team…and I know you didn't get pregnant on purpose and that it takes two for that to happen. I take full responsibility, and I'm sorry I freaked out on you like that."

Claire swallowed. She'd thought she'd come to terms with the hurt he'd inflicted.

Come to terms with them being over.

But talking about it, hearing his apology.

She closed her eyes, which made the tears brimming in her eyes spill over and run down her cheeks. She didn't think she could cry anymore, but here she was…again.

Blake took her hand in his, and his thumb played with the bracelet he'd bought her at a local fair they had visited together.

The green glass pieces, which the artist had collected at the shores of Moon Lake, were smoothed out by the lake, and Claire loved how its velvety surface felt on her skin.

Even though—not quite as good as Blake's rough finger caressing her skin right there felt.

Damn.

His voice choked up when he started to speak again. "Can you forgive me? Please. I want to make this work. I need to make us work." He swallowed. "I missed you so damn much. Missed talking to you. Holding you in my arms."

He paused. "We're a family now, so please, Claire. Can you forgive what happened and give me a second chance? I'll do whatever it takes."

Claire felt a flutter in her belly and moved her hand there.

Holy shit.

She started laughing and crying at the same time, and Blake looked at her with a confused frown. "Is that a yes, or should I continue? I have this whole thing planned out. I'll soften you up now and win you over by overwhelming you with my superb dancing skills later. I'm just not entirely confident my dancing skills are up to par. And if you're already laughing at me now..."

Claire shook her head and laughed even more.

Heat radiated through her chest, and sheer happiness had her warm and tingly.

She couldn't imagine Blake dancing. Sure he had rhythm. But he was also six foot six with 260 pounds of muscle, and his feet compared to hers, were enormous.

So, he didn't have the physique of a dancer, and Claire cracked up at the thought of him making a pirouette in tights.

But those images weren't the only reason for the intense feelings of happiness radiating through her body.

"The baby just moved."

"What?"

"I just felt a flutter." Claire grabbed Blake's hand and led it to her belly.

They waited for a minute, but sadly, the movement had stopped.

Blake looked at her in utter astonishment mixed with rapid blinking, and Claire chuckled again. "Look at the street, Blake."

"But...what...isn't this, kinda early?"

"No, it's okay, normal."

Blake kept his hand on her belly for the rest of the drive and

Soon after, they arrived at the parking lot of the dance studio.

Blake killed the engine but didn't move, still stunned and rendered silent by what happened.

It took him a while to get his act together, and Claire watched, fascinated, how he visibly pulled himself together.

"So, Claire," Blake turned toward her, his eyes serious. "Will you dance with me?"

She watched his Adam's apple bob up and down with his swallow and smiled.

Why did she suddenly have the feeling it was high school all over again? She leaned forward and kissed him on the lips. Just a sweet, short peck. "I will dance with you, but you better not step on my toes, mister."

They both smiled at each other. And Blake acknowledged her request with a slow "Yes, ma'am." Then he signaled for her to stay in the car before he exited.

Lisa and Peter were already waiting for them at the entrance of the dance studio.

Lisa's pinched expression changed into raised eyebrows and a questioning gaze when Blake helped

Claire out of the car, and they held hands all the way toward them.

Peter grinned and slapped Blake on the back before he kissed Claire's cheek. "So, everything okay between the two of you? Because you better be ready to get your ass kicked at ballroom dancing."

Claire looked at Lisa before they both shook their heads. How could it be that almost everything between those two guys ended up in a competition?

Blake chuckled. "Dream on, buddy. I grew up with two sisters. You have no idea."

Claire's eyes widened.

She hadn't believed he was serious about his dancing comment earlier, but maybe she was in for a surprise.

Also, she had seen Peter dancing, and he looked like Claire envisioned a brown bear dancing.

They entered the studio, and after a lengthy training session, where they learned the steps individually, they finally came to the part where they paired up to dance.

And, holy crap, the man had serious moves.

He held her in his arms and led her over the dance floor with sure steps.

Claire felt like floating most of the time, and her fear of missing the steps vanished with his strong lead.

Their eyes locked and stayed that way until the song ended. She felt safe in his arms—safe and secure, and Claire's heart fluttered.

Maybe everything would be all right.

The chemistry was strong between them.

They could make it work.

Claire could feel the heat of his hand on her back permeating through the T-shirt, and his familiar smell surrounded her.

They were nearly at the end of their session when the

door opened, and hooting and hollering broke the spell. Blake's step faltered, and Claire looked at the three men who had entered the room. She knew that the boys would arrive today. Lucas Ford, Christopher Thomas, and Reynaldo Vico. She remembered their names from when they last visited in the summer. They couldn't stay long then, and Claire hadn't really got to know them beyond their names. This time was different. They would stay at the Inn for a week until after the wedding. So maybe this time, she would have time to get to know them better.

Their dance teacher stopped the music and ended their lesson, and Blake kissed her hand before he embraced her and kissed her on her forehead. "Thank you for the dance, ma'am."

Claire chuckled. "You're a great dancer. Something to look forward to at the wedding." She smiled.

Just hours ago, she had dreaded the wedding, but maybe he deserved a second chance. And apparently, she had it in her to forgive him after all.

She rose on tiptoes to kiss Blake on his lips, and as soon as their lips met, he swooped her up and cradled her head in one hand, her ass in the other, while deepening the kiss.

The hooting and hollering resurged, and Claire and Blake both laughed before he released her, and they made their way toward his friends.

22

"Hey, you think he will like her?" Blake watched Christopher "Phantom" Thomas peek into the opened trunk of his Jeep, then up at his teammate Reynaldo "Rage" Vico, who stood next to him. They both chuckled and did a fist bump.

Blake pushed Phantom aside and grabbed a case of beer. "Get going, boys. Hey, Rage, could you inflate the doll?" It was so easy to fall back into their team dynamics.

Phantom, Rage, Motor, Steel, Blaze. They'd been on so many missions together. Had shared highs and lows and everything in between. And developed a brotherhood so tight. No distance in the world could end it.

He turned toward the open front door of his new cabin.

He'd finished the kitchen last week and moved in just yesterday.

The boys wanted to see it, so they'd decided to celebrate Peter's bachelor party up here and not at the bar.

"Hey, Blake, why the hell's your back door ajar?" Peter had been the first to enter the house and blocked the entrance.

Blake looked over Peter's shoulder toward the back door.

"Shit, I left it unlocked on purpose in case the boy needed some food; he's obviously not so good at closing doors behind him. I hope we haven't caught him in the act again."

He put down the case. "Hey, check if there's still food on the table. I left some cookies, bread, and apples for him." He stretched his neck but wasn't able to look past Peter at the table. "Is it still there?"

Peter walked into the house. "Nope, the apples are, but no bread and no cookies." Peter went to the back door and looked left and right before he stepped back in and closed it.

"Have you checked in with Travers—did he find anything?" Peter turned, but Blake shook his head. "No, but I got a picture of the boy, and gave it to the Sheriff yesterday —maybe this helps to identify him."

Peter raised his eyebrows. "You caught him on film— why didn't you snag him?"

Blake grabbed the case again. "Trail cam. The kid's sneaky—wouldn't go near this place if I were here. But he didn't catch the cam—neither did you, by the way. Getting old, Steel." Blake chuckled and pointed at a camera above the back door on his way to the kitchen. "Got him when he left."

After setting down the case, he took a copy of the photo from a shelf and handed it to Peter.

"Hey, nice house. You did this all by yourself?" Phantom entered the house with another case and looked around before he made a beeline for the kitchen and whistled through his teeth. "Never pegged you for a handyman, but really, I'm impressed."

He opened the fridge and started piling bottles in there. "A little small for a family, though."

Blake spun around and scowled at Peter. "You told them?"

Peter grinned. "Well, they're family. They deserve to know."

Blake twisted his mouth into a soured expression. "Asshole," he said before turning his back on Peter.

Rage entered and struggled with the sex doll on the way in. "Hey, Peter, guess this is yours." He threw the doll at Peter, who reached for it reluctantly.

"And the little one for you," Lucas "Motor" Ford, who entered the house behind Rage, said and threw a little redheaded toy doll at Blake, who caught it in midair.

Blake felt a stiffness in his neck when he looked down at the doll in his hand. "What the fuck is that?" He looked up at Rage, then at Lucas, who handed him a pack of diapers.

"There are two ways of doing something—the right way and again. Remember?" Lucas said and grinned at Blake, his familiar gap between his front teeth showing.

Blake looked at the diapers in his left hand and the doll in his right and chuckled after connecting the dots. "And we don't rise to the level of our expectations; we fall to the level of our training." He shook his head. Who would've thought training would ever entail putting a diaper on a fucking doll. "Thanks, guys."

Then their attention shifted to Peter, who held the sex doll like it was contagious. "Same for you, eh, Steel." Phantom chuckled and slapped his hand against his thigh.

"And, now that you're gettin' married, your sex life will probably suffer, so you can keep a go-to alternative in your closet," Blake added, bringing out more laughter.

Except for Peter, who looked at the doll more closely and furrowed his brows.

"We ordered her, especially for you, sent them a picture of Lisa too—made sure that it matches your type," Rage said with a straight face, and Peter looked at him with an incredulous stare.

"Are you shitting me?" he burst out, and the other men in the room laughed even harder, happy not to be in Peter's position.

After Blake and Peter put their respective dolls next to each other on the couch and grabbed their first beer, Peter looked at the picture of the kid again.

"I know the boy. He looks familiar. I just can't put my finger on it."

Blake's heartbeat sped up. "You sure?"

"Yep, I don't know exactly. Gotta think about it." He handed the photograph back to Blake, who glanced at it, before he put it back on the shelf. He turned around, leaned against the kitchen counter, and observed Lucas, who had started a fire in the fireplace, and stared at it.

Motor, they'd called him in the Teams, because he could fix and hot-wire any vehicle he stumbled across.

Which saved their asses more than once on missions when something, as it usually did, didn't go according to plan.

Lucas was being unusually quiet. He wasn't as loud and obnoxious as Phantom even on his best day. But Blake had never seen him that subdued. He wasn't laughing as hard as the others. And he hadn't really joined in the banter that was just part of how they operated.

The fire was burning hot, and Blake wasn't sure if there was enough wood on the porch to keep it going through the evening; he stepped out to check and found Rage sitting in one of the lawn chairs nursing a beer.

"Hey, Vic, everything all right?" Blake leaned against the rail and watched Rage take a sip.

"Yep, I'm good. Smells like snow."

Blake clenched his jaw and nodded. There wasn't much time left before the first snow would fall. The mountaintops were already white, and it was only a matter of weeks before winter would be here.

A sense of urgency welled up inside him.

He had to catch the boy before then. It was freaking cold in winter. Too cold to be homeless and live in the woods.

Even though he didn't know the circumstances, he could feel it in his bones. The way the boy behaved like a deer. His clothes that were far too small for him and dirty and ripped. This boy wasn't living in a home. "I need to get to the boy, get him to safety before it falls. I don't have a good feeling about him."

Vico stared at him without saying a word and, after a sharp nod, took another sip. "Got a plan?"

Blake's stomach tensed, and he grimaced. "Not tonight," he said with a slight shake of his head. He paused for a moment, calculating his next question. "I also have a bad feeling about Motor." Blake looked through the window inside the house and watched Lucas, who still stood and stared into the fire. "What's wrong?"

Vico sighed and crossed his arms. "Last deployment. There was this boy. Local. He hung around the camp a lot. Motor took him under his wings, and did some repairs with him. They just hung around together. We were there only a week. But they made a connection. One day the boy showed up at camp. Tears streaming down his face. He'd been rigged up with a suicide vest." Vico sighed and didn't elaborate on what happened next.

Sadly, he didn't need to. Blake knew. Even without words.

"Lucas...he didn't deal with it well...thinks it's his fault for befriending the boy. Making him a target, you know. He's been brooding ever since. Shut down and quiet, keeps to himself a lot. I think he might be ready to get out."

Blake's eyebrows rose.

War was hard on everyone involved. Especially the innocent who were trapped in a world of hate and violence. And sometimes exploited for evil means. Those stayed with you. Took a piece of you with them, especially if you let them under your skin. He sighed, and Vico took a sip.

"What about you? Becoming a dad? Didn't you always tell us you never wanted children? Thought it too risky. What changed?"

Blake grimaced and then pressed his lips together. The boys knew him, knew his family history. Vico better than the others. He had always been the one everyone talked to if they had troubles.

"It just happened. Not planned or anything. I'm still struggling with the whole concept. But I still got a few months to figure it out."

Vico nodded. "Does she know? Your family shit, I mean?"

Blake's stomach tightened. "Nope...at least not yet." Blake gave a self-deprecating laugh. "Still got that talk to look forward to. Don't I?"

"Yeah, I feel you, man." They both took a sip, and Blake thought about their dancing lesson earlier today. They were good again—solid. He'd missed her this last week. Even though a small part of him still couldn't let go of the feeling of being trapped. Anger about having his whole outlook in life changed.

"Hey, how's your family doing, anyway?" Vico asked and interrupted Blake's thoughts.

"Good, they're doing good. Jessie's here in Moon Lake. Arrived a few days ago. Plus, she's pregnant. Like, really pregnant."

Vico's eyes widened. "You shitting me—is there something in the water around here?" "We better keep our dicks in our pants then. Just to make sure."

Blake raised one eyebrow and gave Vico a glassy stare. "Keeping it in your pants might be a good strategy. But, obviously, Jessie got pregnant, well before she arrived here."

"Thanks for the biology lesson, professor." Vico took another sip. "So, you're going to be an uncle and a father at the same time? That's hilarious." He turned in his chair and opened the front door with his foot.

"Hey, boys, Jessie's here in Moon Lake and pregnant too." His shouting brought Chris and Lucas out to the porch, and Vico chuckled about Blake's pinched expression.

"Don't look so pissed. You know we all fell in love with her, back when we visited your family."

Blake opened his mouth, but Vico stopped him with a gesture. "You made it perfectly clear she's off limits to any of us. So...save it."

Blake shut his mouth, and Peter chuckled.

"Can we meet her?" Chris asked, and Blake shook his head and stared at his shoes.

"She'll be at the wedding, won't she?" Peter asked, and Blake nodded.

"She's living in a barn with her horse right now," Peter added, and all the eyebrows shot up.

"Wow, you are an exceptionally shitty brother, dude," Lucas said, and Blake cringed under the stares of the others.

"I didn't have a say in it, but maybe now that the house is ready, I can convince her to move back into the flat behind the bar."

They all nodded and went inside again to get another beer.

Blake stayed outside a moment longer.

He loved his peace and quiet, but he needed to take care of Jessie, Claire, and the boy.

Their well-being was his responsibility.

His duty.

So he would do everything in his power to take care of them. He left the porch and rounded the house to a small barn he'd just started to build. There, under a tarp, was the material he needed to make two baby cribs.

His family would have a place in his home.

And he would be there for those kids.

Physical and emotional.

He wouldn't shirk his responsibility...not like his own father.

23

Blake loosened his collar with his finger and looked from the kissing couple, in front of the arch, and the smiling minister to Claire on the other side.

Her beautiful dark green bridesmaid dress flattered her womanly curves, and the wreath in her wavy hair, the same one Lisa wore, matched the flowers of the two bouquets in Claire's hand.

She looked freaking beautiful.

A gust of wind made the last colorful leaves rain down on the meadow behind the Inn where the ceremonious part of the wedding took place.

Blake looked at the sky. The weather was holding out, but the wind was picking up, and he was relieved the rest of the festivities would take place inside the Inn.

He turned his eyes back to Claire again, who had started crying.

Why the hell was she crying?

He left his place next to Peter and stepped forward, only to get entangled in all the family and friends who rushed toward the bride and groom like a tide.

He found Claire surrounded by his uniformed friends and nudged Phantom with his elbow to get to her.

"Everything okay?" He put his arm around her shoulders and shot Lucas and Rage a dirty look.

His.

She was his.

Rage looked him up and down, and mischief twinkled in his eyes. Blake just knew they would give him shit.

"So, James Bond, sir. What do you want us to do now?"

He chuckled and glanced down at his tailored tux, which made him feel like a slightly rugged version of James Bond. At least Steel looked the same.

"Grab the chairs—take them into the breakfast room, will ya."

The three of them nodded and turned toward the now empty rows of chairs sitting on the lawn.

He turned back to Claire and cradled her face in his hands. "Everything okay, babe?"

Claire gave him a watery smile and nodded.

"I just got emotional. They're beautiful together. I'm so happy for them."

He turned toward the couple, and they both watched them smiling and talking to the surrounding people congratulating them.

"Yeah. They deserve this. Had a hard enough time gettin' here."

Claire hummed in agreement, and Blake pulled her against his chest.

He enjoyed their newfound intimacy. Even though it was still fragile.

"Let's get inside and make sure everything's ready for them."

Claire nodded, and they made their way toward the Inn.

He stopped when his eyes fell on Jessie being embraced

by Rage and took Claire's hand. "I didn't get the chance before, but it's high time for you to meet someone." He pulled her toward Jessie and stopped right in front of her. He tapped Rage on the shoulder. "Ahem, excuse me."

Rage turned and smiled sheepishly. "Oh, big brother is watching me."

He stepped to the side, grabbed the stack of chairs, and proceeded toward the Inn.

"Claire, meet Jessie, my sister. Jessie, this is Claire."

Claire's eyes went huge when they darted to Jessie's baby bump, but she caught herself, lifted her eyes, and thrust out her hand. "Nice to meet you, Jessie. Your brother talks about you a lot."

Jessie chuckled and shook Claire's hand. "Not as much as he talks about you. And obviously, he didn't tell you I was pregnant."

Claire smiled at Jessie. "Yep, he didn't say a word."

Claire punched Blake in the arm.

He shrugged. "Didn't get the chance."

"Tsk," Claire said and shook her head in disdain before she turned back to Jessie. "Love the dress."

Blake looked down at Jessie's flowery dress. It was loose and layered, so it flowed all around her, but even that couldn't conceal her pregnancy.

Jessie smiled too. "Thank you. Not that I had much choice; this is the only one that is stretchy and wide enough to still fit. So..." She shrugged. "Your dress is astonishing. This rich emerald color suits you. And the wreath is so cute. I always thought I wanted a summer wedding, but now I can see the appeal of having a fall wedding."

His sister wanted a summer wedding.

News to him.

Claire nodded and then tilted her head to the side. "So,

I'm sorry I'm nosy, and you can totally blow me off if you don't wanna answer, but how far along are you?"

Blake loved how Claire sounded so sincere and encouraging and like she really cared at the same time.

He could see in Jessie's genuine smile she didn't feel uneasy at all.

Blake put his hands in his pocket and settled in, happy to just watch the two women in his life hitting it off.

"I'm due in a month. Even though I have the feeling I'm not ready."

A flush crept across Jessie's cheeks, and Claire instantly clasped her hand. "Oh, I'm sure every mother feels that way before the baby is born."

"She's staying here until then."

Claire turned to him. "Of course she does."

Then she turned back to Jessie. "Do you have all the stuff you need? Maybe we could go shopping next week. I'm sure Lisa wants to come too—maybe Julie and Holly, as well. This way, you could get to know the girls, and we could get some things you still need."

Jessie's face transformed into a slow smile, and her eyes started shining. "I would love that." Then her smile disappeared. "But won't Lisa be away on her honeymoon?"

Claire shook her head. "The wife of Peter's boss just died, and another colleague was injured a few weeks ago, so it isn't a good time for Peter to take time off work right now." Claire shrugged. "So they have postponed it to the spring." She grasped Jessie's arm. "See. You can get to know all of us at once. It'll be great."

Blake looked toward the lake; he hated the insecurity in his sister's voice. He should've introduced her earlier. Made sure she settled in okay. He squeezed Claire's hand, grateful she and Jessie kinda hit it off.

There was so much going on in his life, and it felt like he

was dropping balls left and right.

First with not knowing about Jessie's pregnancy, then with how he treated Claire.

He had to up his game, because the way he was showing up right now.

He shook his head.

Not good enough.

From the corner of his eye, he caught Peter waving at him. The wedding photographer stood next to him and Lisa, so it must be time for the wedding pictures.

Lisa and Peter wanted one with him and Claire in it, so he cut the conversation short. "Hey, Jess. Why don't you go inside, get some orange juice, and find your seat? Just relax a little. Claire and I are needed for some photos, and then we have to check on some things. But we'll meet you inside in no time, okay?"

Jessie's face fell a little.

Blake had insisted that she accompany him to this wedding, even though she didn't know anyone in Moon Lake and didn't want to go.

At least Lisa, had her seated at the table with the boys, so she would have someone she knew to keep her company.

"Hey, Jessie, care to join me? I was just about to go in, and get something to drink." Alan joined their group and offered Jessie his arm.

She immediately linked arms with Alan and smiled up at him. "Well then, see you later."

Blake narrowed his eyes and watched them turn toward the entrance of the Inn.

Those two were awfully cozy with each other.

Too cozy.

He turned to Claire when she linked their arms together and steered him toward where Lisa and Peter were already posing to get their wedding pictures taken.

But before they arrived, the other couple, she stopped, turned to him, and hit him in the chest. "Holy shit, why didn't you tell me? I was so shocked I stared at her like an idiot."

He shook his head and then shrugged. She knew exactly why he hadn't told her, why they hadn't talked. And the last couple of days, wedding stuff took over everything.

"Seriously, why didn't you say something?"

Blake kept silent.

He didn't want to bring up the weeks when they'd had no communication because of his dumb-ass behavior.

Claire looked at him, and her smile dimmed.

Blake sighed. "Radio silence. That's why. But I'm sorry, I really am. It was all my fault, and you had every right to be angry."

Claire poked her tongue into her cheek and inhaled a long breath. "It's okay, Blake. We can talk about what happened. The future is what counts. So, when did she arrive? And how is it you didn't tell me she was pregnant before when you told me about her?"

Blake closed his eyes and shook his head before he grabbed Claire and pulled her against him. He caressed her cheek and smiled down at her. "You're the best person I know." Then he kissed her.

In the middle of the meadow, with wedding guests all around them.

But he didn't care.

This was the mother of his future child, and not only that, but Claire was great in so many aspects.

He ended the kiss with a sigh, and the sudden feeling of lightness in his chest stunned him.

"Well." Claire touched her lips as if she could still feel the kiss. "That was nice, very nice...but that doesn't get you off the hook—your sister, here, pregnant. Start talking."

Blake chuckled. "Not much of a story. She showed up at the bar two weeks ago. Like that."

He shook his head. "I didn't know she was pregnant, neither did Mom. She and her boyfriend split. She decided to move and ended up here."

"Does she live with you? At the bar?"

Blake looked over Claire's shoulder at Mrs. Reynolds and Mrs. Brooks, who stood chatting at the entrance of the Inn. How Claire didn't hear any of this was beyond him.

Moon Lake was a small town.

In small towns, people talked.

The last two weeks, Blake felt like every single one of the locals had come into the bar and squeezed him for information on Jessie. He shook his head and concentrated on Claire again. "She lives at Alan's."

Claire's eyebrows shot up. "Alan's as in Alan Radley MD, Alan's?"

Blake nodded. "I told you she's a horse trainer, didn't I?" When Claire nodded, he kept on talking. "She has a horse of her own. Brought it with her and needed a barn for it. Alan's house has one attached that he didn't use, so he offered, and she accepted. Sadly, it came with a small flat. And that's where she's staying."

Claire cocked her head and grinned. "You don't like it, do you?"

Blake pursed his lips. Claire knew him well. "No, especially since I've moved into the house, so the flat behind the bar is empty. But she refuses to leave. Stubborn woman."

This stunned Claire. "The house is done? And you've moved in already."

A sadness slipped over her face but was gone before he could address it.

Then she turned and hurried toward Peter and Lisa. "Let's get those pictures taken."

24

The reception was in full swing, toasts were being made, and Peter and Lisa's wedding dance had been a complete success. Blake leaned against the bar set up in the far left corner of the breakfast room and watched Claire, who was talking to Holly, Julie, and Jessie.

They looked like they were having fun.

But ever since the photo shoot, Claire had been distant to him all through the afternoon.

Blake set down his beer and marched toward her.

Enough.

He'd had enough of them not talking.

Something was bothering her, and he wouldn't risk losing her again after they had just reconciled.

He needed her in his life.

He needed to take care of her.

Needed to fix this. "Would you dance with me?"

The chatter stopped short when he didn't wait for an answer but lifted Claire into his arms and carried her toward the small dance floor. Thank God the band played a slow song because he needed to hold her near.

Her eyes were stormy, and her body rigid when he let her down. "What was that?"

"What?"

"You can't just grab me and carry me to wherever."

He grinned and raised a single eyebrow, then he leaned forward and whispered in her ear. "I can't?"

She sighed and leaned back. "Blake."

He squeezed his eyes for a second and swallowed. "I know you're angry with me. I know I'm at fault. I'm just not entirely sure what happened to cause it. What did I do wrong this time?"

Claire tensed up even more but then sighed and relaxed in his arms. "I'm not angry at you, just...sad. So much happened in the last few weeks, and I wasn't part of any of it. Your sister arrived, and you finished the house and moved. It's just. I hate that, you know?"

He leaned his chin against her forehead and sighed.

He knew the feeling.

He'd found himself wanting to talk to her numerous times. Just talk about the little things that were going on in his life.

Somehow their "taking it easy" had transformed into her being an integral part of his life. Talking to her an integral part of his day.

Without him even realizing it, she'd become his sounding board, his confidant.

"I'm sorry."

Her arms slung around him and they started swaying with the music.

"I know. It's just. It's hard."

He nodded and kissed her forehead, then took her face in his hands. "Promise me from now on we'll talk. Whatever it is. If I piss you off. If I'm being insensitive. Promise me you'll tell me when something isn't right."

She nodded and then smiled.

And he breathed easier. Whatever this was. Whatever the weird status of their relationship right now. He would do everything in his power to make her as happy as he could.

"We're going to be okay. Promise." He smiled down at her and she mirrored his smile.

"And I can't wait to show you the house. It still needs work, of course, but I'm getting there."

"When will you show me?"

"How about now? You up to leave this party? Accompany me home?"

They looked each other deep in the eyes and left the dance floor, and the Inn before the song had even ended.

25

Claire looked out the side window into the pitch-black surroundings of trees.

It should be a full moon tonight, but no light other than the headlights of Blake's Jeep penetrated the thick canopy of the forest.

She swallowed rapidly and turned her face toward Blake.

The dashboard illuminated his face, and as if he could feel her looking at him, he looked at her before concentrating on the road again.

"Wow, this is remote. It never seemed that far in daylight." She had visited the construction sites several times over the summer, but it never seemed that far off the highway.

"It's not. Linear distance it's only a few miles off the highway. But in darkness and with the winding roads, it feels a lot longer."

Claire hummed in agreement and turned to face the window again. She crossed her arms over her belly to suppress the butterflies in her stomach. She shouldn't be this nervous. This was Blake, for God's sake.

They'd had a relationship for months. It shouldn't feel like the first time, but somehow it did. Claire scoffed at herself and wracked her mind for a safe topic of conversation.

"So, you have electricity and all that?"

God, she was so lame.

But Blake chuckled and touched her thigh briefly. "Yeah, got electricity, running water, indoor plumbing. I might like it simple, but I spent enough time in shitholes to want comfort for the rest of my life."

Claire inhaled.

The rest of his life.

He really would be around her and their kid a lot, if they both stayed in Moon Lake.

When they arrived at the house, the security lights went on, and suddenly the oppressive feeling, she had experienced just moments earlier, gave way to awe.

Claire stepped out of the car and walked toward the porch. "It's beautiful, Blake." She loved the lawn chairs on the porch and the wooden exterior.

Blake opened the front door and turned on the lights inside, making it appear even cozier. She could perfectly picture herself in this house.

Even before she ever set foot inside.

When she did step inside, the nervousness returned. She wiped her clammy hands on her dress and immediately crossed her arms.

Blake was already in the kitchen. He'd ditched the jacket on the way and had opened his dress shirt as if he couldn't wait to get out of it.

He and Peter had looked quite dashing today. She'd never seen any one of them this put together, and let's face it, they had looked sexy as hell in their tuxedos.

But not as sexy as Blake looked now, half-undressed. His unruly hair falling into his face.

"Can I get you something to drink? I got that blackcurrant juice you're so fond of."

Claire swallowed and nodded. "That would be great, thank you." Hopefully, she wouldn't spill it all over her beautiful dress.

She followed Blake into the kitchen and slid her hand over the smooth surface of the cupboards.

The open design was perfect for the small cabin.

The arrangement of the appliances provided enough space, and the little bar opposite the stovetop would enable the cook to talk with the guests while cooking.

It was a kitchen right out of her dreams, and Claire looked at Blake from the corner of her eyes.

She couldn't remember them ever talking about kitchen appliances or layouts, but it was so close to her perfect kitchen, it was uncanny.

Blake handed her the glass, and she took one of the bar stools while Blake leaned back against the kitchen counter.

The way he looked at her made Claire's heartbeat start racing.

She hated feeling awkward, but Blake seemed relaxed enough, even though he devoured her with his eyes, so Claire took a deep breath and forced herself to relax too. Then she spotted the picture of a boy behind his shoulders. "Who's that?" She nodded toward the photograph, and he looked over his shoulder before turning back to face her.

"A kid that comes here sometimes. I'm afraid he might live in the woods or something, but I got it covered. I got the sheriff involved to find his identity, and I leave the back door open in case he needs food or shelter."

Claire nodded.

He was a good man—caring.

Even if he didn't want to be involved in something, he just couldn't step away if someone was in need.

Was it the same way with her?

If his initial reaction was any indicator, he really didn't want a family, so then why was she here? And why did he give her that look like he wanted to devour her? That look that made her feel all hot and bothered?

Was it just his overdeveloped need to take care of her that made him change his mind?

She didn't want to think about this right now. It had been a beautiful day, and they were finally on stable ground again. Maybe she shouldn't sabotage this thing before it even started again.

This whole issue was something they had to address sooner rather than later, but maybe just not today.

"So"—Claire tilted her head to the side and blinked—"about that tour of the house I came here for. Will you just stare at me, or will you actually make good on your promise?"

Blake's lips split with a slow smile; he took a sip from his bottle and straightened himself. "Your wish is my command." With a gallant swipe of his arm, he offered for her to precede him. "Shall we start at the front door again, so you get the whole experience?" Blake joked, and Claire laughed when she made the few steps to the front door again before they both turned toward the living area.

Upon entering the house through the front door, Claire immediately faced the whole floor.

Dividing the room was a waist-high stone wall that ended halfway into the room at a huge, round fireplace.

In the living room, to the right was a huge and comfy sofa, and to the left, a dining table and the open-plan kitchen.

The open floor plan made the interior appear huge,

even though this level couldn't be over three, maybe four hundred square feet.

Right at the left side of the entrance was a small walk-in closet that served as a wardrobe and was the only closed-off space on the ground floor.

"When did you finish all of this?"

Blake smiled, but his smile was a little rough around the edges. "I had a lot to think about, and I do my best thinking while working."

Claire nodded but let it drop.

No use in mulling over it again and again.

She'd decided to forgive him, so rehashing his behavior wouldn't help.

Claire rounded the fireplace and crossed the living area, and tried to open the door there. It was closed.

"Garage and barn through there, maybe even a mudroom—just not yet. Back door. Back porch not ready," Blake said and pointed to the door at the back wall of the house.

Claire nodded. Blake had shown her the plans of the house when he started, but seeing it come to life was amazing.

"I'll finish the back porch next spring. Don't need it during winter."

"It's amazing, Blake."

Blake shrugged. "Not very glamorous, but it suits me."

It suited him.

Yes, Claire could definitely see that, even though the three entrances into the house puzzled her a little. "It's great —cozy. And I love your kitchen." Claire smiled at Blake, who beamed back at her.

They passed the kitchen and entered a staircase to the left and two more doors to the right.

Blake pointed to one door. "Toilet." Then he opened the other door.

Claire peeked through the door into a huge finished bathroom with white tiles, a huge tub, an even more enormous shower, and a sink.

Utilitarian, but also comfortably big enough for his large frame.

Blake closed the door again. "Do you want to go upstairs?" He touched her at the small of her back, and shivers ran over her body.

A simple touch that caused her to feel more, to want more.

He steered her toward the stairs. His hand resting on the small of her back. Heat radiating outwards, warming her and infusing her core with tingly warmth.

Her body clearly wanted him, was ready for him.

But what about her heart? And her head?

Was she ready to truly forget everything that had happened?

They still hadn't really talked about their future, about them.

They hadn't talked, period.

And this right now—this—was evidence of that fact.

There hadn't been an upstairs when he'd explained the plans to her. How could he have changed so much in such a short time? "Upstairs? Since when is there an upstairs?"

She looked at Blake, expecting him to somehow explain how he'd missed telling her so much about his house.

"It was a last-minute decision. Peter introduced me to Tara a few weeks back. She owns a construction company in Stone Valley. Some of her men helped me with the roof, and she suggested I raise the roof a little and transform the attic into a second floor. It's not a lot more space, because of the inclinations of the roof, of course, but it actually turned out pretty cool."

He watched her. "It's my bedroom."

He still watched her.

Waited.

He was good that way. Saying a lot without saying anything.

It was an unspoken invitation.

Or maybe it was a blatant one. But he wanted her to know. Wanted her to decide if she was ready to take that step.

Was she?

Ready?

Only one way to find out.

26

She climbed the stairs in front of him and entered the upstairs room. It really wasn't huge by any means, but there it was.

A new bed. A big one.

Not the old one from the bar.

Claire stared at it, a heavy lust settled in her stomach.

She could feel Blake's breath on the fine hairs on her neck. Would he kiss her?

Did she want him to kiss her?

Even though they hadn't really talked about the baby, about how their future would look like?

Claire looked down, then toward the bed again, and closed her eyes.

He wrapped his arms around her from behind, and she leaned back against his muscular frame.

Familiar, safe.

Then he whispered in her ear. "If this is not what you want, we could just go back down and relax on the sofa, maybe play a board game. Just say the word." He kissed the side of her neck, and Claire's muscles went liquid.

She wanted this, him.

Maybe it wasn't the best idea, to have sex with Blake. They still had a lot of issues to talk about, but not now.

Now she wanted this right here. Feel like only he could make her feel.

The sex between them had always been off the charts, and she'd missed it, missed him.

She turned her head to the side to give Blake more access and exhaled, then inhaled deeply—his scent of cologne and starch and uniquely Blake enveloped her.

He pressed his already hard dick against her backside, and she groaned when he nibbled at her ear.

Goosebumps rose on her arms, and she turned around to get her hands on his body, as well.

She struggled with opening the buttons on his dress shirt, and a sigh of relief escaped her lips when she finally made contact with his chest and hard abs.

Finally.

She kissed her way down his skin and nibbled on his abs before going lower.

For a moment, he threaded his hands in her hair and groaned.

He never lasted long in relinquishing control to her before his dominant side took over, and this time wasn't any different.

But having him moan under her ministrations was a heady feeling.

She looked up, and their eyes met.

The fire in his sent a zing right to her core.

God, how she loved how only he could make her feel of being the sole focus of his attention.

He pulled her up and, with a soft nudge and a deep, wet kiss, steered her backward toward the bed.

She was damp already.

He bunched her satiny dress in his fingers and slipped

his hands beneath the fabric. Dragging it slowly, inch by inch, up, torturing both of them.

Her insides clenched, and she closed her eyes.

"God, you're beautiful. I love your skin. Soft as silk," he growled, before he slid the dress over her head.

Her bra followed so fast, she didn't even feel him open it, and when he gently lay her down on the bed, Claire opened her eyes.

Their gazes met, his eyes hot and dark, staring directly at her.

He settled his right knee between her legs, and his gaze moved slowly down her body to her belly.

They both froze.

Her hands flew to her cute little bump, which was clearly visible by now.

Blake hadn't seen her naked ever since the reality of her pregnancy sank in, and the dress had been perfect for concealing her rounded stomach.

"Don't..."

Blake's piercing glance shot up to meet hers, and he swallowed—hard. "You changed your mind?"

Claire's mind raced a mile a minute. No, she hadn't changed her mind. It was just... "I'm already showing," she blurted out.

Blake tilted his head to the side, but never lost eye contact. "I can see that."

He was still holding her loosely at her sides, his thumbs stroking her in little unhurried circles along her hips.

Wow, that felt amazing. "But"—she struggled to voice her convoluted feelings—"I mean...I want to...but..."

Blake clenched his jaw, his Adam's apple bobbing up and down, then he kissed her nose before his face changed into a mask of determination.

He sat back on his heel, leaned down, pulled her left

hand from her belly, and kissed the palm. He repeated the move with her right hand and slowly directed them above her head. His face hovered just inches above Claire's. "Keep them there, 'kay?"

Claire just nodded, completely enthralled by his rough, sexy voice even though her heartbeat raced.

He kissed both her eyelids, her nose, and her lips on the way down. He stroked along the outside of her breast, and Claire's core clenched.

Then he scooted down and just stared at her bump; he touched it with his hands, caressed it, tentatively at first, but soon his hands grew more confident, and his lips joined in.

She gradually relaxed, watching him.

He worshipped her body, her bump, with so much care it made her choke up.

He did that for an extended amount of time, and Claire watched in awe. Then he looked up into her eyes, and she could see a myriad of feelings in his eyes.

Longing, love but torment as well, which left her wondering.

What was behind that? Why was he struggling so much with them having a baby?

"You're beautiful, perfect," he said, before he slipped lower until his mouth was level with her sex.

Claire groaned when his lips met her core, and her hands instinctively grabbed his hair. All thoughts flew out of her mind, and she could only focus on this, him, and the fantastic feelings he so expertly drew out of her.

He had her teetering on the brink in seconds, but expertly kept her there. Always backing off, when she was on the verge of orgasm.

"Blake," she groaned.

Blake intensified the lascivious strokes of his tongue,

paired with just the right suction from his lips, again, but this time he didn't back off, and she came with a sigh.

He slowly made his way up her body, lined up with her body, then hesitated.

"I haven't been with anyone, since... you know."

She opened her eyes. What was he getting at?

"And since you're already pregnant..." he shrugged, then gave her a lopsided grin.

Protection, he was talking about protection. They'd both got tested and ditched using condoms some time ago when they decided to give this friends-with-benefits thing a serious shot, including exclusivity.

Of course, back then, she'd thought she couldn't get pregnant.

And look how wrong she was about that.

Claire looked into his eyes, pulled him upward, and kissed him.

He pulled back. His face hovering inches over hers. "So we're good?"

Claire nodded. "We're good."

They kissed, and what had started as an exquisite little kiss to end a potentially awkward moment turned into more...so much more.

His kisses, sometimes rough and sometimes impossibly sweet, took over her thoughts and body. His fingers played with her, spread her wetness.

And when he finally slid inside of her, deliciously stretched her, there was only feeling left. Feelings of exhilaration, feelings of safety, feelings of love.

She loved him.

For a moment, panic squeezed her chest.

Love made you vulnerable and weak.

Blake must've felt the shift in her because he stopped, looked at her, and raised a single eyebrow in question.

And she relaxed.

This alone.

His awareness of what she was feeling, and thinking.

He was nothing like any other man she'd ever met.

Blake cared, deeply.

Falling in love with him was probably the stupidest thing ever.

It would lead to heartbreak.

But she loved him.

Against their agreement and despite everything.

The thought that he might never feel the same hurt, but whatever his feelings, he'd always put her safety and well-being above everything else.

He put her wants and needs above his own and always cared for her.

He treated her better than any other man ever had.

And she would trust that.

Yes, they needed to talk.

But not now.

Now was the time to feel.

She turned her head and ran her tongue up and down a prominent vein on his forearm. Then she bit him.

His growl made her core squeeze.

And he hissed.

"You wanna play?"

She looked up at him and grinned.

He leaned down. "Tell me what you need." His whispering against her ear made her shiver.

"More."

"More?"

She nodded. "Give it to me."

He nuzzled her neck, intertwined their fingers above her head, and they fell back into the familiar rhythm.

He made love to her like only he could. Rough, then

gentle. Brought her to the brink of orgasm again and again, only to keep her suspended there. A testament to his restraint.

He was a bear of a man. Raw power, barely contained. Dominant, demanding. Wringing everything out of her.

It was deliciously familiar, but also different.

Whenever he was a little too rough, or grabbed her a little harder, he caught himself, slowed down, and became impossibly sweet and caring again.

So unlike him.

And it was driving her insane.

She had to tell him she wouldn't break...later...

But now she needed to come.

She laid her hands on his cheeks. "Now, Blake."

He raised his eyebrow. "Are you being bossy?"

"Hell yeah, and if you don't make me come right now, I'm taking over."

His smile deepened, and it appeared he was contemplating that possibility.

Claire squeezed her core again, and his focus snapped back to her.

"You're playing dirty."

She chuckled. "Well, isn't that the whole point of this?"

His grin was almost evil when he increased his speed, and thrust inside, deep, hard, deliciously stretching her.

Sweat beaded on his forehead, and all she could do was surrender, rock against him, and hold on for the magnificent ride until he pushed her right over the edge into a shattering orgasm.

He buried himself into her one last time before he followed her with a low grunt.

It was hours later, and Blake was fast asleep, wrapped around her when Claire lay awake in bed next to him.

His deep, rhythmic breaths had a calming effect on her,

and she caressed his tattoo of a Spartan warrior, which was illuminated by the moonlight falling through the window.

But her mind circled back to the torment in his eyes. What the hell was wrong with him?

There was something he hadn't told her. And Claire was pretty sure it was something significant.

27

Claire pushed her bike against the wall of the doctor's office. Images of the day she was here last time made her stop for a minute.

Her pregnancy had been a real shock, but so much had changed since. She still got frightened sometimes, but more often, she couldn't wait for the baby to come.

She climbed the first step of the stairs before she thought better. Jessie didn't live in the house with Alan. She would be in the barn.

She turned and, on her way to the side of the house, passed her bike. There was a gust of wind, and Claire pressed her jacket against her.

This was quite possibly the last day she could ride her bike before winter settled in. The weather forecast had reported snow tomorrow.

Claire turned the corner, and before seeing them, she heard laughter—a man's and a woman's.

Jessie and Alan sat on a bench, hidden in between piles of wood, against the wall of the main house.

"Hello," Claire stepped into their view.

They both looked up at her, Jessie still smiling.

Alan jumped up like he'd been caught, then narrowed his eyes. "Hey Claire, what a surprise. Did we have an appointment?" He took a step toward her. "Is something wrong?"

She could hear the concern in his voice, smiled, and shook her head. "No. I'm here to visit friends, not my doctor."

Jessie's face split into a broad smile. "How nice of you to come all the way out here. Come, take a seat."

Alan hovered until Claire sat down next to Jessie.

She smiled up at him.

"How about some tea—can I get you a cup?"

"That would be nice," she said and nodded, and Alan turned toward the house.

She wasn't a big tea drinker, but at least it would warm up her fingers, which had frozen on the ride here, despite wearing gloves.

She watched Jessie, who looked at Alan's retreating back.

Claire's followed Jessie's eyes until Alan turned the corner.

They had been mighty cozy together when she arrived; was there more going on between the two of them?

More than friendship?

It would be good for Alan. He'd shown some interest in Lisa in the summer, but they had no chemistry—according to Lisa—and then Peter staked his claim.

"So, you and Alan…" Claire pointed with her finger back and forth, and wiggled her brows.

Jessie just laughed. "No," she sighed. "He's just being nice to me. He's concerned about me out in the barn alone and wants me to move into the house when the baby is born."

Claire's eyes widened. "I thought there was a flat built into the barn."

"More a room, and heating in winter will be a problem. That's why Alan thinks it isn't a good idea once the baby arrives and winter is here."

She chuckled. "More like he demands me move in with him."

"A room in a barn." Claire frowned. "I'm sorry. If I'd known, I would have offered it earlier—you can come live with us at the Inn. I'm sure Lisa has no problem with that, and we have room enough for you and the baby."

Jessie laid her hand on Claire's thigh. "Thank you for your kind offer. Blake wants me to move into his old flat. But I really like it here, and I think I can manage."

Claire wasn't so sure about that, but she would address this topic another time.

Jessie sipped from her tea, and Claire got the feeling there was something on her mind.

"So, you're dating Sebastian," Jessie said with a stern voice.

Claire's eyebrows shot up, and a flush crept over her cheekbones. "Well, yes...I mean...I hope that's okay for you." She was a grown-up woman—why did she suddenly feel like a teenager again?

Jessie laughed and shook her head. "Gotcha. You should've seen your face." She giggled. "I'm just making fun of you. Of course, it's okay. You're both adults. None of my business."

Claire exhaled slowly. She really thought Jessie would somehow be against them dating.

"How long have you been together?" Jessie asked, and Claire shifted around nervously.

"We've only been casually dating for, I don't know, maybe four months. It's more a friends-with-benefits thing."

Jessie chuckled. "Friends-with-benefits, yep, that sounds like my brother. Ever since he's grown up, he's always been...

let's go with averse to serious relationships. Maybe it's because we were too clingy after Dad died. Even Mom depended heavily on him until we got it together again."

Claire felt her heartbeat slow down. Blake had never told her of his father's death, but she hadn't talked about the difficult topics in her past, as well, so she couldn't fault him for that. She leaned a little toward Jessie.

"I'm sorry for your loss. I didn't know your dad died."

Jessie blinked repeatedly and bit her lip. "It's okay. It was a long time ago. It's just come up again now, with the pregnancy. My emotions really are just hovering under the surface, and there's always a possibility of tears and irrational behavior. It's just..."

Jessie hesitated. "Our family story is shit. So if I go too deep, I always end up crying."

Jessie's face fell, and Claire frantically searched for a topic so the other woman wouldn't start crying.

"I'm pregnant too," Claire blurted out, then snapped her mouth shut.

This was not what she wanted to say.

She hadn't yet decided if and when she would tell other people, and sure as hell, she didn't plan to throw this information at Jessie when she was fighting with tears.

Too Late.

"I'm sorry. I didn't mean... I just wanted to tell you, I get the emotions. And stuff." Claire fizzled out.

She cringed at the uncomfortable silence her outbreak caused.

"Is it Seb's?" Jessie asked after a while, and Claire swallowed before she nodded.

"Wow."

Jessie didn't say anything else. Her reaction concerned Claire, and she searched for signs of clarification in the face of the other woman.

There were none.

Seb and his sister had a superb poker face going.

Her chest tightened, and she shuffled her restless legs.

Her gaze darted from the barn to the pastures to her own feet on the gravel. "I'm sorry, I didn't..."

This was shit.

She hadn't usually had problems with verbal diarrhea. Why now? Why didn't she just keep her mouth shut?

Jessie must've recognized her nervousness because her mouth turned into a big smile, and she grabbed Claire and hugged her. "Congratulations, Claire. Wow, I'm thrilled for you guys."

Claire's body relaxed, and she took a deep breath after the claustrophobic feeling in her chest left.

"I never thought Seb would think of kids of his own, not after Dad, and Paula. Not after he took what the doctor said so hard. But it's great."

She squeezed Claire once more. "Good for him. And my little boy won't be alone growing up. He'll have a cousin the same age right here."

Claire smiled back at Jessie while her mind raced. Dad, and Paula? What did the doctor say? And why hadn't Blake ever told much about his family?

Claire knew Paula needed constant nursing and that Blake's mom was providing it, but he never elaborated on what had happened.

Should she ask Jessie?

Maybe it all tied together; maybe then she would understand Blake's issues a little better, but on the other side of it...no, she wouldn't go behind Blake's back.

She should talk to Blake.

Ask him about all this stuff. And she needed to talk to him about her past too.

About all the things he didn't know.

Claire stopped her fidgeting hands and focused back on Jessie, who was still smiling and sipping her tea.

"It's a boy then—do you know the name yet?" Claire asked.

They both looked up when Alan came around the corner with two cups of tea in his hands. He handed one to Claire and settled in front of them on a tree trunk turned chopping block. "So, do you want company, or do I need to leave you two alone?"

Claire smiled, and Jessie laughed. "You're such a dork. Of course, we want your precious company. We were talking babies."

Alan's eyebrows shot up, and he looked at Claire, who confirmed it with a nod.

"So, do you have a name yet?" Claire repeated the question, and Jessie looked down and twisted her hands. "Not yet. I have a few, that I mull around in my head. But I haven't decided yet."

"Did you do some kind of Lamaze class or anything, you know, to prepare for birth or something?"

Claire wished she hadn't asked as soon as she recognized the panic on Jessie's face and wracked her brain to calm the other woman down. "Not that you absolutely need to. I just wondered, because we don't have such a thing here in Moon Lake, and I thought I would just skip it," Claire rambled.

Shit, why did she say that?

Jessie was still the picture of misery.

"You don't need any of this." Alan laid his hand on Jessie's knee.

"Just read the book we bought, and you will be plenty prepared. No reason to beat yourself up about anything."

Claire pressed her hand to the sinking feeling in her

stomach, and her gaze ping-ponged between Alan and Jessie. Why hadn't she just shut her mouth?

Alan made eye contact and just shook his head. Not in a 'why have you asked such a stupid question' kind of way but in a 'she'll be all right' fashion.

Jessie pressed her lips together in a slight grimace. "I feel like I'm the worst mother ever, and the baby isn't even born yet."

Claire shook her head. "No, you're not. You will be a great mom. Do you know why?"

Jessie looked up slowly with a questioning gaze.

"I know that because you care. That's the single most important thing to being a good mother. To care for your little boy. To care for his well-being, and to care for his happiness. If you do just that, you will be a better mother than many other children get. And look at you. You upped your life to give your boy a good environment to grow up in. You're already a good mother. And the whole birth thing will go as it goes, you'll see."

Jessie's eyes filled with tears, and she pressed her hand against her trembling lips before she grabbed Claire's hand. "Thank you. You will be a good mom too."

Claire swallowed.

She wasn't so sure about that, though.

She hadn't been in the past.

If she'd been a better mom, Anna would still be alive, wouldn't she?

But she'd gotten a second chance. A chance to do it again. A chance to prove that she could be a good mom.

And maybe, just maybe, Blake would see it as a chance too.

28

"Hey, there's my girl." Blake entered the kitchen of the Inn and closed the back door immediately.

Today was a cold one; it had snowed only a little during the night, but the temperatures had dropped to a whopping twenty degrees. It was only early afternoon, but the light was fading fast.

Winter was officially here.

Claire turned toward him from the counter and smiled.

She was in the middle of baking something. Blake looked at the small baby bump that stretched her shirt and the flour, that was all over the shirt. She must have had a batch already in the oven because the delicious smells of buttery sweetness permeated the air. He hung his jacket on to the rack next to the door and crossed the room.

The kiss was a quick one. "Don't get any of the flour on my clothes—I'm dressed for work already."

Claire laughed, and he loved the sound of it.

"I just need a second to finish this, okay?"

Blake smiled at her softly. He loved watching her when she was doing her thing. "So why do you think they want to meet?" He'd gotten a text from Peter, who had asked to meet him this afternoon at the Inn.

Claire shrugged her shoulders and turned back toward the counter. "No clue. Lisa wouldn't tell me. Hey"—she turned around again and pointed toward the coffee maker with her finger that was covered in dough—"help yourself, will you? And could you pour me a glass of water, while you're at it?" She turned back to her dough, and Blake focused on the task at hand. He took down Claire's favorite mug and prepared her tea before he did the same with his coffee.

He liked how they were back on solid ground.

Easy and fun.

He'd missed this; he had missed Claire's kindness and their companionship. He kissed Claire's neck on the way to the breakfast nook, and she giggled in reaction.

Then the door that connected the kitchen to the rest of the Inn opened. Blake spun around and watched Peter and Lisa step inside.

Blake blinked and examined them. They were holding hands, but they both smiled and looked relaxed, so Blake relaxed too. "Hey, you two."

They greeted him back, and he put his coffee and Claire's tea on the table and turned toward the coffee maker. "Can I get you two a coffee?" He fetched two more cups.

"Yes, please," Peter said, but Lisa instead went to Blake's side and selected a tea for herself, which she handed him before she went back to Peter, who had settled at the table. "Thanks, Blake."

Meanwhile, Claire had exchanged the cookie sheets in the oven and brought a plate full of hot cookies to the table, where she settled opposite Lisa and Peter.

"So, what did you wanna talk about?" Blake asked and bit into a cookie.

He moaned.

It was delicious, even though it was hot enough to burn his mouth. "Those are delicious, baby." He turned to Claire, and they smiled at each other and kissed.

Everything else fell away when he was kissing his woman.

His woman.

His responsibility.

She smiled at him and he lost himself in her eyes, until Peter cleared his throat.

Only then did both Claire and him turn back to Lisa and Peter.

Lisa grabbed Peter's hand and took a deep breath. "We're pregnant. And we wanted you to be the first to know."

A smile split her face, and Peter grinned from ear to ear.

Claire jumped up, squealed, and pulled Lisa off her chair and into an embrace. They both jumped through the room, hugging each other and screeching like little girls.

Infectious, happy little girls.

Blake stood up, as well, and rounded the table where Peter mimicked his movement.

They shook hands, both somewhat serious, until they both cracked up, hugged each other, and patted each other on the back. "Wow, you're not one for wasting time, are you?"

Peter grinned. "When you know, you know. No need to delay anything. Plus, we've already lost decades. We're not getting any younger."

Blake nodded and grinned while he returned to his seat.

He sipped from his cup and watched the girls, and his smile wavered.

Peter and Lisa would be great parents. Their kid really would be lucky.

He looked at Claire's bump again. He'd made his peace with becoming a father, but...

He looked back at Peter, who was also watching the girls; Peter's face shone of happiness and pride, both things Blake didn't feel when he thought about becoming a father.

Blake lowered his brows and, after contemplating his feelings, or lack thereof, rubbed his face.

Shit.

The girls sat down again, and Peter pulled Lisa to his side and laid his other hand on her belly; they looked at each other and shared a small smile.

Blake felt a prickling of his scalp and glanced quickly at Claire, who stared at him, before he stared back at the dark remnants of cold coffee in his cup. She had been watching him and she hadn't looked happy. Did she know about his conflicted feelings?

A knot built in Blake's stomach. He took another cookie, even though he didn't want it, and avoided looking at Claire again. Luckily that wasn't hard to do.

Peter and especially Lisa's chatter filled the void for the time being.

"We got an ultrasound, and the baby is the size of a plum. Look how cute." Lisa handed the picture first to Claire, and when it was Blake's turn to take it, he hesitated.

Then Blake looked at the ultrasound picture, and all air left his body like a deflating balloon.

Claire hadn't shown him any ultrasound pictures of their child. He swallowed hard.

He really was as shitty as his dad had been, not caring about anyone but himself.

He'd been so busy seducing Claire they hadn't even talked about their future.

Maybe Claire and the baby would be better off without him.

Maybe the baby would turn out better if she raised it alone, if he had no negative influence on its life.

Blake's throat closed up, and he forced a breath through it, and another.

His heart raced, and cold sweat trickled down his spine.

He had to get out of there.

It took him a second to connect the ringing in his ears with the phone in his pocket, and, after looking at the display, he murmured something like an apology to Claire and Lisa before he shot up, jerked his jacket off the rack, and rushed out the back door to take the call.

From the corner of his eye he could see Claire's solemn face. He also got a glimpse of Peter's face, his pinched mouth and hard expression telling him everything he needed to know.

He was a damaged piece of shit.

Not worth such great friends and not worth the love of a woman like Claire and the love of a child.

He walked toward the parking space while he called back the unknown number. A small, red, beat-up car entered the gravel lot of the Inn and stopped with screeching brakes.

Julie Brooks hopped out of the car and floated, more than walked toward the Inn. She passed him with a quirky wave that made Blake nearly smile back at her.

Moon Lake really was the home of some original folks.

He startled when a female voice answered the phone.

"Hey, Blake, I'm glad you called back. I wanted to take you up on that dinner. Would tonight be okay?"

"Oookay." Blake frowned. Who the hell was on the other side of the line? He knew the voice; he just couldn't place it. Dinner. Was there any woman he had promised dinner? There hadn't been another woman in his life besides Claire for the better half of this year. Which made this quite possibly his longest relationship, in like—ever.

He shook his head to get his mind back to the caller, who laughed into his ear.

"You don't know who I am, do you?"

She laughed again, and the image of a resolute young woman rushed into Blake's mind. Tara, that's who he'd promised dinner to.

"Tara, tonight would be perfect. There will be a table for you."

He ended the call and looked at the back door.

Blake rubbed his neck.

He had to get back in there.

Had to get a grip on his fucked up emotions.

He owed it to Claire and to their relationship. Even though all he wanted was to get away as fast and as far as possible.

When Blake entered the kitchen, the atmosphere had changed completely.

Everybody was happy, relaxed, and there was a heated conversation going on.

Blake walked toward the counter and joined Peter, who watched the women over his steaming cup of coffee.

"Julie here got herself her first high-profile client. Hockey Player. Will come here for rehab and not only from an injury. Apparently, he'll be staying at the Inn and working with Julie at her new PT center."

Blake's eyebrows shot up, and Peter chuckled. "Formerly known as the garage of the Brook's residence. Julie and Paul's dad are working on it as we speak."

Blake contemplated this new information. A hockey player? Staying at the Inn? "Who's the guy?"

Peter shrugged his shoulders. "Julie wouldn't say. But.

My best guess? Most likely one of Paul's teammates. And the only one in the news about substance abuse on top of rehab for his blown-out knees is the goalie of the Hamilton Hailstorms, Kevin Reyes. But he'll arrive in a few weeks, so we'll see soon enough."

Peter took a sip from his cup, swallowed, and cleared his throat.

"You gotta get a grip, you know."

He looked at Blake sideways, and his voice was so low, Blake could hardly hear him, so nobody else would understand what he said.

Blake swallowed, his Adam's apple bobbing up and down. "I know. I'm just…"

Peter turned to him and gripped Blake's forearm. Hard. "Look. I know you got it tougher than most. I know you struggle with your whole family disaster. But this kid is happening, and if you don't get your shit together, you will not be part of its life, or Claire's."

His body tensed as he looked down at Peter's hand and then up at his best friend. "Let go."

Peter sighed, let go, and leaned back against the counter. "Do more research. Talk to Alan, get a fucking therapist, but for Christ's sake, Blake, get your friggin' mind right. You're hurting Claire, and you're hurting your baby. And quite frankly, this might just be the happiest time of our lives, and you're fucking it up for all of us." Peter took another sip and then poured the rest into the sink.

Blake stood rooted on the spot; his anger had subsided as fast as it had flared.

He looked at Claire, who was still in deep conversation with Julie and Lisa, a smile constantly on her lips and her eyes glued to her friends.

She deserved to be happy.

His kid deserved to be happy.

He deserved to be happy.

Blake rubbed his chest, right where the pain was back, with full vigor.

He needed to deal with his shit.

And he needed to do it now.

29

"Thank you for taking the time to see me. I'm sorry for your loss." Claire shook hands with Sheriff Travers as soon as they met just outside the sheriff's office. He looked pale, and she could see the grief that had etched itself into his face.

"No, problem. Thank you. It was a long fight. Theresa was ready to go." He shook his head. It was obvious to Claire that his wife's death had hit him hard, no matter the circumstances. News in town was that she'd had lung cancer for a long time. She died two days before Peter's and Lisa's wedding—the reason why the sheriff didn't attend the wedding and why Peter and Lisa had postponed their honeymoon.

Sheriff Travers opened the door and invited her inside. Claire hadn't been inside a police station for a long time. And even back then, they had visited her in the hospital more often than she'd been at the station.

The sheriff led her through the open floor plan of the front office to his small office right at the back, past a very surprised-looking Peter, who jumped up and stormed toward them, but stopped short when the sheriff closed the door in his face.

"So, Miss Gunterson. What can I do for you? Is this about the break-in?"

She'd called earlier to make this appointment. She looked toward the door. Maybe this was a mistake. Her heart raced, and she rubbed her ice-cold fingers.

"Ahem. I want to—" Claire took a deep breath. "I want to make inquiries about my ex-husband."

Sheriff Travers's eyebrows shot up and he stopped for a split-second, before he continued to sit down behind his desk. "Why would you do that via the Sheriff's Department?"

Claire's face turned red. "Well, the officer who handled my case back then, he actually told me if I ever needed to, I should go through official channels."

Sheriff Travers nodded and opened a small notebook. "So, I need his name, your name at the time, the place where you lived, and a date." He looked up at Claire, and a muscle twitched below his left eye. "I know this is extremely personal and you don't have to answer, but...what happened?"

Claire immediately stopped the replay of the events in her mind. Some people's minds blocked out the bad, so they couldn't remember, but that never happened to her. She could still recall the whole day her world nearly ended in glaringly bright colors... She remembered everything, until she blacked out. Claire shifted in her seat. "My ex-husband, Jeff, and I married right out of high school. My mother wasn't"—Claire hesitated—"able to raise me, so I lived with my granddad for a while and was glad to escape the first chance I got."

The sheriff nodded and scribbled something in his notebook.

"Jeff was pretty popular in high school, but he drank a lot. Then he lost his job, and then another one. Drinking

173

was the only thing he did consistently. I worked as a server at a restaurant in the afternoon and evening and in a bakery in the mornings. Both belonged to the same grumpy, old owner. He taught me how to cook and bake and constantly fed my mind with business books." She smiled at the memory of old Mr. Soothers.

"Home life became worse and worse; the abuse started verbally at first. Jeff belittled me for everything I did. Then, after a while, he turned physical. He was always so sorry after it happened. Made promises, even quit drinking for a few days, but then the pattern would repeat itself. We lived in a little town, so everybody knew what was going on."

"So, you were eighteen?"

"We both were."

The Sheriff pushed his notebook toward Claire. "Can you please write down your old address?"

Claire did as he asked and returned the notebook. Sheriff Travers studied it for a split-second, before he looked up at Claire. "Gunterson your maiden name?"

Claire nodded. "His name is Bellows, Jeff Bellows."

Sheriff Travers wrote that down. "Then, what happened?"

"Then I got pregnant. I didn't plan for it. It was the worst possible timing, but it got me going. It took me a while, but when I started to feel the baby, it gave me the strength I needed." She smiled. For the first time in her life she knew she deserved better, and she knew she would do everything for her baby.

"I made plans to leave him. I had my bags packed one evening, ready to leave. I don't know why, but he came home early. He knocked me around, smashed my head against the wall, and kicked me in the belly. At least that's what the doctors told me." She hadn't felt that kick, had no recollection of what happened after her head had hit the wall.

"And that's what they wrote in the police report. I lost my child that night, and I nearly lost my life. After that everything's a little hazy. The hospital staff and police were extremely helpful. I got a permanent protective order. Then a divorce. Then I packed my bags and took a job in a hotel in the Caribbean, where I trained to be a cook. I didn't care for anything, only that it was as far away as possible. I think he went to jail, but I didn't wait around. I worked there for some years and afterward I signed on a cruise ship as a cook. That's where I met Lisa. And then, we came here early summer."

Claire took a deep breath and looked from her hands, which were clutching her purse, to the sheriff, who was scribbling into his notebook. The sheriff finished writing and looked up at her. His eyes were soft when they darted to her belly and back to her face again.

"You're pregnant again."

Claire swallowed and nodded.

"That's why you want to know?"

Claire nodded again. "I need to play it absolutely safe. I just need to know where he is. Nothing else."

"Did he ever contact you again?"

Claire shook her head. "But I was far away, then. Now I'm within reach again, and—I just want to make sure."

"Do you think the break-in could've been in connection to him?"

My head jerked back, and my breath caught.

I'd never even thought of this.

I shook my head. "I don't know, but I don't think he'd had any motive."

"Did anything suspicious happen since?"

I shook my head. Apart from the emotional rollercoaster Blake and I had been on, nothing had happened.

The Sheriff nodded and snapped his notebook shut. "I

will make some inquiries. But I want you to know that it could stir up unwanted attention. Wake up any sleeping dogs. Are you sure you want to do this?"

Claire shifted in her seat, unable to get comfortable. The walls seemed to close in on her, and her chest tightened. Did she really want to know? Did she want to risk it? Wasn't it better to just hide and hope for the best?

Stop.

Hiding was what she'd done before. Hoping everything would turn out okay. Somehow. She'd waited too long. She wouldn't make the same mistake a second time.

This time she would be proactive. Claire nodded once and tightened her fists. "I'm absolutely sure I want to know about his whereabouts. I'm done hiding. I'm not that person anymore."

She stood up and Sheriff Travers mirrored her movement. They shook hands, and the sheriff nodded.

"You are a fighter. Good for you. Maybe you should now go talk to Peter, because the way he's hovering outside the office, he needs some kind of story for your visit today."

Claire turned around and watched Peter read some report just outside the glass panels that divided the small office from the main office.

Then he looked up with his eyebrows drawn, and Claire could see the questions on his face as well as the determination. He wouldn't stop bothering her, until she gave him a good enough reason for her being here.

Claire turned back to the sheriff and thanked him again before she grabbed her jacket and opened the door.

Peter had strong protective instincts.

Claire loved that every time she saw them in action around her best friend. But Blake was the same way.

Duty, responsibility, honor, protection.

That's what made them the men they were. But was it

the same thing that made Blake stay with her even though she could see him struggle?

Even though Claire had the strong feeling he'd rather leave.

Maybe that was the only reason why he came back to her. Because of his honor and sense of duty, not because he wanted to or because she was what made him happy.

Claire came to a standstill right in front of Peter, who had discarded the file and leaned against the desk with his arm crossed in front of his chest. "Talk! My shift has just ended."

She deliberately softened her pinched lips and gave him a sharp nod. "You can give me a ride home, while we do."

He bowed and pointed his arm to the back door of the office, his actions in stark contrast to his piercing eyes and clenched jaw. "Or, better yet, why don't I give you a ride to the bar, while we talk, because I'm pretty sure there's more to say than a simple chat."

Claire raised one eyebrow and gave him a glassy stare.

Peter stared back at her. Not mean or anything. Just firm, unmovable, and silent.

She knew the type.

Blake was the type.

In fact, she fell in love with the type.

Claire sighed heavily and focused her gaze on the door at the back of the office, where Peter, with his hand behind her back, carefully pushed her forward.

He was unmovable, silent, and pushy—she'd forgotten pushy.

Claire stopped.

She hated being pushed. She looked up at Peter and saw the silent plea in his eyes that got her moving again.

On the other side she loved the motivation behind his

actions. Peter always cared for all of them and wanted them to be okay.

As did Blake.

She gave a sharp nod and Peter led her to a parking lot at the back side of the building and toward his car.

They left the parking lot in silence and drove to Moon Lake.

Claire cleared her throat before she started talking. "It's about something that happened in my past. Nothing that affects the present or the future. But I needed to be sure—that's why I had a chat with the sheriff. I'll talk to Blake about it. But—" Claire hesitated "—I need to tell Blake before I tell you, so you have to wait."

She looked at Peter who was concentrating on the streets and driving. The silence ticked Claire off and she wracked her brain for something more to say. "Look, I was married, it had gone bad, very bad—that's all I can say right now."

Peter exhaled and shot her a look. "Okay, good enough for now. But you need to talk to Blake about it."

Claire nodded and looked out of the window.

She had to talk to Blake, not only about her ex but also about their relationship. And Blake's motives. She didn't want Blake to force himself into something he just didn't feel.

He was a good man.

A man who honored his commitments. But she didn't want to be just a commitment.

She wanted to be the love of his life. She wanted him to love her just as much as she loved him. She wanted an unshakable and mind-blowing love affair.

And a family.

That's what she deserved. That's what she'd promised herself: she wouldn't settle for less. Not for lukewarm affection. Not for the sensible thing.

But she feared the outcome of that conversation.

And she could feel her heart breaking a little, just thinking about the possibilities.

If she told Blake all of this, it might be too much, and he might retreat.

Maybe at first, he would even try to give her all of that. But gaging from his reaction to Peter and Lisa's news, there was just something missing.

Some wounds that never healed. Or he wasn't able to heal.

She had to face that now.

No more hiding. No more pushing.

She was a fighter. That's what the sheriff said.

Now she only had to believe it herself.

30

Blake looked up when the door opened and stopped wiping the bar for a second. He greeted Jessie and watched her waddle toward him. She was really huge now. He couldn't believe it would be three more weeks.

"Hey, Jess. How're you doing?"

Jessie plonked down right in front of him with a deep sigh. "I'm done. Really, pregnancy is shit. My body hurts in places I didn't even know existed before." She gripped her back and groaned. "See, I got back pain all day long. I haven't slept in days because I can't, for the life of me, get comfortable anymore."

Blake frowned. He didn't know the first thing about pregnancy, but Jessie looked miserable. Shouldn't she be this ethereal happy, glowing woman, who was the epitome of life? "Maybe you should go see a doctor."

Oh oh.

Jessie's face contorted into a real scary mask like she was about to kill him or something. She pushed her hand to her side and spoke through clenched teeth. "I already did, smart-ass. I live right next to one. Alan says it's normal to feel uncomfortable. Plus, I got Braxton Hicks. Also, completely normal."

The way she was imitating Alan was pretty accurate and Blake cracked a smile.

Then, a few seconds later Jessie visibly relaxed again and even smiled back a little. With that the tension in Blake's body evaporated fully. "Can I get you something?"

"I read outside it's burger night, so can I please have a cheeseburger with fries, and an orange juice?"

Blake turned, shouted the order back to Milan, and filled a glass with juice.

"So, I hear congratulations are in order...Daddy."

Blake's eyebrows shot up. He hadn't told her. Not that he intended to keep it a secret. He just flat out forgot—or maybe he avoided thinking about the whole thing a little too much. "Who told you?" Surely Alan wouldn't break his medical confidentiality, would he?

"Claire came to visit me a few days ago. She's such a nice person. We talked about my pregnancy and I got emotional and then it kinda slipped, so..." She tilted her head to the side, squinted, and studied him until a prickling started at Blake's scalp.

"So?"

"So...what's the deal, big brother, not happy?" She stared him down, and heat climbed up Blake's neck until he started sweating.

"What do you mean?" Maybe if he played dumb well enough she would drop the topic.

"Something's not quite right. I thought, after Claire's reaction she was...torn—but you..." She stared at him a little longer, nodded once, as if she'd figured it out, then she leaned closer.

Blake leaned back against the bar and crossed his arms

in front of his chest. He didn't want to have this talk with anyone, least of all his sister.

"Let me guess. Getting pregnant was an accident. You're freaked out of your mind, giving Claire a hard time, and you want the whole thing to just go away. But it doesn't so you pretend you are okay with it all, but you are not. Not at all." Jessie gave a terse nod, as if she'd made her conclusion. "Am I close? I'm spot on. I know it. I know you."

Blake swallowed which did nothing to take away the sour taste in his mouth. He should've known she wouldn't let it go. She'd always been like a bloodhound, even as a teenager. Had snooped around his stuff, and once she caught a hint of something going on in his life, she'd latched onto it until she found out the truth and everything there was to know. Jessie always knew when he was lying and never let him get away with anything, so more often than not, they'd gotten into huge fights and quit communicating for days.

"I'm fine...don't know what you're talking about. Don't project your own feelings onto me, Sis."

The door opened again and Tara Patterson entered the bar. She'd been a regular guest, ever since they met at his house. She looked around at the other customers and came straight to the bar where she sat down right next to Jessie.

"Hey, Blake." Her tone was soft, and she smiled at him. "I need a whiskey and a beer and something to eat. I'm starving. But I need the whiskey first."

He smiled and winked at her, which made Tara's smile deepen and Jessie frown.

"Hey Milan..."

"Yeah, boss?" Milan stuck his head through the door. "Oh, hey, Jessie, Tara." He greeted the ladies then looked back at Blake.

"A cheeseburger with fries for the lady." He looked at Tara who confirmed his order.

Milan grinned, nodded, and disappeared back into the kitchen.

"Tough day?" Blake placed the whiskey in front of Tara.

"The worst. There's this company. They started a drilling operation in Stone Valley. Do you know anything about fracking?"

Blake's forehead wrinkled. "Not much—just what's been on the news—never really dug any deeper."

Tara sighed and grabbed the whiskey. "Well, never mind. It might not be as bad as I think. Maybe I'm being a drama queen."

He never pegged Tara as being very high drama. But then he didn't know her too well.

"So, I guess you're my stress relief guy now. I seem to get through the day a little easier with the prospect of coming here afterward."

Blake's eyebrows shot up. Was she flirting with him? He chuckled. "Better watch out about that alcohol then. Because...you know, when your relief is a bar, that ain't good."

She laughed and Blake grinned back.

Jessie's frown had deepened during their conversation and she looked between the two of them like a visitor at a tennis match. Then she straightened her spine, dismissed Tara, and concentrated on Blake again.

"I know what you're doing. I know you're hiding. But if you continue this path, you will mess up everything. I'm not concerned about you. You'll land on your feet, you will be miserable as hell, but you'll endure it. That's your choice—just don't drag her down. She deserves better. They deserve better. And I want my burger on the go, please." She took a sip of her glass and awkwardly hopped off the bar stool.

She waddled away toward the bathrooms, and Blake watched her retreat while rubbing the back of his neck. Well, shit.

Then the door opened again, and Peter and Claire entered. Peter said something that made Claire giggle and Blake felt a pang. She hardly ever laughed with him anymore since she told him she was pregnant and their subsequent radio silence. Yes, they were getting along just fine in recent weeks, but Blake couldn't shake the feeling of Claire tiptoeing around him, like she was afraid he would crack if she said something or made one wrong move.

He might as well just let her go. Give her back the opportunity to find happiness and joy and love. Maybe he wasn't ready for a family, a baby. And maybe she was better off without him. He didn't want to hurt her, but what if he couldn't deal with his shit. What if he was just broken beyond repair?

Maybe if he would step back, end their relationship, maybe she would find everything she deserved in life.

Just not with him.

The thought alone made his chest squeeze in.

He just couldn't.

He made his way around the bar and touched her arm. "Hey, baby, can we go talk for a second? Behind back?"

Claire pinched her lips, and Peter's eyebrows shot up. Peter scrutinized Blake, but Blake didn't give him a chance to interfere. He led Claire to the now-empty flat behind the bar and sat with her on the sofa.

It was time to come clean.

Let her decide if she even wanted to be with him.

"I gotta talk to you about something." Blake swallowed —should he really? He hated himself for the pain he'd already inflicted. And now he planned to dump all of his family history on her?

Claire looked relieved. "Oh, I do too."

"I'm not sure if I'm the right guy for you. I know I'm not good enough for you...or the baby."

Blake stopped.

That was not what he'd planned to say. He'd planned to beg her to give him more time. To trust that he would get his shit in order.

Every single fiber inside of him screamed that he wanted her. That she was it and he would get there.

But that's not what came out of his mouth.

And what if he didn't get there?

What if she was better off without him.

She deserved to be happy.

Was what he was asking of her selfish?

He was a burden to her, hadn't Peter told him that?

The honorable thing would be to step away, to set her free.

But he just couldn't do it.

When he finally looked up again, Claire's face was a stony mask, but tears streamed down her cheeks.

Then she swallowed, took a deep breath, and nodded once. "Maybe you're right. Maybe it's better if we remained just friends. Distant friends."

Blake's chest tightened. Fuck, what? Was she really thinking that?

That they should stay distant friends?

What ever the fuck that even meant?

He inhaled. It hurt.

She was giving up on them?

Not that he hadn't given her enough reason.

He tried to gather his thoughts.

He didn't expect this. Didn't expect that curveball.

But he wasn't ready to give up just yet.

He'd been a warrior most of his life.

He knew how to fight.

Knew when to cut his losses, and he knew when to step up.

Now was the time to step up.

And even though her words stung, he would prove it to himself...and her.

He just needed a plan.

A knock on the door startled them both, and Blake got up, which took more effort than it should.

Peter stepped inside, and his eyes darted between them. "Hey, sorry to interrupt, but I think Jessie's in labor."

Blake's head jerked back, and he stared at his buddy. His mind felt fuzzy when he looked at Claire.

He couldn't go. He needed to talk to her first, needed to tell her why he was so fucked up, needed to beg her for forgiveness, and beg for another chance.

Tell her he loved her.

She stared back at him and wiped at her silent tears. "Go, Blake, get her to the hospital, now."

He gulped in some air and passed Peter on the way out. He had to get Jessie to the hospital.

He had to focus.

Jessie first, Claire later.

When he entered the bar, his glance fell immediately on Jessie, who was bent over, supported by Tara in the middle of the bar.

When Blake closed the distance, he could hear her breath sawing in and out.

He touched her back and talked to her in a soothing voice.

She didn't react.

Shit.

He darted behind the bar to grab his keys and wallet. Then he picked her up and walked to his car.

Tara assisted him in opening the door of the bar and the passenger door of his jeep.

After Blake made sure she was as comfortable as possible, he buckled her up, sprinted to the driver's side, and flung himself behind the steering wheel.

He was visualizing the way to the hospital, mission-focused, until he saw Claire through the windshield of his car.

She was crying, and Peter had his arm around her shoulders.

Blake's lungs constricted.

He pinched his lips to keep them from trembling, but the pain in his chest was agonizing.

They were not over, they couldn't be.

Because if this, if staying friends, was the right decision for all of them, why did they both feel like shit?

He turned on the ignition, started the car, and rolled out of the lot, but not without taking one last glance at Claire in his rear-view mirror.

He would do whatever it took to be good enough.

He just had to prove it to her.

Because this, this was agony.

And if he knew one thing, it was what agony felt like.

He'd lived through it.

His father's death, and his sister's suicide attempt.

He'd had teammates and friends die in his arms.

And now, losing Claire...the pain was excruciating.

31

"Ahh." Jessie released the side rail of the hospital bed and gripped Blake's hand, her fingernails almost piercing the skin. She curled the other one around her belly with her face red and contorted.

In the last twelve hours, since arriving at the hospital in Whitebrook, they'd moved from walking up and down the hallway to a room in the maternity ward to here.

As soon as Jessie relaxed again, Blake groaned under his breath, inspected his hand, and rubbed at the crick in his neck.

Fucking hell.

He looked at Jessie, and his stomach tensed. Her face was red, and her hair sweaty.

Her energy was fading fast.

He looked at his watch. Twelve hours. This had been going on for twelve hours already—without serious progress.

Jessie had been in serious pain every five minutes for the last hour, but their nurse/midwife, Abby, was still unfazed.

She'd flitted in and out of their room repeatedly but now had stayed with them and watched the last contraction.

Blake looked at her on the other side of the bed.

Abby stood, frowning at the apparatus that recorded the baby's heartbeat and the strength of the contractions.

Blake swallowed when he looked back at Jessie's exhausted face. He'd faced multiple situations during training and war, that he wouldn't want to repeat, but he couldn't, for the life of him, recall a single moment in one of these situations when he'd felt this helpless.

And it was killing him.

Abby tore the paper printout off and walked out of the room without a word, but her frown never changed, and Blake's muscles tensed.

Blake had just turned back toward Jessie when a knock at the door stopped him in his tracks.

"Knock, knock. May I come in? I brought your hospital bag."

Jessie opened her eyes and smiled at Alan, but it was a tired smile, barely there before she closed her eyes again.

Alan crossed the room and caressed Jessie's head before he put a stray strand of hair behind her ear. "You holdin' up okay, sweetie?"

Blake's eyebrows shot up.

This was mighty friendly behavior for someone whom she had just met a few days ago.

But Jessie seemed to relax under his caress, so Blake let it go—for now.

Alan turned to Blake and watched him, his brows drawn. "You don't look so good, as well. Everything good?"

Blake shrugged his shoulders.

No...not really.

But he wasn't the one in pain. He wasn't important.

He looked at Alan, shrugged, and shuffled his feet.

Wasn't childbirth supposed to be the most natural thing in the world?

Didn't look like it to him.

And in a few months, Claire would be in the exact same situation as Jessie.

Shit.

Blake recalled her tear-stricken face.

He needed to fix this once and for all.

He needed to be there for Claire. Needed to step up.

Because not being there when his baby was born—not a fucking option.

Blake's stomach hardened, and bile rose in his throat.

He'd fucked up.

He'd just fucked up the most important relationship in his life because...because he was indecisive and scared.

Blake took a few steps back and sank down on a chair.

What a dimwit he was.

Even if everything went to shit. Even if he was the worst father on earth. Claire would straighten him out. She would call him on his bullshit.

Just chickening out?

That was not the man he grew up to be.

Alan came over to him and gripped his shoulders. "It's hard to just watch them in pain. But it will be okay."

Blake inhaled deeply. "How the hell do they do this, and why would anyone go through this multiple times?" he asked.

Alan opened his mouth when Abbie came back accompanied by a doctor. They both stepped toward Jessie and signaled at Blake to join them.

"We're a little concerned about your baby. The heart rate went down during the last contraction, and there is too little progression."

Blake grimaced and clenched his jaw. He looked from the doctor to Alan, who nodded.

Well, at least one of them knew what they were talking

about because he didn't understand what that meant, and a short glance at Jessie made it obvious to Blake that she didn't either.

"And this means what exactly?" Blake moved his feet shoulder-width apart and crossed his arms in front of his chest.

"This means, we think a C-section would be the best way forward," the doctor said, and Alan nodded once while both of them looked at him expectantly.

Blake's throat closed up. Did they want him to make a decision?

He had no clue about any of this.

Didn't know the risk involved.

But one look at Jessie's pain-ridden face—apparently the next contraction had arrived, affirmed she clearly couldn't in any way, shape, or form make that decision.

Blake looked over to Alan. "Your opinion, Doc?" Alan cared about Jessie, his display of affection earlier proved that, so he would have Jessie's best interest in mind.

Alan grabbed the medical file from the doctor and, after seconds of excruciating silence, nodded.

"Yep, same opinion." He turned to Jessie and caressed her head again, while talking in her ear.

Blake narrowed his eyes, but Jessie grabbed Alan's hand and clung to it.

Her voice was so hoarse that Blake leaned forward to understand the intimate conversation between them.

"Will you"—she took a deep breath—"stay with me?"

Alan caressed Jessie's soaking-wet hair and made eye contact with Blake as if he was asking his permission to comply with Jessie's request.

He swallowed and nodded once—anything to keep his sister safe.

Alan turned to Jessie again and pushed a strand of hair

behind her ear. "I'll stay with you. Don't be afraid. This is routine and you will hold your boy in your arms in no time."

Jessie visibly relaxed, and the nurse started preparations for what was to come. Alan turned to the doctor and Blake leaned down to kiss Jessie's forehead. "You're doing great, Jess. I'm proud of you. Alan will take care of you and I'll see you real soon, okay?"

Jessie nodded weakly while the nurse released the brakes and set her bed in motion.

Blake watched them push Jessie out of the room and sagged into the only chair. He closed his eyes briefly but opened them when he felt Alan watching him.

"I'll take real good care of her, Blake. Trust me."

Blake nodded but didn't reply, and Alan left.

Did he trust Alan?

He thought about the tenderness and familiarity he had witnessed. He had to talk to Alan about that, but not now.

Now it was about Jessie and her baby.

Everything else had to wait.

Blake's muscles tensed at every approaching footstep in the hallway, only to relax again when the person passed by the room they'd relocated him in. He was alone here, Jessie's hospital bag on the chair next to him. He twisted the watch on his wrist. Time ran agonizingly slow. He should've asked Alan how long a C-section actually took.

Blake looked up when he recognized Peter's voice in the hallway. His heart skipped a beat when it was joined by Lisa's.

Claire...would she be with them?

He rolled his shoulders.

He desperately needed her to be here. He had toyed

with the idea of calling her on and off, and he really didn't even know what the hell came over him to leave her like that, let her think being apart would be better for them.

He missed her more with every breath he took.

The door opened and Peter held it open for Lisa to enter.

When Peter released the door, Blake offered them a weak smile.

"Hey, where's Jessie?" Peter looked around the empty room, narrowed his eyes, and attached the silly-looking unicorn-shaped balloon to the nightstand.

Lisa stood rigidly right next to the door and licked her lips.

"C-section. Something about too little progression and the baby's heartbeat." He shrugged his shoulders and looked at his watch again.

Fifty-five minutes.

He looked up at Lisa, who was silently sniffing.

"It's going to be okay. Alan is with her and he said it's routine, not an emergency."

Blake watched Peter take Lisa in his arms and his ribs seemed to squeeze tightly together.

They'd really come a long way as a couple in just a matter of a few months. But then again, they had known each other since they were both teenagers.

Blake rubbed at the pain in his clenched jaw, before he forced himself to loosen it.

He wished Claire was here.

Maybe then he wouldn't feel envious of his best friend.

The door opened again, and Blake's heart skipped a beat before it settled into a gallop.

He stood up when Alan made his way toward him. Blake searched for a clue in his face but couldn't figure it out.

"So?"

Alan's face was serious, and Lisa as well as Peter huddled closer.

"It was a closer call than I would like to admit. The baby had a so-called nuchal cord. The umbilical cord was wrapped around his neck, which caused the decrease in heart rate with every contraction. But both son and mother are well and on their way here."

Blake exhaled deeply and closed his eyes.

The release of all the tension made him weak in the knees and he smiled at Peter, who patted his back. Lisa hugged Alan first and then him before she went back into her man's arms.

There was just the place right around Blake's heart that stayed tight. A vise around his heart that cast a shadow over the joyous moment.

32

"Hey, Sis, how're you and Junior doing?" Blake juggled the flowers, the balloons, and the present in his one hand and closed the door to the hospital room with the other. He'd driven himself home to Moon Lake as soon as Jessie had been settled back in her room. Just to get a shower and get changed before talking to Claire.

Instead, he woke up six hours later, still sitting on his sofa, with one shoe untied.

He shook his head. He'd survived on far less sleep in the Teams. And now he couldn't even get through thirty-six hours?

Embarrassing.

He looked at Jessie, who watched him with a smile.

"I'm good. How about you?" She held her little boy in her arms and Blake turned his gaze to the small crib, when he realized she was breastfeeding him.

"I'm good. I got you something." He dropped the magazines next to her bed and turned around in search of a vase for the flowers.

There was already a huge bouquet, full of vibrant-colored flowers on the small table.

"Vases are outside—I don't know exactly where, but Alan got one outside."

Blake's jaw clenched.

Of course, Alan had already visited. He released the tight pressure on his teeth and smiled at Jessie. Alan had been perfect the day before. He had cared for Jessie. He had helped.

Blake had to accept this.

But they sure as hell would have a talk.

He left the room, found a vase, and positioned his flowers on the windowsill. Not quite as colorful as Alan's, but he'd bought tasteful yellow and orange chrysanthemums, the flowers of junior's birth month, or so the florist told him.

"So, do you have a name for the little one, yet? I don't have a problem with Junior. But I think he needs a proper name."

Jessie chuckled. "You're absolutely right. I already named him, though."

Blake's eyebrows shot up. "You did?" He dropped on the chair right beside the bed and tried to decipher the small band slung around the baby's impossibly tiny arm.

"You are not far off with Junior, though." Jessie smiled cryptically and Blake's stomach hardened in anticipation. She wouldn't choose the name of their father, would she?

"His name is Sebastian. Named after his uncle and godfather."

Blake inhaled sharply. Did that mean? "You want me to be his godfather?"

Jessie nodded.

Blake looked at the baby.

Sebastian.

He had stopped drinking and was fast asleep by now, his dark lashes surprisingly long. "I'm honored, Jess. Clueless but honored. Have you called Mom yet? I talked to her on my way home yesterday. She cried—don't know why."

Jessie chuckled. "I called—she cried with me, as well." She shrugged. "It's her first grandchild. I guess that's why she's a little sentimental. Hey, would you hold Seb for a minute?"

Blake froze, but Jessie already leaned forward and laid Seb in his arms.

Warmth flooded Blake as he looked into the baby's face.

The boy's eyes were still closed, and his mouth was a small pink pout.

"I'll just need a second. Be right back."

Blake leaned down to kiss the baby on the forehead and was startled by the smell of the little bundle.

He had never smelled something quite like it before.

He couldn't remember the birth of his sisters even though he was quite a bit older than them. Then the baby's eyes opened, and his heart started racing.

He looked up to where Jessie had left for the bathroom.

Panic settled into his chest. What if the baby started to cry? What should he do then?

But Seb just smacked his lips a little and closed his eyes again. Tenderness swamped him.

This was scary and exhilarating at the same time. He would do anything to protect this little child.

Blake looked up when Jessie returned. "Aren't you afraid?"

Jessie looked at him strangely. "Of course I am—everybody is. I have no clue about parenthood."

Blake swallowed; his voice was hoarse when he spoke the next words: "What about depression?"

Jessie furrowed her brows then released them. "Depression? What the hell, Seb? Is that what got you so freaked out?"

Blake leaned down and kissed little Sebastian's forehead again.

"So is that the reason you have such a hard time dealing with Claire's pregnancy?"

Blake didn't respond—instead, he touched Seb's little hand—impossibly soft.

Jessie reached out and touched Blake's forearm, which caused him to look up at her. "You think because Dad killed himself and Paula tried to, it's in our genes, don't you?"

Blake shrugged. "There is scientific proof that depression runs in families. So, it's not only us—it can affect our children as well."

"Did you ever deal with depression? Any suicidal ideations?"

Blake broke eye contact and shrugged.

He'd gone through quite some emotional times. Had seen and done things that weren't always easy to deal with.

Sometimes he'd wondered, but he'd always come out of these episodes mentally stable.

His father had gone into depressive episodes so often.

Blake had been angry about it as a child. Had often had the feeling his father didn't fight it enough.

Didn't love them enough to fight.

What triggered this for his sister Paula he didn't know, but he would always feel responsible for not seeing it, getting her help, and for not being there to hinder her from what she'd done to herself. "No."

Jessie got up, went to the windowsill, and smelled his flowers.

Then she turned and looked at him with sad eyes. "I haven't either. I always struggled to understand. A part of me thinks it's more a decision to let yourself slip into the darkness instead of fighting for the light. But I have no clue how it feels."

Jessie was still at home when Paula tried to kill herself. She must've seen how their sister lapsed into depression.

"Did you..." Blake hesitated. "Were there any signs? I mean, with Paula?" Blake's stomach was rock hard.

They'd never talked about this before. He'd never talked to anyone about this. Not because he had no one to talk to but because he didn't know how.

Jessie hugged herself. "Well, she was moody a lot, but she never wanted to talk much. So, after a while, I stopped asking. She changed after Dad left us. But we were all grieving. Maybe I should have seen it. Done more." Jessie shrugged.

"But I was a teenager. Self-absorbed to a fault. I'd just lost my father, and I was struggling myself. I still don't know what I could have done."

"I didn't mean to imply..."

Jessie moved toward him and cupped his cheek. "I know. Ultimately, it's nothing I could control." She sighed. "And neither could you."

She kissed his cheek softly, then she picked up Seb and sat back down on the bed.

"It's our past, our history, but I don't think fear or regret should rule your life. Every one of us gets to decide how we want to live and what we want to focus on. Me, I'm terrified. I'm a single mother, with no place to stay; I need to get working soon. This is not the best environment to raise a child. But, it is what it is, and I will make the best of it."

Blake crossed his arms in front of his chest. "You're not alone—Moon Lake is your home now. There are great people here, and it's a great place to raise a child."

"And Seb will not be alone, either. He will have a cousin who is the same age and lives in the same place. And he has his uncle and godfather right there, who can help him whenever he needs more than I can give him."

Blake hesitated. Jessie made it seem so easy. As if he could be all that. As if she didn't think he could mess this up. But what if he did? What if something went wrong? Could he deal with losing another loved one?

"You're a warrior, Blake. You care deeply and protect those you love. I've never known you as a coward. So why are you so hesitant when it comes to Claire and the baby?"

She stared at him, her gaze inquisitive to the point of uncomfortable. "Don't you love her?"

She raised a single eyebrow.

And he could feel every single word of her hit him right in the chest. Of course, he loved her.

"Because from my viewpoint, at the wedding, it sure looked like you do. So, correct me if I'm wrong, but if you do, if you love her, you have to fight for what you want. Not jiggle around like yesterday's jello."

Jiggle around? Jello? He swallowed. She was damn right.

"And you have to fight for the kind of life you want. Otherwise, you're just existing, not living; even though it might feel safer right now, in the end, it will leave you miserable and lonely."

Blake cringed.

When did his little sister become the wise one?

He would never tell her, but she was right.

The things she said made perfect sense to him.

He was hiding.

He was being a coward when it came to Claire and the baby.

He was being hesitant because of his family history. But he couldn't let his past influence his future.

He owned his future, and it was his decision how he wanted to show up.

Claire made him happy.

She evoked a sense of belonging and home that he hadn't felt in a long time.

He loved her, deeply.

And fear was the destroyer of dreams.

He'd learned how to walk through fear again and again.

He just forgot to apply it to this.

This was the most important thing.

Their future and their future family. Everything would work out okay. He owed it to himself and Claire to give it his best.

And maybe it didn't work out. Then he would be miserable, but without Claire, he already was.

Blake stood up, kissed the baby and then Jessie on the forehead, and grabbed his jacket. "I gotta go. I'll see you tomorrow, okay?"

He turned and grabbed the handle of the door when it was pushed open from the other side, and he came face to face with the woman who occupied his thoughts and owned his heart.

Claire looked as surprised as Blake felt and pressed the little blue teddy bear against her chest. "I'm sorry. I didn't know you were here. I can come back later."

She turned, but Blake grabbed her elbow and led her into the room.

"Don't be silly," Jessie said from her position on the bed, "I'm glad you're here and he was just about to leave."

Claire hesitated, and her gaze ping-ponged between Jessie and him.

Blake just nodded and gave her a half-smile. "I was just leaving anyhow, so it's actually great timing." He waved goodbye and left the room.

When the door closed with a silent click, he turned and laid his hand on the frame.

He should have never fought his feelings for Claire.

He recognized his racing heart as what it was.

Claire took his breath away with just her presence.

She made everything better, brighter, and worth it.

Blake made his way to a group of chairs that were positioned in the hallway, just a few steps left of Jessie's room.

He would wait until Claire left, and he would fight for their future.

A future together.

33

Claire embraced Jessie and kissed the baby before she put on her jacket. "If you need anything, just call. I'll try to visit tomorrow, okay?"

Jessie beamed at her. "Thanks, Claire."

Claire nodded and pushed the door open. As soon as she stepped out into the hallway, her stomach tensed when Blake straightened from leaning against the wall.

He must have waited for her.

Butterflies erupted in her stomach, and she immediately pressed her hand there. The little one kicked, and it was almost too much. She had to stop dreaming of what might have been and deal with reality. They were friends.

He didn't deserve, nor wanted butterflies, or anything else from her, really.

Blake made his way toward her, his face a taut mask of determination, and Claire's whole body tensed.

When he reached her, he touched her elbow and his face softened. "Can I talk to you for a sec?" His voice was scratchy and his whole demeanor was more hesitant than she'd ever seen him before.

Claire's brain screamed at her to get away from him.

He'd hurt her enough. Sadly, her bruised, yet still hopeful heart wasn't on board with her brain.

While Claire still struggled on how to react, Blake turned toward the elevator and gently pushed her along with him.

It took Claire the whole way to harden herself against the mesmerizing effect his delicious smell had on her.

She shrugged off his hand and crossed her arms. "I don't think there's anything left to say."

She witnessed a gamut of emotions cross over Blake's face, before it settled on pleading. "Just one last talk. If afterward you still think the same way, I promise I will not bother you again."

Claire hesitated but when the elevator's doors opened, she nodded once and preceded Blake into it.

They arrived at ground level in complete silence and both turned toward the exit as if they had the same goal.

Outside, the harsh wind blew Claire's hair in her face and she hastened to close her jacket over her baby bump.

Blake did the same and, after looking around, stepped forward and laid his right hand on the small of her back.

Then he turned and positioned himself so she was sheltered from the wind. "I'm sorry. I didn't think this through. It's too cold outside. Either we go sit in my car or we could go back into the cafeteria. Your choice."

Claire bit her lip. She didn't want to talk with him in the cafeteria but the prospect of the confined space in his car wasn't appealing either.

Another gust of wind—from a different direction—blew her hair in her face, and it felt like tiny stings in her face. "Your car is fine—at least we'll be out of the wind."

Blake cast her a long sideways glance while he steered them toward the parking lot and didn't slow down until they reached his jeep. His car was a fairly new model, and Claire was thankful when he turned on the heating and the seat-heating system.

Claire stared through the windshield, not looking at him in the driver's seat. "So, what did you wanna talk about?"

Blake shifted around in his seat, trying to get comfortable. "I..." He cleared his throat. "I'm actually...I wanted to tell you I'm sorry, and I-I made a mistake."

Claire's stomach tensed. She had never seen Blake like this before. Unsure, hesitating. Not with his usual quiet but unshakable self-confidence.

She watched him out of the side of her eye, her head still angled straight ahead.

"It's okay. Kind of. It's not like we were in love or anything. We were friends, we had fun together, and it's okay if you don't care for more. Better to end it now, then—" Claire stopped herself before she said it—better now, then after the baby was born.

Better now, than for their baby to get to know him and think she's not worthy of her father's love.

Claire felt her eyes well up.

Bloody tears.

She didn't want to cry, not in front of Blake.

"No, you don't understand. I'm sorry for being a coward."

A coward? Blake was many things. An arrogant ass, too-good-looking for his own good. Too charming, too intense. But a coward? No, that didn't match the picture Claire had of him. He was a goddamn warrior. No coward could ever face war and make a career out of it.

"There are some things in my past...about my family...I need to tell you, but first I need to tell you, that I love you."

Claire pressed her hand against her mouth but couldn't contain a whimper.

"I really do. And I didn't want to, you know. I had a plan for my life. I decided a long time ago how my life would be like. But that's not what I want anymore; that's not what I need anymore."

Claire's eyes spilled over.

How could he say one thing one day, then make a complete U-turn the next day?

What did he want from her, playing with her feelings like that?

She sniffed and wiped at her tears. "I'm sorry, but I can't."

She still didn't look at Blake, but she could feel his shoulders sag right next to her. "I don't think you know what you want or need. And I can't wait around until you figure it out. I got a baby to think of. Kids need stability in their lives. This roller coaster we've been on these last couple of weeks." She shook her head. "This is not what I want or need for my life."

Claire looked up for the first time.

She could see the pain in his eyes but steeled herself against it. "But I'll listen. I want to understand where you're coming from. Moon Lake is a small town. We need to stay friends, and somehow, we'll manage to do just that."

There was a long silence between them. Her tears were still trickling down her face, and she searched for a tissue until Blake handed her one.

"My dad committed suicide when I was seventeen." Blake took a deep breath before he continued, and she grabbed his hand.

He entwined their fingers as if he needed someone to hold on. "He set himself on fire...right in the backyard of our house. We never knew why exactly, but...he battled with depression for years. There was no letter. No explanation. He just...it was..." Blake hesitated. "Difficult for all of us... but especially for Paula."

Claire leaned a little closer. "Were you still home, when it happened?"

Blake nodded. "I stayed home for two years afterward. Mom"—Blake swallowed—"she had a hard time dealing with things, and Jessie and Paula were only six and eight at the time."

Claire stayed silent; she had a hard time wrapping her head around what Blake had just told her. Who would do something like that? Who would leave his children like that? And in such a horrible way.

There were so many questions running around in her mind.

But before she could sort out her thoughts, Blake continued.

"That's not all. Mom and Jessie dealt with it okay, well, after a while. But Paula...Paula tried to kill herself too."

Blake scrubbed a hand over his face, but left the other one in Claire's grip. "I wasn't home when it happened; my little sister fought with depression, as well...and I never knew."

He looked at Claire and his eyes were brimming with tears. "She jumped off a bridge, but survived. A quadriplegic with severe damage to the brain. But she survived."

Claire caressed Blake's forearm.

She couldn't even process the tragedy Blake and his family had gone through.

What a horrible tragedy.

How he came out of this the kind, caring, and stable person he was, she didn't know.

"She'd written a letter. Didn't see a way out. She'd never gotten over Dad's death. Was battling depression just like him."

He sniffed. "The doctor told us there's strong evidence

that depression can run in families. That means Jessie and I might have it in our DNA, as well."

Blake looked her deeply in the eyes. "That means we could pass it on to our children."

He scraped his hand through his hair and leaned back in his seat. "I decided then and there that I wouldn't be responsible for more pain and heartbreak, that I wouldn't have children of my own. That it ended with me."

Realization dawned on her.

That was why he'd been so furious with her, on that boat, when she told him she was pregnant. He believed his child would be predisposed, just because of his DNA. Claire took deep breaths to handle the rising panic in her body. She had never heard of that, but it could affect her child. "Did you ever?" Claire swallowed, not knowing how she should breach the topic. "Battle with it? Depression, I mean."

Blake shook his head. "Never...neither has Jessie." He shrugged and turned his head away from Claire. "But there's always the possibility..."

He didn't elaborate, but Claire had a pretty good grasp on what he was thinking. They both sat there in silence for a good long while, both staring out of the windshield, with their hands still connected.

What if her child had a genetic predisposition for depression? Would it change anything? Claire remembered her ex-husband. She was pretty sure domestic violence ran in his family.

They'd never talked about it.

He'd had broken off all contact with his family, but from the bits and pieces she knew about his parents, she was almost sure.

Would that have affected Anna? Was that something that ran in families, as well?

And what about Claire's own mother? She'd been an alcoholic—was that genetically disposed, as well?

Claire put her right hand on her belly.

She rejected that thought.

Life, how you lived your life, was something anyone could decide, whether to drink, to be violent, or to succumb to depression without searching for help.

"I don't think so."

Blake turned his head and looked at her. His eyebrows were squished together. "You don't think what?"

"I don't think that nothing can be done, even if a child has these predispositions. Look at you. You are mentally stable. You went to war. I guess there were ample times to be depressed about your circumstances, about things you've seen. But you didn't. And I haven't."

Blake's face turned into a frown. "What do you mean? You haven't?" He spoke the last words very slow, distinct.

Well, time to come clean.

34

Claire took a deep breath. "I haven't given up. My mother was an alcoholic. But I'm not." She hesitated, but this was the moment. He'd opened up, so it was time for her to tell him.

Everything.

"I made mistakes, though. I've been married before... and pregnant."

She paused.

Waited for Blake to react. To say something.

Anything.

Agonizing seconds ticked by, but when he remained silent and motionless, she went on.

"My ex was a drunk and abusive, and I lost my child because of him."

The ache settled deep in her heart. Dull and familiar, not sharp like in the beginning, but it still reverberated through her body until she could feel it everywhere.

What would he think of her?

Would he think she was weak?

Because she had been.

Had waited too long to leave. Risked her baby and lost...everything.

"I'd already decided to leave him, but he caught up with me. Angry and drunk."

Claire looked up, and her speech fizzled out when she registered rage on Blake's face.

His jaw was clenched tight, a vein pulsed at the side of his neck.

But despite all that, he still held her hand softly. Cradled it in his much bigger hand. Infused her with warmth.

So much warmth.

He squeezed once, then drew a slow circle with his thumb.

Such a little movement, but powerful enough to beat back the ache, beat back the pain she still felt, whenever she thought back... and the lingering shame that would never go away.

"I divorced him and got on with my life. The doctors told me I wouldn't be able to get pregnant again. And I didn't want to have children again after I lost my Anna. The pain, was just too much, you know."

"I'm sorry, babe." His voice sounded hoarse.

Clearly shaken by her news. "I... I didn't know. I just wish..." he swallowed, "I could do something, anything to make it better."

He squeezed her hand once more.

Clearly, hearing that was hard on him, just as hard as it was for her to talk about it.

Blake was used to fix problems.

That's what he did for everyone else.

But some things couldn't be fixed. Some things stayed broken.

And you just had to learn to live with them.

She let go of Blake's hand and crossed her arms in front of her chest. "And here we are. Full fucking circle."

Blake raised his eyebrows at her swearing, then a small smile scurried over his face.

He leaned back against his seat. "Full fucking circle."

There was silence again. Blake's breath hitched a few times, and Claire thought he would ask her a question, but Blake remained silent, and she did too.

"So, you don't think my DNA or my presence will fuck our kid up?"

Claire smirked. "I think neither your DNA nor your presence will fuck up our kid any more, than my DNA or my presence. If we both decide to give it our best."

"So, you take me back, give me another chance?"

Claire's face turned serious, and she shook her head. "No, I won't."

She could feel the air leave the room.

Feel Blake stare at her, but never moved her eyes from looking out the windshield. "That doesn't mean I never will. Just not now. I think we're a long way from having the kind of relationship that makes a family, and I don't know if that's even in the cards for us. But... Honesty is a good start, don't you think?"

She half shrugged her left shoulder and finally looked at Blake with a sad smile, only to encounter Blake's laser-focused stare.

"I will fight for us, you know."

Claire's eyebrows shot up at the determination in his eyes and voice.

Now, that was more like the Blake she got to know since she arrived in Moon Lake.

Not hesitant or desperate, or wobbly in his actions.

"There's one more thing I need to tell you."

She remembered her conversation with Peter. Had it been only two days?

"I went to the sheriff's office to ask them to find my ex-husband. I need to make sure the baby and I are safe, so I want to know where he is and what he's up to. Peter knows, so I thought you should know too."

She watched Blake's face. His lips were pressed tight into a slight grimace, and he drew his eyebrows; he looked angry and conflicted at the same time.

Then he gave her a curt nod. "I understand. Don't like that I haven't been there for you. And you not telling me sooner. But I understand."

Claire nodded too and released a shaky breath, she hadn't realized she'd been holding, and sank against her seat.

There was a lot she had to think about.

"Can I come by the Inn for a coffee later?" He asked, and she almost smiled.

He sounded so hesitant. He'd never asked for permission to come by before, even before they became intimate.

He knew he'd fucked up.

Was this his way of telling her she had all the power? "Yes, you can come by the Inn later."

Then Blake took her hand and guided it to his lips, holding her gaze the entire time.

The kiss he pressed against the back of her hand, no matter how sweet a gesture, made her stomach flutter, and when he turned her hand and placed a kiss on the inside of her wrist, right on her pulse point, her body tingled all over.

Maybe they still had a chance. They'd always had the attraction part right. And if they could work out everything else.

They had a true shot at happiness.

Together.

35

"Hey, you ready? We gotta head out now to make it in time before the ladies arrive."

Blake tied his left running shoe and smirked at Peter. "You in a hurry, old man?" Peter was three years younger than Blake but ribbing him with the aches that were part of the job and life they'd chosen, was a lot of fun.

They both were huge guys, so running hadn't been a favorite part of their workout routine. On the contrary, timed runs had always troubled him the most. He'd chosen drown-proofing over running any day.

But now, apart from weight training, it kept them both in shape, and running cross-country through the woods was just the right challenge to make it fun.

"Does Lisa know they can get in through the back door for the party later?" Blake had established the habit of locking the front door of his house, but he always left the back door unlocked in case the boy needed some food.

The boy hadn't visited for quite some time, and Blake was worried about him. Winter had officially arrived in Moon Lake and snow covered the mountains and woods.

"She knows—hurry. It's getting dark already. We don't have more than an hour left."

Blake chuckled. "You just have to run full out, then drag your ass back here—wouldn't take more than half an hour this way."

Peter stuck out his tongue and jogged toward the edge of the clearing.

Blake checked his shoes one more time before he launched himself after Peter.

It was on.

And afterward, he would see Claire again.

He couldn't wait. He already missed her. Even though he constantly showed up at the Inn. Her coming here, to his house, having agreed to a date, was special.

These last couple of days had cemented what he'd probably known all along. Claire was his future. His chance to get everything.

He just had to let go of his fear.

And convince her, he was done running.

They reached the creek, where he'd lost the tracks of the boy last time, and stopped to catch their breath. It was cold enough that they were steaming, and their condensing breath created a cloud around each of them.

"Holy shit, it's freaking cold."

Blake shot a sideways glance at Peter but concentrated on slowing down his breathing.

Peter looked up and down the creek. "Which way?"

Blake pointed to the left. "There's a passage down there, where we can cross. The stones might be slippery, so prepare."

They both set out alongside the creek and soon reached the narrow passage, where they could cross the rapidly flowing water.

"Hey, what's that down there?" Peter pointed farther down the creek, and Blake searched the steep embankment.

There was a piece of cloth impaled by a branch just a few feet down on the other side.

Peter and Blake crossed the creek, and Blake nearly slipped on the icy surface of a stone.

They reached the piece of cloth. It was a sweater, small, child-sized, and the hair on the nape of Blake's neck stood up.

"See what I see?" Peter picked up a stick from the ground.

They were both cowering at the edge of the precipice. The creek gurgled ten feet below them. And the sweater hung maybe three feet down in the embankment, completely entangled into the branches of a bush.

Peter poked at the frozen sweater and turned it a little. Blake's heart sank. "Blood."

Peter nodded.

Blake straightened and scanned the area. This happened no longer than a day ago; there were quite a few tracks in the snow on the slope. Most likely the boy had slipped on the stone and tumbled into the creek, but managed to get out.

"He fell in, but got out." Blake took a step and examined one footprint and a trickle of blood next to it, then turned back to Peter.

Peter stood up and nodded. His eyebrows were drawn, and his face a tight mask. "Must be wet to the bones; the sweater is frozen solid, and the blood...maybe he cut himself."

Their eyes connected and Blake's mind raced. "Gotta find him, if he's still alive."

Peter got his phone out and frowned at it. "No, reception. I gotta get back to the house."

Blake nodded and looked in the direction of the footprints, then up into the canopy of trees. "It's getting darker by the minute. Better split up. You call in reinforcements; I'll follow the tracks."

Peter nodded and turned back the way they'd come.

"Flashlights are in the kitchen, first drawer to the left. First aid kit is in the cabinet below."

Peter nodded again and made his way across the creek.

Blake set out following the tracks.

While every fiber in his body screamed at him to hurry.

36

Claire was just about to walk up the stairs and follow Lisa through the back entrance into the kitchen of the Inn when a guy came out of nowhere.

He stopped a couple of feet from her.

She stopped on the steps, turned around, and eyed him. She didn't appreciate being side-tracked. She was usually more attentive than that.

"You, Claire?"

She studied his face but was pretty confident he wasn't from around here as far as she could assess as he was bundled up into a jacket with the hood drawn deep into his face.

"Yes, are you looking for a room?"

They didn't get a lot of visitors at this time of year. Not until the slopes opened.

She waited for a response.

Somehow the way he studied her made her uncomfortable. She looked over her shoulder, the door was still open, but Lisa was nowhere to be seen.

"Hey, Claire,"

Julie Brooks danced across the parking lot and stopped beside the stranger.

"Hey Jules, long time no see," Claire said and relaxed marginally.

She loved how everybody popped in all the time here in Moon Lake.

Just like one big family.

But she'd never been more glad than right that moment. This stranger gave her the creeps.

At least she wasn't alone with him anymore.

"Would you please go around to the main entrance? We'll be with you in a minute," she said to the man.

Julie moved closer to her, and together they watched until he rounded the corner.

"Who's that?" Julie whispered.

Did she feel the weird vibes as well? He shouldn't have even been back here. "Don't know. Just a visitor."

"Maybe we should call Blake." She said.

And Claire's breath hitched.

Everybody just popped in all the time.

Except for Blake.

Blake always called and asked if it was okay before he came by, even though he'd been coming by at least once every day since their talk at the hospital parking lot four days ago.

He was courting her and flirting with her shamelessly.

And boy, it was a heady feeling to be courted by Sebastian Blake.

She still hadn't committed to getting together, but who was she kidding?

The way he showered her with attention showed that he wouldn't give up quickly.

And spending time with him just made her happy.

When Jessie was released from the hospital yesterday,

they brought her home together, and to her's and Jessie's surprise, all of Jessie's things had been moved from the barn into Alan's house.

Jessie had burst into tears when she'd seen the lovely room Alan had prepared for her and baby Seb.

Big enough for Jessie to be comfortable and with enough details for the baby, like a changing table, a crib, and a mobile above it, that had horses dancing around.

Claire had suspected Blake had been part of the surprise. But he wouldn't admit to it.

Even afterward, when they were alone in the car.

"Hey, Jules," Lisa showed up at the door. "How about the two of you come in and not let all the warm air out?"

Julie chuckled and bounced up the stairs.

The girl had entirely too much energy.

Claire followed, but suddenly she lost her footing and slipped.

She scooted in limbo, then grabbed the handrail and bumped against it before she slid into a sitting position underneath.

"Everything okay? Lisa and Julie were by her side in seconds.

"Yes, I think so," Claire said but held her belly where she bumped against the handrail. A dull wave of pain came and went.

"Let's get you inside," Julie said, and they both helped her inside and into a seat.

"You sure you're okay," Lisa asked, and Claire nodded since the wave of pain had subsided.

"Yikes! It's freezing out there. My lungs hurt, just from walking the short distance from my parents. That stairs are a hazard, you should take care of the ice. Hey, Odin." Julie leaned down and patted Odin, Peter's dog, who was walking around the kitchen, alert and a little nervous, while Cookie, Lisa's old dog, didn't even move an inch when they entered.

Lisa nodded. "The weather forecast even predicted more snow in the next days. I'll make sure to have Peter take care of the stairs."

"There's someone out front. Can you take care of him?" Claire said. "But don't put him in the house."

Lisa stared at her for a beat, then nodded and exited the kitchen.

After five minutes, she came back. "There's nobody there," she said, looking at Claire as if she'd lost her mind.

"Did you look outside?" Claire asked, "he was there just a minute ago."

Julie nodded.

"Yes, of course, I looked around," Lisa answered and shrugged.

She went to the counter, filled the electric kettle, turned it on, then plated some cookies and carried them to the table.

"Perfect timing." Julie grinned and snapped one of the cookies Claire had baked earlier.

She'd put aside a batch for Blake as a present for later.

Their first date—part housewarming party, part date. Just the four of them, Lisa and Peter, and her and Blake.

Maybe Blake had engineered it this way for her to feel less awkward in his house.

To ease her into it.

She was still unsure if this...them dating was a smart idea. But she couldn't deny the jump in her heartbeat she experienced every time he stepped through the kitchen door.

Like earlier today, when he brought her a present.

Lisa had made fun of it, but the whisk he'd made for

Claire—from the top section of one of the trees he'd cut—was perfect.

She still couldn't believe how he'd made a complete 360 after their talk.

Gone was his hesitation, the trepidation in his eyes every time they talked about the future.

Replaced by an enthusiasm for the baby and a single-minded focus on her.

Flirting with her. Touching her.

Stealing kisses and courting her.

Claire got up when the kettle was done.

She gathered cups, then prepared a teapot. When she carried it over to the table, her step hitched, and her hand flew to her belly.

Something wasn't right.

"Everything okay?" Lisa took the pot from her hands and put it on the table. "You have the same expression as you did earlier. Something's not right."

Claire shook her head and proceeded to the table. "It's okay, just a little hiccup. No problem at all."

Maybe it was just nerves.

She'd had belly flutters ever since she'd agreed to their date night.

Claire zoomed back in to the ongoing conversation in the room.

"So, when will he arrive? We gotta know exactly, so the room is ready for him." Lisa bit her lip.

And Claire knew the feeling. They were both a little nervous about the big NHL star, who would stay with them.

"It's fine. He'll arrive mid-December and stay with you until he finds a house, or cottage to rent nearby. We just have to make sure he can climb the stairs; otherwise, we'll need to put him in one of the cottages," Julie said.

Lisa's eyebrows shot up. "You never told us he's disabled.

The cottages don't have heating. And we're not equipped for that. There are stairs everywhere."

It was a topic they'd been discussing. But it was complicated—and expensive—to make adaptations to the old structure of the Inn.

Julie laid her hand on Lisa's on the table. "Don't freak out. I don't know how agile he'll be. He's scheduled for surgery in a week, and it's still a month before he comes here."

Lisa nodded, and Claire shook her head and chuckled. "So, who exactly is this guy and why the hell does he come here for rehab? Don't they handle stuff like that in-house?"

Claire didn't know hockey at all. It had been all football where she grew up, so even if Julie would tell her about him, she would have to look him up on the internet.

Actually, that wasn't a half-bad idea. She picked up her phone and waited with her thumb hovering in the air. "So? His name?"

Julie grinned. "His name is Kevin Reyes. He's"—Julie hesitated—"was the goalie for Paul's team, the Hamilton Hailstorms." Julie looked at Claire expectantly, who just shrugged—the name didn't ring a bell—and entered his name in the search bar.

"Oh, he looks like a cutie," Claire said, when the first search results showed a picture of an attractive man in his thirties, maybe even younger.

Hard to say with the beard he had going on.

"Or not." Claire glanced away from a vomiting man in the next picture.

There were tons of photos of the man: some were professional shoots; some showed him visibly drunk; then another when he was writhing in pain while holding his knee on the ice. "Ouch."

Lisa grabbed Claire's phone. "Let me see. Oh, wow. I'm

glad Peter didn't make it to the Pros. He would be damaged all over by now."

Claire looked at her with one brow lifted.

Was she serious?

Peter had gone on to be a Navy Seal—nothing more dangerous than training like a lunatic and getting shot at in between.

Claire scoffed. She was pretty sure being a hockey player was a piece of cake in comparison.

Another wave of dull pain settled in her stomach, and the feeling of something not being right grew stronger and stronger.

Lisa still held Claire's phone in her hands when her own phone rang.

"Hey, babe." Lisa's smile fell. "Okay, I understand. We will get there ASAP."

Claire and Julie watched her while she ended the call.

"We gotta go." Lisa pushed herself up. "Blake and Peter found the boy. Well, not yet, but he fell into the creek and left a bloody trail." Lisa inhaled sharply. "They need Odin."

Claire's heart started racing. She remembered the small boy from the picture in Blake's kitchen.

It was freezing outside, and he fell into a creek?

Holy shit.

Claire jumped up and looked around the kitchen. "I gotta go to the bathroom first. Then I'm ready to go. Can you grab the food?"

Lisa nodded, and Claire said goodbye to Julie before she left the kitchen.

She grabbed their coats from the office and threw them on a chair in the hallway. Her mind was so preoccupied with images of the child, freezing, hurt, and alone in the woods, that she nearly missed it when she pulled up her panties.

Blood.

She was bleeding.

Claire's breath hitched, and she shook her head. "No, no, no," she whimpered, and her breaths rasped through her lungs.

She didn't recall how she got back to the kitchen, but there she was, in the middle of the kitchen.

She squeezed the coats to her chest, but her whole body was shaking.

Lisa looked at her as if she'd seen a ghost. "What's wrong? You're white as a sheet."

Claire didn't react. She just stood there with her chin trembling. "Blood, there's blood."

Lisa lifted her brows. "Yes, I told you there was a bloody trail. Peter told me to just let Odin loose at the house. He would find his and Blake's tracks."

Claire shook her head. "No"—she squeezed air into her constricted lungs—"I...I'm bleeding. There's blood."

Lisa's eyes widened, and she let out a yelp. "Shit."

She pressed her mouth shut. "We need to get you to the hospital." She turned the phone in her hand and dialed Peter again. "Shit. He's out of reach." She looked at Claire again.

Claire could see her head spinning. "Let's go. You shoot him a text while I drive. Go, go, go."

They both slipped into their jackets and zipped them up.

Claire's stomach roiled. "Wait, can't we just get Odin to them and then go to the hospital?"

Lisa looked at her like she had a third eye growing on her forehead. "This would take half an hour. Do you really want to risk your own child, just for that?"

A ringing in Claire's ears tuned everything else out, and dark spots appeared in her vision.

She was going to faint.

Claire took a deep breath and another one.

She looked at Lisa, who looked back at her with her head cocked to the left.

Was she willing to risk her own child for another?

Blake and Peter were good. They were trained to do such things. They would find the boy.

With or without Odin.

Claire swallowed hard, nodded, and went to the door. "Let's go to the hospital."

They both entered the car, and Claire typed a text to Peter. At the same time, she prayed that everything would be fine. For the boy in the woods, and for her and Blake's child.

She put her hand on her belly after she finished with the text.

What if she lost this one too?

Maybe it just wasn't in the cards for her. "What if I'm just not supposed to be a mother?" Claire didn't realize she'd spoken out loud until Lisa scoffed.

"Bullshit. You were meant to be a mother. Look at you, you're caring, nurturing, you cook like a goddess."

She shook her head, while concentrating to keep them safe on the snowy road. "If anyone was born to be a mother, it's you. So, stop thinking this kind of bullshit. We'll get you to the hospital and everything will be fine."

Claire swallowed hard.

Lisa was right.

She would be a great mother and Blake would be a great father. She thought about the child in the woods.

Where were his parents to take care of him?

Why was he all alone out there?

37

Blake watched Peter traverse then concentrated on the small footsteps in the snow.

There were trickles of blood here and there, but not too much, so Blake wasn't concerned about that.

But hypothermia was a real concern.

The fading light wasn't making things any easier so he stopped. He had only minutes left and if he turned back, he needed to cross the creek while he was still able to see.

His gut told him to hurry, but he was without equipment. He turned back and met Peter halfway between the creek and the house.

"Got you a jacket. Search party is on their way. I called Lisa too—they will bring Odin with them. Should have taken him anyhow. Shit."

Blake zipped up his jacket and pulled the cap over his frozen ears. If he was fucking cold like that, how much worse must the boy be?

"Let's roll." They both took off on a run. It was a lot more difficult to maneuver the roots and underbrush with so little light left.

They switched on their flashlights at the creek and left them on.

"How far did you make it, before you turned around?" Peter's breath puffed up next to Blake.

"Not far—couldn't see the tracks anymore and wanted to make the creek before darkness."

Peter kept the cone of his flashlight on the small footprints.

They followed the tracks for another ten minutes.

Darkness ensconced them completely now. "I wonder where the hell he's going," Blake said.

Then he and Peter halted.

The tracks ended at a pile of rocks.

"I know this place," Peter said, his flashlight dancing across the boulders. "There was a mudslide here before I was born. A lot of the boulders built up to a pile at the end of the slide. It's the endpoint of a hiking trail." He directed his flashlight downwards.

"We must be east of that point. A little higher up too. Not that many boulders here. Let's search for a cave or something—maybe he's hiding somewhere."

Blake and Peter fanned out, and Blake was about to stop looking when his flashlight highlighted a dark spot on the surface of a boulder in front of him. He shone his light directly on the spot and touched the stone with his finger.

Blood.

He slowly searched farther up, until his cone of light encountered a bloody handprint. The child was far too small to be out here in the woods. Hurt and alone.

He looked up when Peter's phone beeped.

"Got something," Blake said and shone his light at Peter ten feet to his right, slightly higher up the pile.

Peter's face looked strange, his eyes huge like saucers, and his look dazed.

228

"What's wrong?"

Peter looked down at Blake then back at his phone. "There's...I got..." Peter stammered and Blake raised his eyebrows.

"What the fuck is wrong?"

Peter hesitated. "I got a text from Lisa—they're on the way to the hospital. Claire's bleeding."

Blake pressed his eyes closed.

His heartbeat raced, and he shivered from the sudden coldness that hit his core. "Are you sure?"

Peter looked down at his phone. "Positive."

Blake hitched a breath, but couldn't suck enough air in. Dark spots appeared in front of his eyes.

He put his hands on his knees and forced a breath, then a second. Slowly the dark spots faded and his breathing returned to normal again. He needed to get his shit together.

"Can you call?" Blake straightened and looked up at Peter.

His rasping breaths making his voice all raspy. He wasn't steady enough to climb the rocks himself and watched Peter climb farther up to the top of the rocks.

Peter dialed and held his phone to his ear. "Lisa, what the hell happened?" Peter was quiet for a long time, and Blake could hear the blood rushing through his body.

"Hospital in Whitebrook?"

Blake squeezed his eyes shut. Claire was losing the baby. He didn't know much about pregnancy, but he knew you weren't supposed to bleed.

Bleeding was a bad sign, a terrible sign.

"Shit, fuck, damn it."

Blake opened his eyes again.

"I lost the signal. Claire had an accident earlier. She slipped on the frozen staircase and caught the handrail on her belly—now she's bleeding. They are on their way to the hospital in Whitebrook right now."

Blake couldn't see Peter's face in the darkness, but he could hear the sorrow in his voice. "I'm sorry, bud." Peter looked at his phone again. "I got our coordinates."

Peter shone his cone of light at Blake and blinded him from above.

"Get your fucking beam out of my face."

Blake swiped at the wetness on his face.

They had been so close. Their talk last week had cleared up all the conflicting feelings inside of him.

He loved Claire and he would love their little baby. Blake hesitated. He didn't want to be stuck here in the woods. He wanted to go to Claire as fast as possible.

Protect her.

Her and their baby.

They would go through this together.

He looked around.

Maybe they could return and search for the boy in daylight. Even as the thought ran through his mind Blake immediately dismissed it.

The boy wouldn't make it until daylight.

Blake slowly picked up his flashlight from the ground. He must have dropped it, but he couldn't remember. Then the bloody handprint came into the light again.

So small.

Another child, in danger.

He forced his eyes from the handprint and up to Peter.

Peter had climbed to the left, so now he was right above Blake. "Got something. Looks like a cave."

Blake immediately stuck his flashlight between his teeth and climbed up the boulders to Peter's level. Peter was hanging headfirst between two stones.

"I see something down there. Can you hold me back?"

Blake grabbed Peter's jacket and waistband while Peter angled himself farther down.

"Got him. Can you pull us up?" Peter's voice was muffled between the stones.

Blake pushed his feet against the rocks and pulled until Peter was able to get his footing again. Then he grabbed the small bundle. Holy hell, cold as ice, his T-shirt wet and frozen in places.

This wasn't good.

Together, they got the boy down from the boulders and Blake checked for a pulse.

Hardly there, and his breathing was so shallow Blake nearly missed it.

Blake's finger came away bloody and he searched until he found a bleeding head wound.

Nothing he could do now, not when he needed to carry him.

He looked up at Peter, who shone his flashlight onto the boy.

They'd both been trained in combat medicine. But hypothermia was no joke. "Gotta get him to the hospital. Fast."

Blake took off his jacket and started taking off the boy's clammy clothes. "Peter, find a route back, and establish comms, fast."

Peter climbed back up the rocks and fiddled with his phone.

Then he disappeared behind the boulders and Blake concentrated on the boy.

He took off the boy's wet T-shirt, then his own, which he slipped over the boy's small frame. He put his jacket back on, pressed the boy against his bare skin, and closed the jacket behind the boy's back.

His skin broke out in goosebumps.

Fucking freezing.

Blake stood up from his sitting position and took the boy with him. It was an awkward position, but he couldn't weigh more than a feather.

Blake hadn't dealt with the boy's trousers, but now that he carried him, he maybe should have.

"We gotta roll," Blake hollered and Peter neared him from farther down.

"Let's go—shortest way down is via the hiking trail—called the sheriff—they'll meet us there. Do you need help?"

Blake shook his head and nodded for Peter to take point.

They settled on a slow run and Blake's thoughts returned to Claire, and their baby, who were fighting without him.

Be strong. I'm coming.

38

Blake wasn't sure if the boy was still breathing until he felt the soft bump of his heart against his chest.

Now and then, he caught a whiff from the boy's hair.

Like copper mixed with wet dog.

His last shower must've been ages ago—not good for the head wound, though the cold was.

They'd scrambled along the tail end of the landslide, down the mountain.

Until they'd arrived at the hiking trail ten minutes ago, the underground had changed into a slightly less bumpy trip, even though the snow made it really hard to walk.

Blake's running shoes were soaked, and he hadn't felt his toes in a while.

Embrace the suck!

"Where are they? Shouldn't we've met them by now?" Blake huffed.

His grip on the boy was awkward, and his right thigh must've had a bruise the size of a shoe where the boy's feet tangled out of the zipped-up jacket.

"I don't know where the fuck they are. I was spot-on with my coordinates," Peter replied.

He handled both flashlights and illuminated the ground in front of them.

They walked around the next bend and were blinded by light.

"Finally. We thought you might have had your position wrong." Sheriff Travers pulled his hat from his head and rested his hands on his knees.

Peter scoffed.

Two EMTs pulled their rucks from their shoulders and Blake stepped toward them.

Just then, he discovered the wheeled rescue basket behind them.

He unzipped his jacket and gently went down on his knees to secure the boy from falling.

Together with the paramedics, he placed him on the litter. "He slipped into a creek and knocked his head. Hasn't been conscious. He's wearing my T-shirt, but his trousers are still wet."

For a split-second Blake's heart stopped.

What if the boy was dead?

He watched one of them searching for a pulse And loosened his jaw, when he went on to check his pupils.

"Okay, let's package him up." They bundled the boy up and strapped him on the litter in no time and started their descent.

Blake went alongside, but never far away from the boy.

He didn't want to talk to anyone anyhow.

Not that he could.

The pain in the back of his throat intensified, every time his thoughts drifted from the boy to Claire and the baby.

He lit up his watch for the hundredth time. Their descent was slow.

Too slow.

Maybe he should have just carried the boy down.

Claire must have arrived at the hospital by now.

He looked back at Peter, ready to tell him to call again, but decided not to.

It wouldn't help.

And he was going there anyhow.

Finally, they arrived at the parking lot and loaded the boy onto the stretcher of the waiting ambulance.

Blake climbed in after the EMT, as well.

Peter and the sheriff stood outside, ready to pop the doors closed.

"We'll clear the way to Whitebrook for you," Sheriff Travers told the other EMT, who nodded, closed the doors, and sprinted to the driver's seat of the ambulance.

Blake fastened his seat belt and stared at the boy. Now, in the harsh light, his skin was waxy, and the wound on his forehead looked far more severe.

The paramedic checked his pulse. It took nearly a minute until he nodded, and Blake released the breath he was holding.

The boy'd had a pulse when they found him. But with hypothermia, anything could happen.

The paramedic took his temperature and showed it to Blake. Ninety-two.

"Fuck." Blake rubbed his eyes—the boy was still too cold to even shiver.

The paramedic took several heat packs and placed them in his armpits and on his groin, before he fastened the blanket again.

"Why isn't he conscious?" Blake tapped his fingers on his thigh.

The paramedic shrugged. "Might be the cold, or the wound on his head. But he's stable as far as I can tell. His heart rate is slow, but that is to be expected. Now he just has to pull through." The paramedic cut the kid's shorts away, and Blake gasped.

A girl.

Blake wrapped the blanket around her feet as soon as they'd removed the clammy cloth and shook his head.

The thought never once entered his mind.

But at this age, kids pretty much all looked the same.

They arrived at the hospital, and Blake was eager to get to Claire.

He turned to Peter, away from the girl, when a small whimper made him rush back.

She was awake.

The girl didn't open her eyes, but her whimper glued Blake to her side.

"Can you go check on Claire for me?" Blake looked at Peter, who stood next to him by the stretcher. "I can't leave her alone."

"Her?" Peter cocked his brow.

Blake looked back at him, puzzled. "Yes, her." He pointed at the little girl on the stretcher. "So, would you please go check on Claire for me? Now?"

He scraped a hand through his hair. His arms were sore. His chest hurt and he still didn't know anything about Claire and the baby.

Peter turned away without another word.

Blake sighed.

This day was already going on too long.

He followed alongside the stretcher into the ICU.

There, he was pushed aside by a flurry of people who worked around his girl. Blake positioned himself to the side, his back against the wall, out of the way of all the professionals, but his eyes were trained on her face and never lost focus.

A nurse handed him a clipboard with a form attached.

He glanced at it repeatedly and filled out all the information he could. But his focus never left his girl. He narrowed his eyes when he came to the field for her name and left it empty. Ground his teeth. He hated filling out these stupid forms.

Hated not knowing.

Why was she up there?

Why was she alone?

And why hadn't he investigated this earlier?

Followed her.

Trapped her.

Did something.

A female doctor stepped up to him, right in his path of sight, and Blake adjusted his position slightly. "We'll move her to get a CT scan done. Then we will know more about her head injury. You need to wait here, but two nurses will always be by her side."

Blake's face tightened. He glanced at the name tag—Dr. Michaels, but looked up again when the doctor squeezed his arm.

"Don't worry, we'll take good care of your daughter. We'll do everything we can for her."

Then she turned around and Blake watched the bed pass him.

He needed to get to Claire. And his baby, who hopefully was still alive.

He stepped out of the room and up to the nurses' room.

A sour-looking old nurse sat there and hacked at the keyboard of the computer using one finger from each hand. She huffed repeatedly and swore under her breath but didn't react to Blake's presence.

"Excuse me, I'm here to see Claire Gunterson."

The nurse looked up and flattened her lips. "And you would be?"

Blake's muscles tensed and he pressed his hands flat on the counter. "I would be the father of her child. Can you please tell me where she is?"

Blake took a deep breath in through his nose and out through his mouth. This evening was the most challenging he'd faced in a long fucking time, and he barely hung on by a thread.

He moved his hands to the edge of the counter and gripped it.

The nurse must've realized he was on edge, because she gave him a hard look, and after a short nod, focused on her screen.

After a while her pinched expression cleared up. "Ms. Gunterson is in room 1." She pointed in the direction he came from. "The first room on the left."

Blake nodded, murmured a quick, "Thank you." and turned toward Claire's room, but then his step faltered. "Can you come get me, when the little girl gets back from her CT?" He asked, and she nodded.

He sprinted toward the door, his heartbeat pounding in his ears.

Please let Claire and the baby be okay.

Blake knocked and entered the room.

He immediately was hit by a strange sound, that reverberated from the walls of the room.

Claire looked frail in the white hospital bed, and Lisa sat on Peter's lap on a chair next to the bed.

Claire smiled when he closed the door behind him and moved toward her.

"How is the girl?" Claire asked softly, and Blake swallowed the lump in his throat.

"They moved her to get a CT scan. She's still unconscious." He leaned down and carefully kissed her forehead. "What about you, and our little girl?"

Claire furrowed her brow. "What makes you think it's a girl?"

Blake shrugged. "Just a hunch. So?"

Claire took a deep breath. "We don't know for sure yet. They took some bloodwork and we're waiting for the results. The baby's heartbeat is steady though. No signs of distress."

She pointed at the monitor next to her, which showed multiple graphs of some sort on its split screen.

Not unlike the thing that monitored Jessie during her delivery. The noises he'd heard upon entering came from this machine too.

"Listen. It's our baby's heartbeat."

Blake inhaled sharply, closed his eyes for a second, and just listened. Until now, the concept of having a baby had been exactly that.

A concept.

Now, with her heartbeat all around him, Blake's eyes started watering.

He opened his eyes and stared at Claire. "That's our baby?"

She nodded and Blake sniffed.

Then he put his palm on her cheek and slowly leaned in for a kiss. When they looked into each other's eyes afterward, he could see her face had turned soft.

A wave of heat hit him. He would be a dad.

He would have a family.

And he loved this woman.

He wiped the tears from his eyes. "When will we know for sure?"

Claire shrugged and tears clouded her beautiful eyes. "I don't know. They're checking if any of the baby's blood is in my blood."

She sniffed. "I slipped on the staircase and knocked my

belly against the handrail." Tears started to flow down her cheeks and Blake wiped them away gently.

"Shh. It will be okay."

But Claire only cried harder. "I'm sorry I didn't take better care of our baby. I tried. I really did."

Blake felt more than saw Lisa and Peter leave the room, but he focused fully on Claire. "I know, baby. This was a freak accident. Accidents happen. Shh."

He positioned himself next to Claire on the bed, careful not to touch any cables, or move the sensor on her belly. He took her in his arms and caressed her head.

After a while, the sobs subsided and soon, her breaths got regular again.

"I was so careful. And so afraid something would happen to this child. And look at us now."

Blake nodded, but she couldn't see it. "It will be okay. We will be okay."

Claire relaxed against him even more, and soon her breathing pattern told him she fell asleep.

Safe, in his arms.

Blake listened to the heartbeat of his child, calmer and happier than he'd ever felt in his life.

His thoughts turned to the girl.

She would be okay too.

He just knew she would.

39

The door opened and Blake snapped his eyes open and his body tensed.

He focused on the door.

He must've fallen asleep. He looked down at Claire. Her head lay on his shoulder and he could feel her steady breath on his neck.

Still asleep.

The door opened wider and Peter and Lisa tiptoed inside as soon as they saw Blake awake.

Blake chuckled at their antics, but when reality hit him again, his face tightened.

Peter watched the changes in Blake's facial expression and stopped, but Blake waved him forward.

They sat down on the single chair, Lisa on Peter's lap.

"How's the girl? She all right?" Blake asked under his breath,

Peter shrugged and whispered back. "She's not back from the CT scan, and they wouldn't tell us anything more. How are things here?"

Blake stared down at Claire who was still sleeping. A pained expression swept over his face. "We're still waiting for the bloodwork to come back. But the heartbeat is steady —no hiccups."

The heartbeat was what had lulled him into a light sleep earlier. It was strong and steady and somehow very soothing.

He smiled.

Who would've thought hearing the sound of his child's heartbeat alone could change everything. In a heartbeat he'd reached a whole new level of love and protectiveness .

He looked down at Claire's body again. She'd wrapped herself around him from head to toe, their unborn child safely wedged in between.

No distance, not an inch of space between them...and Blake loved it like he'd never loved anything ever before.

The door opened again, and Dr. Michaels came in with some files in her hand.

Blake rocked Claire slightly to wake her up. "Baby, you need to wake up. The doctor's here."

Claire woke up with a start and sat up. The tenseness in her eyes made Blake's muscles jump under his skin.

It would be okay, it just had to be okay.

Lisa and Peter left the room, and Dr. Michaels cleared her throat as soon as the door closed behind them. "So, Mr. And Mrs. Gunterson, I have good news for you. The amount of blood from the baby detected in your blood is minuscule. There are no signs of any severe injuries to the baby. The heartbeat is strong and steady, this too is an indicator every-thing should be fine." She smiled.

"We want to keep you here for a while longer to monitor the bleeding. But after that you can go home..." She paused for a moment. "We got lucky. Accidents happen, but with this one, we got off lightly."

Blake's mouth went dry, and he uttered a soft "Thank God" under his breath.

He squeezed Claire with his left arm, then shook the doctor's hand. "Thank you, Doc."

Dr. Michaels shook Claire's hand, as well, turned around, and left the room.

Blake drew a deep breath and let his head fall back on the pillow.

Safe.

His girls were safe.

After a second he looked up at Claire who hadn't moved from her sitting position.

Blake sat up and bent toward her to get a better look into her face.

Tears were streaming down her face.

"You okay, honey? What's wrong?"

Claire pressed the palms against her eyes and her mouth changed into a wobbly smile while she nodded her head. "I'm fine. We're fine."

Blake swallowed again.

They were fine.

Claire...the baby. His family.

"I love you, Claire." He leaned toward her belly, which wasn't the easiest feat in the small hospital bed. "I love you, little one." He kissed her belly and Claire's crying intensified.

This was it.

The perfect moment.

He climbed from the bed, stepped around the other side, and went on one knee.

He took Claire's left hand in his and cleared his throat. "Will you marry me, Claire Gunterson? Will you make me the happiest man alive and build a family with me?"

Claire's watery eyes shone when she nodded. Her wobbly smile turned into a big grin and her, "Yes." evoked a sudden lightness in Blake, unlike anything he'd ever felt before. He grinned at Claire and their eyes locked for a moment.

They would be a family.

His very own family.

The door opened and Peter and Lisa stopped in their tracks. Lisa yelped and Peter reacted with a bark of laughter.

They both stepped inside, and in a flurry of motions, embraced and congratulated first Claire and then him.

When Peter patted him on the shoulder, Blake had to look way up at him which made him realize he was still in this awkward on-one-knee posture, so he straightened.

"Copying my moves, hmm?" Peter laughed and gripped his shoulder. "Smart move—gotta get them while they can't get away."

It took a while for Blake to make the connection.

Peter had proposed to Lisa in the hospital, as well.

What a strange coincidence.

Then Blake's eyes shot back to Claire immediately.

Claire smiled at him, but her smile wobbled when his eyes narrowed.

He'd forgotten to kiss Claire after the yes. Shouldn't there be a kiss to seal the deal?

Their eyes were still connected and even though Blake was vaguely aware of Lisa and Peter in the periphery of his vision, his focus was solely on Claire.

His Claire.

The mother of his child and the love of his life.

He leaned down to her and kissed her.

"I love you," she whispered against his lips and heat radiated through his chest.

"Love you, too."

The door opened again and Alan and Jessie entered. The newborn was bundled up against Jessie and looked like the Pillsbury dough boy in his white snowsuit.

They stopped and looked around at all the smiling faces before they stepped farther into the room and relaxed.

"So, good news, I guess?" Alan zeroed in on Claire, moved across the room, and sat next to her on the bed, then took her hand in his.

Claire nodded. "They want to monitor me a while longer, but the baby's fine."

Alan smiled. "That's excellent news."

"Plus, they're getting married," Lisa said in a singsong voice like it was high school all over again.

Alan nodded and glanced at Blake.

And Jessie, who'd claimed the chair to work little Sebastian out of his snowsuit, stopped for a second.

She looked at Blake and a cocky smile lit up her face.

Blake just grinned back at her. The silent communication between them must have been palpable, because Claire nudged him and laid her hand in his.

"So, is the girl back?" Blake sat down on the other side of Claire's bed and Alan vacated his spot and moved to Jessie and little Sebastian.

Peter shrugged his shoulders. "No. I spoke to Nici Michaels though. She woke up a few minutes ago. Seems to be clear in the head—just frightened. I told them to get her in here with you, since you're listed as her dad and all," he raised a single eyebrow, "but they need to finish some tests first."

Blake's ears felt impossibly hot all of a sudden and he didn't dare look at Claire. "Why would they list me as her dad?"

Peter shrugged his shoulders. "Maybe because you were with her the whole time? Maybe because you acted like a dad?"

He gave him a lopsided grin. "Or maybe, I don't know, because you wrote your damn name on her sheet?"

He narrowed his eyebrows. He did?

"Anyway, she'll be here in a little while," Peter said with a half-smile.

Blake nodded and looked at Claire who had a soft grin on her face.

"What?" His eyes narrowed.

"Well, for someone who didn't want any children as of not that long ago, you're really piling them up now, bro," Jessie said and Blake's head snapped in her direction.

Claire chuckled softly. "I think we need to talk about how many we want then because that could be a deal breaker. I'm not that young anymore and I have an Inn to run."

Blake's head shot back to Claire and his eyes narrowed.

How did he get to be the butt end of the jokes around here?

40

They were still waiting for the girl to come back when Claire had fallen asleep five minutes ago and their friends had filed out.

What took them so long? Was something wrong?

He was slowly coming down from his adrenaline rush and had a hard time concentrating.

He'd used the woodworking magazine Peter had conjured up to keep his mind occupied and his ass in the chair instead of pacing—what he really wanted to do—or go out there and demand to see the girl.

He'd already decided to build a crib for Jessie's boy and their own children, as well as a rack for his wardrobe. But he welcomed the inspiration, and distraction.

A soft knock on the hospital door caused Blake to look up.

A nurse opened the door and Blake jumped up when he saw the hospital bed behind her.

The girl looked small and very pale in the huge bed, and her gaze shot from him to Claire and roamed around the room. She was nervous and Blake sat back down again to not intimidate her more than necessary.

"Look who we have here. Your mom and dad," a second nurse said in a cheerful voice.

Blake cringed and clenched his jaw when he saw the devastation and the tears building up in the little girl's eyes.

Fuck.

The two nurses positioned the bed on Claire's other side, then left the room.

Blake cleared his throat.

The girl had a white bandage wrapped around her head to cover her wound which made her look even more frail.

"I'm sorry they thought we were your mom and dad."

The girl shrugged, but the tears were still rolling down her cheeks, and she clasped her hands around the edge of her blanket.

"I'm Blake and this is Claire. I found you in the woods and brought you here. You hurt your head. We met at my house—remember the cookies?"

He was rambling, he knew that, but he was afraid to stop.

Blake grabbed Claire's arm and shook her gently to wake her up.

Claire was groggy at first, but pushed herself up when she registered the presence of the girl.

"Oh, hey. You're finally awake, and here. We've been waiting for you." Claire's soft voice seemed to calm the girl down a little, the death grip she had on her blanket loosened, but her eyes were still wet.

"You know, Blake thought you were a boy at first. How he got that idea, I really don't know. Anybody who looks at you can clearly see what a beautiful young lady you are."

Claire shook her head and the girl seemed to hang on her every word.

"What's your name? I'm Claire and this is Blake."

The girl didn't answer the question, but her body relaxed even more and her eyes got droopy.

Had they given her something before, that had just kicked in now?

Blake's phone rang, and he looked down at the display. Milan.

He stood up.

"I gotta take this—be back in a minute." He moved toward the door and left the room.

"Everything okay?" He asked Milan.

"Of course, everything under control, boss."

He'd asked Milan to cover for him at the bar tonight.

He'd been so excited when Claire agreed to their little double date.

He sighed. So much had happened since.

"We just heard. How's our girl—everything all right?" Milan asked while Blake watched Sheriff Travers move toward him.

"Claire's fine—they just want to monitor her a little while longer. How's the bar?"

"Busy. Sharon was swamped, so I'm behind the bar and closed down the kitchen for tonight."

"Good call. Appreciate it, pal."

"No factor, boss. Tell Claire I said hi."

Sheriff Travers stopped in front of him and Blake waved.

"Will do. Hey, I gotta go, thanks, Milan. I owe you one."

Blake ended the call and slipped his phone into the pocket of his track pants.

He shook hands with Richard. "They just brought her in."

Richard nodded. "And I got a hit."

Blake raised his eyebrows and crossed his arms in front of his chest. "Wow, already."

He swallowed. A strange wave of possessiveness flushed through him. "That was fast."

"Name's Sunnie Davis—made the news two years ago. Apparently, her father shot her mother in a domestic dispute and disappeared with the child. They remained missing ever since."

Sheriff Travers took a folded sheet of paper from the breast pocket of his uniform and handed it to Blake. The girl in the picture was a happy little girl, her brown, curly hair in a ponytail, playing with a cute white dog in the grass.

Blake scrunched up his face then released it. "You think it's her?" The girl in the picture looked quite a bit younger.

Carefree and happy.

Sheriff Travers handed him another sheet of paper. "This is her. Artificially aged and with shorter hair."

Blake gasped.

Yep, this picture was spot on.

"Holy shit, it's her." He looked up at Richard, who nodded.

"We just need to know what the hell she's been doing in our woods."

Blake looked down at the picture again and rolled his neck.

"She hasn't talked. I don't think she's ready to answer your questions. They brought her in, like five minutes ago."

Sheriff Travers contemplated this for a minute. "Let's try, anyway."

Blake ran his hands through his hair. He didn't want to frighten the girl any more than she already was.

"What about relatives, grandparents? Aunts and uncles?"

Sheriff Travers shook his head. "No one besides the father. Grandparents are dead and there are no aunts and uncles."

Blake's shoulders slumped.

He couldn't stop Richard, but the need to protect the girl was strong. "Just...let's make this really gentle, will ya?"

He nodded. "Child services are on their way."

Blake preceded him into the hospital room.

The moment the sheriff entered the room, the little girl jumped out of her bed, and in a flurry of motion, scrambled into Claire's bed and under her blanket.

Claire's eyes were huge as saucers, and her mouth opened.

What the hell had just happened?

Blake exchanged a look with Sheriff Travers, who shrugged his shoulders, unsure of the situation himself.

"Hey, Sunnie." Blake's tone was soft and Claire's eyebrows shot up. "This is Sheriff Travers—he helped me find you. He has some questions—do you think you could help him out?"

Claire peeked under her blanket and whispered something Blake couldn't hear.

He moved next to Claire's bed and sat down on his chair again. "He's a good man, Sunnie. You don't have to be afraid. Claire and I won't let anything bad happen to you."

Did she even understand what he was saying? Sheriff Travers hadn't told him where she was from, so maybe she didn't understand their language.

Claire was still under the blanket, whispering with Sunnie and it seemed like Sunnie was whispering back.

After a while the small face emerged from under the blanket. Sunnie pressed herself against Claire's side and Claire wrapped her arm tightly around her.

Sheriff Travers was still at the door and made no move. "Is your name Sunnie?" His voice was so low and soft that Blake had to smile. Richard was a good man.

The little girl nodded and Blake clutched the armrests of his chair.

"Do you live in the woods?" Sheriff Travers asked once more and Sunnie nodded again.

"Is your dad there with you?"

Tears appeared in Sunnie's eyes and Blake's chest tightened.

"Did your dad bring you there?"

Sunnie nodded, tears dripped down her chin, and Claire looked like she was about to cry too.

"But he isn't there anymore?"

Sunnie shrugged her shoulders.

"So he's still up there?"

The girl nodded.

"What happened?"

The girl shrugged her shoulders again. She whispered something in Claire's ears and Blake leaned toward them.

He caught the words "move," "speak," and "stares," but not the whole sentence.

Claire's chin trembled, and she squeezed Sunnie even tighter against her side. "Sunnie said he's sitting in the cave, but he doesn't move or speak anymore—just stares at the rocks." Tears were running down Claire's face and Blake slid to the edge of his seat to reach her hand.

Claire glanced at his open palm and laid her left hand on it. Then she leaned down and kissed Sunnie on the top of her bandaged head.

"I see." Sheriff Travers nodded, and Blake and him exchanged a knowing look.

"That's it for now. Thank you, Sunnie. You were a great help."

Travers turned around and opened the hospital door.

Blake stood up, kissed Claire's hand, and followed him out the door.

When the door closed, Sheriff Travers turned around, his lips pressed together in a slight grimace. "Shit, shit, shit."

Blake nodded and patted Richard's shoulder.

The other man stared down at his feet and shook his head. "How can it be, that they were hiding in my woods and I didn't have a clue?"

Blake shrugged and crossed his arms over his chest. "Maybe he was good at hiding."

"I need to organize S&R."

Blake nodded. "I'll need a minute. I'm coming with you."

Richard nodded.

Blake slipped back inside.

His eyes found Claire's. And she knew.

"You need to go, don't you?"

He nodded. He didn't want to leave, but he and Peter were the only ones who knew the terrain.

Then she smiled. "We'll be fine for a couple of hours. Go."

He kissed Claire's forehead, then left his two girls behind.

But just for a short while.

41

Claire was resting with her arm around Sunnie when the door opened.

Blake hadn't been gone long, so she was surprised.

She'd expected him to call in Lisa or someone else to keep her company, but she didn't expect company to arrive just so soon.

But the man that entered was just another nurse checking in on them.

She just hoped they didn't have to wake Sunnie again since she'd just fallen asleep right there beside her in her bed.

She looked down at her peaceful face, barely visible because she'd snuggled into her side and under the blanket.

She must be exhausted and needed sleep more than she needed another nurse prodding at her or taking her temp.

Wow.

Claire smiled, and heat radiated through her chest.

She was already feeling intensely protective of the girl.

Her motherly feelings had just been lying dormant.

She laid one hand on her belly and could feel the movement.

Her baby was moving a lot—if it wasn't asleep—and she couldn't wait until it was born.

Now, with Blake by her side, her happiness was complete.

He'd asked her to marry him.

Giddiness bubbled up until her whole body was flooded by next-level happiness.

She sighed, then pulled Sunnie closer.

Blake loved her.

She would have a family.

Another shot at what she secretly wished for but thought she'd never have.

"Can I help you with something?" She watched the nurse come in.

Somehow his movements were a little hesitant—entirely unlike all the other nurses coming in and out of her room and caring for them.

The nurse closed the door and took a couple of steps in her direction before he suddenly rushed to her side, grabbed the emergency button, and jerked it out of its socket.

Claire blinked once, twice. It took a while for the action to sink in.

Then he retreated a couple of steps, threw the cable on the chair, and pulled a scalpel out of his pocket.

What the fuck?

Claire couldn't move. Paralyzed she stared at his hand.

The scalpel.

Her mouth gaped open but she couldn't form any words.

Didn't have words.

Her mind raced.

What was going on?

The guy seemed equally surprised. He focused on the

scalpel in his hand—as if he had no clue how it came to be there.

Or maybe he was unsure about his actions?

Claire's stomach tightened. What did he want?

She blinked, but the image remained the same.

Distance, she needed distance.

She took a shaky breath, then tightened her arm around Sunnie, pulled the blanket up until her head was fully covered, and slid them both farther to the opposite side of the bed.

In response, the guy stepped forward, wielding the scalpel like a sword.

Coldness hit her core. She shrank even farther back.

Shit.

"Don't remember me, hah, bitch."

Remember him? Her heartbeat galloped in her chest while her field of vision scaled down to the scalpel in his hand.

Her pulse raced.

There was nowhere for her and Sunnie to go.

Her breathing turned sketchy. Black spots appeared in her vision. They would never make it out of the room.

He would catch up with them. Or hurt them.

She clenched her jaw.

Forced a breath through her nostrils.

A move so achingly familiar it grounded her.

She was not helpless. She was not a victim.

Could she use something as a weapon? Her eyes darted through the room.

There was an IV stand. She could use that.

And the bed.

The only possible barrier was the hospital bed.

Could she use it?

They could drop out of the bed and hide behind it.

But then what? What good would that do?

Damn.

She needed a plan. Something. Where was her phone?

Stay calm.

She took another breath that got stuck somewhere in her throat.

Okay, calm down. You can do this.

He'd asked her a question. What was it again? If she remembered him? "Should I remember you?"

Her voice was squeaky. She needed to pull it together.

For Sunnie.

She focused on the man. He looked pale, almost see-through, his movements erratic, and he seemed...out of it.

His eyes were feverish and scary. His gaze flitted across the room and back to her faster than she'd ever seen.

She got a sinking feeling.

It was the same guy she'd met earlier today.

At the Inn.

Right before her accident.

"Of course, you don't remember. You've always been too good for the family," he snarled.

His open hostility jarred her.

Family?

What family?

She'd been an only child of a not-in-the-picture father and the worst kind of mean drunk mother you could imagine.

Was he mistaking her for someone else?

What if he had the wrong Claire, the wrong room, what if all of this was just a misunderstanding?

She shook her head.

Didn't change a thing.

Whatever his reasoning, he stood just feet away from them, wielding a scalpel.

Openly hostile.

Probably drugged up.

"Claire."

The way he said her name made her skin tingle. He'd showed up at the Inn, and knew her name.

What if this wasn't a mistake?

But what would he want from her?

Time seemed to slow down.

He was close to her age, maybe even a little younger, though his skin stretched across his bones, making him look like a living skull.

Her mother's face had always been a little puffy, so alcohol probably wasn't his drug of choice. And there was no resemblance to the single picture she had of her father.

"Well, I guess it's just fitting that you'd don't remember me since you left Jeff and never looked back."

Jeff?

Her ex-husband Jeff?

Suddenly as if her brain had just waited for her to make the connection, an old memory popped up.

Jeff had a half-brother.

Somebody, he had no real connection with, somebody she only met once in passing.

Jeff had hated him. Said he was the reason for his family falling apart.

She didn't remember the name, something short and snappy, Drew maybe?

She'd spent years trying to forget all of this, get rid of the memories. His half-brother must've been in high school when she left Jeff.

What could he possibly want from her now? "So you're Jeff's brother?"

Somehow a strange kind of giddiness arose in her.

This whole situation was utterly surreal. How could she

sound so normal when she was scared shitless, and shivering inside?

He nodded. "I was his brother, all right. Didn't do me any good, though." He scowled. "Just give me my half of the money, and I'll go away."

There was another knock on the door, and his head flew around. He hid the scalpel behind his back and stared at the door as if he couldn't fathom someone coming in.

The door opened, and hell, Lisa's head, appeared.

"Hello, I heard someone was in need of company," she singsonged.

Shit.

Adrenaline shot through Claire's system and made her sit upright. She looked from the guy to Lisa and back.

She couldn't have Lisa in here.

She needed to leave.

Claire's mind was racing.

She needed to get rid of Lisa and, at the same time, tell her something was wrong.

How?

Just tell her?

But what would the guy do if she told her outright?

Would he jump her?

Hurt her?

Lisa's gaze zig-zagged from the guy to Claire and back.

She needed to stop her, say something, anything. "I'm sorry, ma'am, but I think you're in the wrong room. I don't know you," Claire said, then prayed her best friend would get the message and get out.

What followed was a beat of silence and another.

Lisa's eyes bulged.

Claire's heart bounced in her chest, and she fisted her blanket.

Please, leave.

Come on.

Lisa still hadn't moved.

Go, please turn around, go and get help.

Claire prayed that she would get the message, but she focused back on Jeff's brother and tensed her muscles.

If he jumped Lisa, she would come up from behind.

Two-on-one.

It would at least give them a fighting chance.

Lisa looked one last time at her, then nodded. "I'm truly sorry. I didn't want to disturb you."

She backed out of the room and closed the door, and even though that was precisely what Claire had prayed for, she felt utterly alone again.

Alone and defeated.

Her heart pounded slowly, and heaviness settled in her chest. Despair spread through her body like she was slowly sinking into ice-cold water.

Slowly drowning.

She couldn't escape the situation; there was no chance in hell she could fight Jeff's brother without risking injury if he caught her with that scalpel.

Or Sunnie.

She had to protect Sunnie.

The only thing she could do was keep him talking.

Hopefully long enough for Lisa to get help.

"What money?"

"Hey Lisa, are you on your way?" Blake asked as soon as the call connected.

"Is Travers with you?"

He could hear the shakiness in her voice and immediately tensed in the front seat of Richard's truck.

They'd barely made it out of Whitebrook. What could've happened in the twenty minutes since they'd talked?

"Yes, what's wrong?"

"Put me on speaker," she said, and he did just that.

"I don't know what any of this means, but I just went to the hospital as you asked me to, and there was a nurse in the room with Claire. Claire looked scared, and she pretended not to know me. I don't know what's going on, but I'm scared. What do I do now?"

Blake's eyes met with Richards, and his heartbeat sped up. Something was not right, and he had a bad feeling about what Lisa told them.

The night of the break-in flashed through his mind.

What if it wasn't a coincidence?

But it had been weeks ago.

And nothing had happened since.

"We're 10 minutes out," Travers activated the emergency lights and siren and made a U-turn.

"We're on our way, just stay there, call 911, and inform the staff," he said.

Blake ended the call and listened to Richard operating the radio and coordinating his people. These were the cons of being in such a rural area and having such a small team. They were already spread thin because it was night, and most of the guys on duty were heading to Moon Lake to search for Sunnie's father.

Shit.

He should've stayed.

If he would, Claire wouldn't be in this situation.

His mind was reeling. What was going on?

Why would she pretend to not know Lisa? And why would she be afraid?

"Any ideas?" Richard asked him.

Blake shook his head. "None. Maybe it's because of Sunnie?"

Richard shook his head. "Don't think so. Nobody knows she's there. There was no press release or any other statement."

"Coincidence then?"

"Let's hope for the best." Richard turned down the siren when they approached the hospital, and they both were out of the truck and on the stairs in seconds.

Blake focused on the rhythm of taking two steps at once and used it to calm down his breathing.

He needed to focus.

Whatever the situation, he wouldn't let Claire down.

I'm coming, babe. Hold on tight.

42

"What money?" Claire asked and held her breath.

He was still staring at the door. Did he even hear her?

And what did he mean, his half? Half of what?

The little money she had in savings wasn't something to write home about.

And even if, why would a virtual stranger think half of it belonged to him?

"Jeff's money."

"Jeff's money?"

He snorted. "You can play dumb as much as you like, but I know better." The color of his face turned from pale to a yellowish red, and he got more agitated.

If that was even possible.

"You got the letter a couple of weeks ago. I took it." He grinned, and suddenly she felt like vomiting.

He took a letter she got?

Was he the one behind the break-in? He'd been in her office when she was alone at the Inn?

For a letter?

She was suddenly freezing cold.

"Got sidetracked there for a little. Stupid cops. But they

didn't even ask about it. They didn't know." He chuckled, but it had a hollowness that made shivers run down her spine.

He pulled the scalpel back out and tested the sharpness of the blade against his fingernail. "Don't tell me they haven't contacted you again because I don't believe you."

Claire didn't know what to say or do.

Nobody had contacted her about anything. She never knew she got a letter regarding Jeff; this was the first time she'd heard about any of it.

But how could she make him believe her? She needed more time.

Stall him for as long as possible.

By now, Lisa must've called in an emergency, right?

But what if the cops didn't believe her?

Sunnie, next to her, slipped her hand inside Claire's, and for a split second, she looked down.

The girl's big eyes stared at her from under the blanket.

Visibly afraid.

Didn't she go through enough? The girl had just survived alone in the woods.

And now this.

Heat flushed through her body, and her muscles tensed.

She hated this.

She'd promised Sunnie she would be safe.

No way in hell would she let this dimwit destroy the little trust Sunnie had in her.

She squeezed her little hand, pushed her farther to the edge, then focused back on Jeff's brother.

"Your name's Drew, right?" She said, suddenly ultra-calm.

She'd experienced violence.

She'd handled Jeff's mood swings for a long time, learned to walk on eggshells, and gauge every micro-action.

She could keep him calm for as long as she needed.

She felt Sunnie slip from the bed to the floor, but he didn't notice. Or maybe he did but didn't think Sunnie was a threat.

He scoffed, "Dew, you mean."

Dew. Really?

"I'm so sorry, Dew. For a moment there, I didn't know what you were talking about. Of course, I can give you the money. I just don't have it yet."

Was lying a good tactic, or would it worsen their situation?

When they arrived at the floor of Claire's room, there was mayhem already. Hospital staff, doctors, nurses, a couple of EMTs, and two deputies crowded the corridor.

"Deputy Graves."

The female deputy came forward.

"What's going on? Give me a SITREP." Richard said.

Blake remained quiet. As much as he wanted to storm in, take over, and make sure Claire and Sunnie were safe, he couldn't.

And wouldn't.

This was his ego talking—and if he learned one thing in his years in the Teams—checking your ego was the most crucial thing on and off the battlefield.

They needed more intel, needed to know what exactly was going on.

And they needed a plan.

"Apparently, there's a guy in there with her dressed like a nurse. We had the staff ensure everybody is accounted for, and nobody on shift is missing."

"So he's not on staff?" Blake asked.

Belinda shook her head. "No, but that's all we know. Nobody tried to go in. We haven't called it in yet."

She looked at Richard, who seemed deep in thought.

Called it in? As in, called in a SWAT team?

"What about Sunnie?"

"Sunnie?" Deputy Graves' eyes turned big.

"Sunnie, the little girl? She's in there with Claire."

Graves grimaced. "I'm sorry, I didn't…"

Richard tapped her on the shoulder. "It's okay. The hospital staff should've told you. Do we have anything on the guy?"

Graves nodded. She gestured to someone who stood to the side with a laptop in his hands.

"This is Colby. He works in IT, I had him pull the CCTV, and Lisa verified it's him."

Richard and Blake watched a short feed.

He could feel a presence behind him and opened his arms. Lisa stepped into his embrace.

"I'm so sorry. I didn't know what to do."

She'd been crying and pressed her face against his chest, which muffled her words.

"It's fine; you did good. We'll get them out of there. I promise."

He just wished they were in a better position. The room only had one entrance and was on the third floor.

Their options were severely limited.

"Did you see any weapons on him?" Richard asked Lisa.

She looked sideways at him but shook her head. "But he looked… freaked out, or maybe high."

She shrugged. "And Claire was scared…I don't know. It all happened so fast, and I didn't understand what was going on."

Travers nodded. "It's okay."

"Can we get someone up on a roof to get some visuals?" Blake asked.

It was dark out, but maybe.

He needed to do something, or he would go insane.

His sanity, his life depended on it.

He would go in there in a heartbeat.

But he needed to evaluate the situation first. Needed to know if any action would put Claire in danger.

"Already on it," Graves said, "I sent Hopper up the building."

Travers got on the radio. "Hopper, come in."

"Hopper, do you copy?"

When nothing happened, he grabbed his phone and dialed.

"Hopper, Travers here."

Travers listened, and Blake could feel the restlessness swipe through his body in waves.

All of their eyes were on Richard, who shuffled his feet.

"Okay, anything else?"

He nodded, which made Blake twitch. He loathed being inactive.

Richard ended the call, and his gaze clashed with Blake's. "Hopper has eyes on the guy. He's by the windows. He could see Claire as well. They appear to be talking. No sign of a threat or a weapon."

Blake's mind raced.

Was it a misunderstanding?

But if this was just a regular guy, why would Claire be scared?

"Okay, so I can go in, check out the situation?" He asked.

Richard furrowed his eyebrows. "That's not what I said."

Blake let go of Lisa and straightened. "Then what do you suggest?"

Travers rubbed the back of his neck. "Calling her cell would be a start."

It might be, but why would he call if he could go in there and make sure she was safe?

He nodded anyways.

Travers dialed and waited.

For a second, Blake wondered why the sheriff had Claire's number. Then the realization set in. Her ex. She'd talked to Richard about her ex.

"She's not picking up," Richard said to him, his phone still on his ear.

"Then I'm going in."

Travers gave him a long look. Contemplating if he should hold him back, then he focused on his phone and made another call.

"Hopper, where is he now?" Travers looked back at Blake. "Same position. No movement. They're still talking. No visible threat."

He nodded but kept the phone to his ear. "Talk me through everything you see." He nodded at Blake, and they both started walking toward the room.

Blake took a deep breath. He would go in and pretend nothing was amiss. But he would be prepared to jump the guy as soon as he made a single move.

It was risky, but what else could they do? Wait for a SWAT team?

That would take hours.

Try to establish comms?

They didn't even know if the guy was a threat.

Speed, surprise, and violence of action.

All three were on his side.

Which was better than nothing.

43

Dew believed her. He really did.

She still didn't know why she would have money that belonged to Jeff.

But she hadn't asked for clarification.

Instead, she'd pretended to know exactly what he was talking about and would give him anything he wanted.

And at the same time, she prayed she could drag their conversation out long enough until help would come.

"How's the family?" Not that she was interested, but she needed to keep him talking.

"The family?" He laughed. But it was high-pitched. Maniacally.

Like a thousand tiny icepicks piercing her skin.

The sound of her heartbeat thrashed in her ears. She needed to find a safe topic—something to keep him talking —not agitate him further.

"What will you do? With the money?"

She prayed this was a better topic. Safer.

He bristled with anger. Stomped.

Shit.

"I owe some bad people."

She was so surprised he started talking. She could only blink.

Then nod.

"It's really not fair, you know. There was this one game. One lousy game."

He began reciting a whole night of poker. Play by play. Hand by hand. Which cards he had, how he thought he got it, how his winning streak slowly turned into a catastrophic loss.

Poker was never her game, so the cards and hands he recited didn't tell her anything.

So she nodded.

And he kept talking. Focused on something else.

Giving her a second to breathe.

She um-ed and ah-ed. Feigned interest. Kept him talking.

"They set me up, you know. I just can't prove it."

Claire nodded.

Gambling debts.

When he was done with his story, he stared at her.

He never mentioned anything about drugs, but the longer he talked, the more it became crystal-clear.

He was high on something.

His eyes were still freaking her out, and his speech was a-mile-a-minute.

But he'd calmed down and even leaned back against the window. The scalpel loosely held at his side.

Silence stretched until she couldn't not say anything.

"So, what do we do now?" I can get you the money when I'm out of here. But not before tomorrow—how did you know I was in the hospital?"

He shrugged. "I listened."

How comforting. He hadn't left. Instead, he'd been eavesdropping.

Claire shivered again.

Sunnie shifted; she was still hiding on the side of the bed on the floor. She must be cold as hell by now.

They needed help.

Blake, we need you.

She pushed the blanket off the bed and buried Sunnie in it.

Dew didn't comment.

He hadn't answered her question either.

So she racked her brain for another topic, something, anything to keep him talking.

But she got nothing, which made her nervous as hell.

What now? What if he demanded she go with him right now?

What if he psyched himself out and hurt her with that scalpel?

Suddenly the door flew open with a bang.

Claire saw Blake, froze for a split second, then immediately rolled off the bed and dropped to the floor next to Sunnie.

He came!

There was a blood-curdling scream, and she curled her body around Sunnie and pressed her eyes closed—as if that would do her any good.

There were a few grunts and a shuffle. Then Dew started spewing expletives.

Her heartbeat thrummed in her ears, and she stayed on the floor, her body protectively wrapped around Sunnie and her unborn child.

Seconds ticked by, stretched impossibly long. She was so scared. What should she do?

What was happening?

There was suddenly a lot of commotion.

A lot of people swarming into the room

Then she felt a hand on her shoulder.

And when she looked up, she looked into the most expressive and vulnerable arctic blue eyes she'd ever seen. She could see fear but also care and so much love.

Blake.

She could see every ounce of love she felt for this man reflected in his eyes, and every ounce of tension left her body.

"Are you okay?"

He dropped to the floor, grabbed her and Sunnie, and pulled them into his lap.

And all she could think was.

Safe. We're safe now.

Sunnie started crying, and their focus shifted.

Blake's hand and hers touched Sunnie's head, both eager to comfort her, and ultimately, they ended with her hugging Sunnie and Blake hugging them both.

Safe.

44

It had taken a while until everyone was settled again. The three of them had spent the remaining hours until morning huddled together.

Blake hadn't slept, instead, he'd watched over Sunnie and her.

Had been their rock.

She'd told Travers everything she knew about Jeff's half-brother, which was nothing since she didn't even know his last name.

She repeated everything he'd told her, how he'd been behind the break-in, and had followed her.

Wanted money.

Travers promised to come back as soon as he had more information.

Child services had shown up as well but had left after Travers had vouched for them to keep Sunnie company through the night.

At first light. Peter and Lisa had shown up with coffee and cupcakes. A little while later, Jessie and Alan arrived—with bagels and more coffee.

She'd never before had friends like that. Friends who

stood by you, who closed ranks, when you needed it, and were there for each other.

No questions asked.

It felt like she was part of a big, caring family.

For the first time in her life.

The search for Sunnie's father would start later today. But Blake wouldn't be on it.

He'd already said he wouldn't leave his girls again.

His girls.

The door opened, and instead of Sunnie—who they'd taken for yet another exam—Sheriff Travers entered the room again. He looked around and his eyebrows rose.

"Shouldn't I be invited, if there's a party going on?" He smiled and focused back on her. "Claire. There are some things I'd like to talk to you about." He looked around. "Maybe I come by later? When it's more convenient?"

"Wait. Can you..." Claire grasped Blake's hand. "We can talk now...I mean...if you've got time."

She watched Blake shoot a gaze at Peter and Alan, who both nodded.

The men immediately got up and ushered Lisa and Jessie to pack their things.

Sheriff Travers nodded and Peter and Lisa made their way to the door. "We we'll check on Sunnie again." They escaped through the door and Alan and Jessie bundled up the baby stuff and left too.

The door clicked closed behind Alan and Sheriff Travers rocked back and forth on his feet.

"Why don't you take a seat?" Claire pointed to the chair next to the bed.

Travers cleared his throat and rubbed the back of his neck before he nodded decisively and walked toward the chair.

He glanced at Blake, who hadn't moved from his place next to her on the bed before he focused back on Claire.

"Mr. Brown, Dew hasn't talked," he said with a sigh. "But I'd reached out to the officer who handled your case back then."

She nodded.

"He still remembered, and he'd made some inquiries about your ex-husband."

Claire clutched her tingling hands and Blake laid his arm around her shoulders, which felt strangely soothing to her.

"Turns out your husband died of cancer a couple of weeks ago."

Claire's breath exhaled in a swoosh. He was dead. He couldn't harm her or her baby.

She turned down her eyes to avert Sheriff Travers' gaze.

She was ashamed of her feelings of relief.

Certainly, she should feel some empathy, something else, something more than relief at the death of someone who was once her husband.

But there wasn't anything.

She cleared her throat and looked up. "Thanks for your effort, Sheriff."

Sheriff Travers nodded. "Apparently he sobered up after the divorce. He faced the charges. Did his time, did therapy, and became a reformed, upstanding citizen afterward. He even got married again. Unlike his half-brother."

Claire nodded and crossed her arms over her chest. She wasn't sure if she even wanted to hear any of this.

She'd made her peace, well, maybe not peace, but she'd sure made an effort to leave her past in the past.

She'd moved on.

Before Dew showed up yesterday.

Before that blast from the past threatened to wreck her future.

Threatened the happiness and calm that had engulfed her since they knew the baby was okay and Blake asked her to marry him.

She looked up at Blake who gave her a little smile, which intensified the soothing effect his presence had on her.

Everything was fine.

"I've got a letter." Sheriff Travers took an envelope out of his breast pocket and handed it to Claire. "It arrived yesterday, I just didn't..."

Claire inhaled sharply and stared at the extended hand with the letter, mesmerized, like it was a snake ready for attack.

Gone was the calmness.

A thousand different thoughts raced through her mind, pulling her in all different directions.

Should she take it?

Did she want to know what that bastard wanted to tell her? Why didn't he just leave her alone?

He'd never written her a letter back then.

Did he beat his second wife, too?

Her mind raced but her body was frozen.

She watched, like in slow motion, how Blake took the letter, and Sheriff Travers leaned back again.

"You don't have to read it, baby. You don't have to do anything. It's just a letter. Nobody can hurt you anymore and nothing in there can change anything about our life right now."

Claire swallowed.

Blake was right.

This was her past.

Nothing could touch her or hurt her, if she didn't let it.

And especially not Jeff.

Dead Jeff.

Claire took the envelope from Blake, snuggled back into his embrace, and looked at it.

"Claire Gunterson" it said on the envelope. No address, nothing else, just her name.

He'd used her maiden name, which made breathing suddenly a little easier for her.

She opened the envelope and found a single sheet of paper.

"Maybe I should leave you alone for this." Sheriff Travers straightened from the chair, but Claire indicated him to stop, and started reading.

Dear Claire,

I know I have no right to contact you, and for you to even read this letter is a sign of what an amazing person you are.

I'm not asking for your forgiveness because I don't deserve it and I'm afraid you'd give it anyway.

But what I want you to know is how sorry I am for what I did. I killed our child. I hurt you, even though I loved you.

There is no forgiveness for acts like that. There is no forgiveness for me.

Maybe that's why this cancer is eating me alive.

It's penance for what I did to you.

I hope you have a good life now. Good people around you, who love you and care for you and cherish you, the way I should have.

I wish you all the happiness in the world. And I

hope you're a mother by now. Because the way you cared, the way you love and don't give up on people, even though you have every reason to do so, would make you a magnificent mother.

This is what makes you special, and this is what makes you deserve everything you ever want.

Jeff

Claire had started crying while reading the letter, and when she finished, she turned her head onto Blake's shoulder.

Gut-wrenching sobs shook her whole body, and Blake stroked her spine and made soothing noises against the side of her head.

After a while, her sobs quieted down and her chest stopped hitching.

She dried her tears and focused on the reverberations of Blake's deep voice which echoed through his chest to her ear.

She didn't follow the conversation between the sheriff and Blake but just enjoyed her warm cocoon. After a while Sheriff Travers stood up and Claire looked at him again.

"There are a few more things, but we should maybe continue this in my office, sometime later."

Claire tilted her head to the side. "What else is there? He's dead, isn't he?"

Sheriff Travers nodded. "He left you money, though. So, there is some more paperwork waiting for you. And that's what Dew was after."

Claire shook her head. She didn't want any of his money.

Sheriff Travers moved to the door but turned around one more time. "You don't have to make any decisions right now. Just rest, and we will talk again, when you feel a little better."

Claire released the breath she didn't know she'd been holding. "What about the girl?"

The sheriff exchanged a long look with Blake. Claire didn't understand, but she would ask Blake about it later. "I don't have anything new right now."

"Can she...can you..." Claire hesitated. "Can she keep staying with us?"

Sheriff Travers gave a sharp nod, and a soft smile transformed his face and smoothed out the harsh lines around his mouth. "I'll do my best."

She mirrored his smile, then relaxed back into Blake's arm and watched Travers leave. His wife had just died a few weeks ago. It must be hard for him to concentrate on his job right now.

"Why did he look at you like that, when I asked about the girl?" Claire turned her head toward Blake, and he chuckled.

"We were talking about the girl just now while you were crying, but you were obviously somewhere else with your thoughts."

Claire nodded.

She looked into Blake's soft, blue eyes.

She loved this man with all her heart.

What Jeff said in his letter was true.

She didn't give up easily on the people she loved. And sometimes, she got rewarded for it.

She kissed Blake, and the timid kiss she intended turned heated pretty fast.

45

Claire laid the woodworking magazine to the side, onto her packed bag, and stood up from the chair.

Sunnie fell asleep again ten minutes ago. She slept a lot, and Claire had worried about it, but Dr. Michaels—who had taken a special liking to Sunnie—told her it was perfectly normal and good for healing.

Claire went to the window and crossed her arms over her chest. The snow had continued nonstop these last few days, and had transformed everything—even the small city of Whitebrook.

She longed to go out.

She wasn't a nature-loving kind of girl. But she'd been trapped in this room for days now and really longed for the feeling of wind on her face and the crunching sound of the snow under her shoes.

A soft knock interrupted her thoughts, and she turned to face the door. Her heart leaped when Blake smiled at her softly.

"Hey, babe. You up?"

"Shh." Claire stepped toward him and kissed him on the lips. It didn't take long for Blake to take over the kiss and when they both came up for air again, Claire whispered against his lips, "Sunnie's sleeping."

Blake nodded and led her out the door. "Why are you dressed, and why is your bag packed?"

Amazing how nothing ever escaped Blake's attention.

"I'm being released. The bleeding has stopped, the baby is okay. There's no reason for me to stay any longer."

She suspected they kept her in longer than necessary, just to make sure the stress of her encounter with Dew wouldn't cause any complication—which it didn't.

Blake scrunched up his face. "Are you sure?"

Claire nodded. "I just don't know if I can leave. I don't want Sunnie to be alone in here. So I don't think I will go. Sunnie is scheduled for another CT scan later. So..."

Blake planted his feet in a wide stance. "So, you'll come home with me? After we take care of the situation with Sunnie?"

Claire's stomach tensed. They had never spoken about moving in together.

She loved Blake's house. She could see herself reading a book on that comfy sofa of his.

But what about Lisa and the Inn?

She was responsible for breakfast, and her early mornings wouldn't work well with Blake's late evenings.

Claire bit the inside of her cheek and searched for a response. "I need to talk to Lisa first."

Blake nodded.

"I need to be at the Inn early. To prepare breakfast."

Blake nodded again. "Come here."

Claire stepped into his open arms and leaned against his shoulder. "We'll find a way. Don't worry."

Claire inhaled Blake's woodsy scent and nodded. She loved Blake and he loved her.

They wanted to build a family together.

Somehow they would find a way to intertwine their lives and build something new.

Together.

Claire relaxed against Blake's strong body. Amazing how much she loved this man.

"We need to visit the sheriff's office before we leave Whitebrook."

The letter. She'd read it again and again, last evening, after Blake left.

She couldn't connect the man who wrote that letter with the man she knew as her ex-husband. And she didn't want to. It was the past, and that's where it all belonged.

"Maybe we should do it, while Sunnie is getting her scans. We could be in and out, and she wouldn't even notice.

Claire straightened when she saw Lisa and Josephine coming toward them.

She smiled at the stuffed bear in Lisa's hands and stepped out of Blake's embrace.

Her friends had all adopted Sunnie just as much as she and Blake had.

"You ready for visitors?" Lisa grinned and placed the bear in Blake's hands, who looked a little awkward holding the toy.

Claire hugged first Lisa and then Josephine.

"Why are we meeting out here?" Lisa looked Claire up and down. "Oh, you ready to come home?"

Claire nodded but Lisa's face turned into a frown. "What about Sunnie?"

She shrugged. "She's asleep—that's why we're out here."

Lisa nodded.

"She'll get another CT scan to check on her brain—hopefully we can talk to a doctor afterward."

Claire paused.

Had she heard something?

She went to the door and was sure there was a sound coming from the room. Claire was reminded of a wounded animal and immediately opened the door.

"Hey, sweetie." She entered and marched toward the bed. "I'm here. Did you have a bad dream?" She sat on the hospital bed, and Sunnie crawled into her lap.

"Shh, everything's fine." She caressed the little girl's hair and soon Sunnie relaxed again.

Claire hummed under her breath. The big bandage, that had covered Sunnie's hair at the beginning, had been removed the day before and Claire let her short hair slide through her fingers.

She'd zoomed out of the surrounding conversation between Blake and Lisa and enjoyed the calmness and connection with Sunnie.

Her Anna would have been quite a few years older than Sunnie.

"Hey." Claire looked up at Josephine. Her head was heavy and she felt a calm drowsiness in her body.

"Why don't we look after Sunnie, so you and Blake can go out, visit the sheriff, and get some shopping done?" Josephine smiled at Sunnie who smiled back.

Claire was proud of her little girl. She was getting more courageous every day.

"Maybe we can play some games?" Josephine focused fully on Sunnie. "Do you know any games? I have a niece who loves to play UNO. Do you know it?"

Sunnie shook her head in Claire's lap.

"Well, look, since you never know, I always keep a stack in my purse. Maybe I could teach you. What do you think?"

Sunnie nodded, straightened, and climbed back into her own bed.

Claire immediately missed the soft feeling of her head in her lap but was glad Sunnie was opening up to other people. How had Sunnie's life been like these last two years? Claire couldn't even imagine what her little girl had gone through.

The door to the hospital room opened, and a nurse appeared. "Time for your head check, little princess." Sunnie looked first at the stack of cards on her bed, then at Claire.

"It's okay, you can play afterward. Now you need to be brave one last time. Okay?" Claire said.

Sunnie nodded and Claire and Josephine stepped back from her bed.

"Claire will go out for a little while, but we're waiting here for you, ready to play when you come back from going with the nurse."

Claire glanced from Josephine to Sunnie, unsure if she should really leave the little girl alone.

But when the nurse drove her away, Sunnie nodded and even waved goodbye at them.

"Peter and Odin are still with the S&R team," Lisa told Blake.

Claire's eyebrows shot up. They were still searching for Sunnie's dad? "Still?"

Lisa shrugged. "It's the damn snow."

Blake came toward Claire with her jacket in his hands. "Let's get going, babe. Maybe we'll beat Sunnie back here."

"Thanks for taking care of our little girl." Claire zipped up her jacket, and Blake escorted her to the door.

"No, problem," Josephine and Lisa replied in unison.

Claire was glad that Blake saw the need to move fast. She didn't feel comfortable leaving Sunnie in the hospital, and neither did he.

They arrived at the sheriff's office in record time.

"What if he isn't in his office? Shouldn't we have made an appointment?"

Blake looked at her strangely. "I did. I called. Didn't you hear me talking on the phone?"

Claire shook her head. Did she fall asleep on the bed with Sunnie? She sure had felt calm, maybe a little drowsy.

They stepped into the office and Claire was reminded of her last visit there. Was it really just a little more than a week ago? So much had happened in between.

Sheriff Travers welcomed them into his office.

"I hope you made it here okay. We got some serious snow these last couple of days."

Blake nodded and Claire swallowed and looked out the window.

So much snow.

Thank God Sunnie was safe and sound.

"So, your ex-husband left you the letter I already gave you, plus an attorney contacted me. He left you some money too. I have his information right here, so why don't I step out so you can contact him?"

Claire nodded. She took the contact information from Sheriff Travers and the phone he gave her.

The conversation with the attorney was short.

Apparently Jeff came into a lot of money, legally.

How, Claire didn't even want to know, but he'd wanted her to have some.

Claire's head jerked back when the lawyer told her just how much and Blake raised his eyebrows, slid closer with his chair, and took her hand in his.

She was still dizzy when she ended the call. "He"—she hesitated—"I don't know why he would have that much money—we never had a lot."

Blake laid his hand against her cheek and Claire focused on his eyes. "Calm down, baby. Deep breaths. In and out."

Claire consciously forced her body to relax. And after a minute of deep breathing, felt calm again.

"He left me just shy of a million dollars."

She snapped her head to Blake.

"Now I get it. That's what Dew was after."

Blake nodded.

"But I don't want the money. Maybe we can donate it?" She took a deep breath. "Yes, to some missing-child search foundation or something. That's what I want to do."

Blake leaned in and kissed Claire softly on the lips. "You are an amazing woman, soon-to-be Mrs. Blake."

Claire's head jerked back. "But, oh God, I never thought about that. Everyone calls you Blake all the time. But after the wedding."

Blake frowned at her until his face cleared into a smile. "You can call me whatever you like, Claire: Blake, Sebastian, Seb, man of my dreams, Adonis, God. I don't care as long as you're mine."

They kissed again until a soft knock on the glass door interrupted them. "Sorry to interrupt. But it seems like what you came here for is done, so could I maybe have my office back?"

Blake chuckled and Claire could feel by the sudden hotness that her ears must have turned red.

"Claire inherited money from her ex, that was what Dew was after," Blake told Travers, who nodded.

"That gives him a clear motive," Travers said.

"But how did he know?" Blake asked.

Travers shrugged. "Maybe he'll start talking now," he said, and Blake nodded.

It wasn't that she wasn't interested in what would

happen with Dew. But she refused to spend any more time thinking about him than she had to.

Everything else would be handled by whatever the court would decide.

"He skipped bail, so he might get transferred."

Claire shrugged. She really didn't care.

She was ready to leave it all behind.

Focus on her future.

Their future. "Do you know of any missing-child search foundations in the area? I want to donate some money to them."

The sheriff looked at her for a moment, then smiled. "Of course, there's a foundation right here in Whitebrook. Have you met Dorothy?"

Blake and her shook their heads.

"Just contact her, and she will steer you in the right direction. We might even have her card up front. Let's take a look."

"One more thing," Blake said—his voice took on a serious tone that made Sheriff Travers stop in his tracks and look at Blake.

"How is the S&R going? Did they find him already?"

"It's still ongoing, as far as I know. The snow has delayed the effort." Sheriff Travers stepped out of the office, and Claire and Blake followed him to the front, where he took a business card from a holder and handed it to Claire.

"Hey, chief. I got Peter on the phone. They found him." The woman, who worked in the back office, held her receiver up in the air, and Sheriff Travers turned around, crossed the office, and took the call.

Claire grabbed Blake's hand, who squeezed hers gently. No chance in hell she would leave the office before she knew exactly what had happened.

She studied the business card while they both waited for the call to end.

"Okay, just wrap everything up," Sheriff Travers said before he ended the call and squeezed his eyes shut.

"So, what is it?"

Claire looked from Blake to Sheriff Travers.

"He's dead. Broken neck, most likely. They found him sitting in the cave. The kid must have lived next to him for quite a while."

Claire gasped, then her breath left with a whoosh, and her chest caved in.

Sunnie had lived next to her dead father.

Most likely, she didn't understand at first what happened. Tears formed in her scratchy eyes and her nose started running.

"How long?" Blake's face was like ice. She couldn't see any reaction or emotion on it.

Sheriff Travers shook his head. "Don't know yet. Frozen solid."

Blake nodded and put his arm around Claire's lower back. "We'll see you," he said to the sheriff. Then he turned them around and steered Claire toward his jeep.

"Custody." Blake opened the car door for her and waited until she got settled in. "I need one second." He closed her door and ran back to the sheriff's office.

Claire sat in the car, pondering his actions.

Did he say custody? Custody of Sunnie? She thought about all the difficulties this could entail. But they couldn't turn their back on the girl.

Social services had already been a bit iffy about letting Sunnie stay with her in the same room.

After a while Blake returned to the car and entered on the driver side.

"What was that about?"

Blake looked straight, then over his shoulder, then started driving. "I need to ensure her safety. Sheriff Travers will look into our options. Guardianship or temporary custody. We will have to go to court for it."

Claire nodded when understanding dawned on her. Yes, they would. Go to court—do whatever it took to get their girl to safety.

46

Blake was pacing in the small hospital room and never moved his eyes off the door.

Sunnie was cleared to leave the hospital, and now they waited for Sheriff Travers and Social Services to arrive.

Blake had been to court and had filled out and signed hundreds of forms, and he still didn't know if they would be granted guardianship for Sunnie.

He watched Claire and Sunnie. Sunnie wore the new clothes he'd bought for her.

It had been rather uncomfortable for him as he'd stood in the shop, with no idea what size of clothes he should buy. The nice lady that had approached him had obviously seen the terror in his eyes.

And the clothes she helped him choose fit Sunnie perfectly.

He'd even gotten her a nice warm winter jacket, in hot pink, and Sunnie loved it so much she had it wrapped around her lower body even though it was already hot in the room.

At least it was hot to him.

He slumped down in a chair just to jump up again a second later and resume his pacing.

He was sick of the room.

Sick of the smell of antiseptics.

He wanted to go home. And take his girls with him. Yesterday evening, after Sunnie had fallen asleep, Claire and Blake had made plans about their foreseeable future.

So technically, they wouldn't go home at first, at least not his home. They would move into the Inn.

All of them.

That would give him some time to adjust the house to make room for Sunnie and the baby.

Blake chuckled. His house was hardly finished, and already he would be adding two rooms, one for Sunnie, one as a nursery. And in spring, they would all move in together. Like a real family.

He couldn't wait.

Blake stopped in his tracks when the door opened, and Sheriff Travers led a petite woman inside.

"Sebastian Blake, Claire Gunterson." He nodded at them. "This is Dorothy Cleaver. She's the head of Child Protection Services."

Dorothy Cleaver—Blake recalled the name from the business card Travers had given Claire. She was the chairman of the missing child foundation, Claire wanted to donate the money to.

"Dorothy needs to talk to Sunnie for a while. Why don't we step out for a minute?" Sheriff Travers held the door open for Blake and Claire.

Blake nodded and helped Claire from the bed, and they walked to the door.

But Sunnie scrambled from the bed, as well, and clung to Claire who stopped in her tracks. "It's okay, baby. I'm right outside. Don't be afraid. You know, Mrs. Dorothy helps to find missing children."

Blake smiled.

Claire had studied the card meticulously and had even gone online and researched the organization.

Sunnie squinted from behind Claire at Mrs. Cleaver, who had squatted down to be below eye level to meet Sunnie's gaze.

"Did you help Blake find me too?"

Mrs. Cleaver swallowed hard and shook her head. "We didn't know you were here, in our woods."

Blake appreciated the honesty.

Sunnie pondered the answer, and he suspected came to the conclusion that Mrs. Cleaver was at least honest.

"Would you tell me how you came to live in the woods?" Mrs. Cleaver's voice was melodic and soft, and Claire and Sunnie relaxed. "Claire can stay if you need her to."

"Your hair is nice."

"You think so?" Dorothy Cleaver touched the golden-brown locks that framed her face.

Blake and Claire exchanged a look. Ever since Sunnie started talking, they were even more in awe of her. She was funny, straightforward, and an all-around adorable little girl.

"Mine is short, but Claire said it will grow back in no time."

"Claire's right. Maybe one day we'll get together and braid our hair."

"Okay."

"I'll wait right outside the door, while you talk to Dorothy, okay, sweetie?" Claire said.

Sunnie nodded and Claire reached out and touched Sunnie's head, amazement and pride written all over her face. "I'll be just outside." Then she stepped away from Sunnie, who let her this time.

Sheriff Travers still held the door and closed it after Blake and Claire stepped through it.

"Dorothy is good, don't worry," Travers said, and Blake nodded.

"Does she decide if we can take Sunnie home with us?" Claire clutched Blake's hand and looked at Travers, who shuffled his feet.

"No, I'm pretty sure the court has already assigned temporary custody. I guess she just wants to make sure this is what's best for Sunnie. Don't worry."

"We need a car seat—do we need a car seat?" Claire's gaze ping-ponged from him to Travers.

"Calm down, baby." He laid his hand on the small of her back and his fingers found a way under her T-shirt to her warm skin. "I got it covered. I got her a booster seat. I bought enough clothes, a toothbrush. Everything I could think of." Claire relaxed under his caress. "And if I missed something, we can always get it."

Claire nodded and Travers grinned knowingly.

"Spoken like a real dad."

Blake recognized the gleam in Travers' eyes and grinned back. It had taken him some time. Hell, he'd done everything to avoid a family or kids of his own for the last seventeen years of his life.

But now.

This.

This expanding feeling in his breast.

Once he'd went all in, his mind felt at ease for the first time in a very long time.

Blake squeezed Claire's side and she turned to face him.

He loved this woman so much thinking about it scared the shit out of him.

But the alternative—there really wasn't any alternative.

He inhaled and his grin deepened when he felt the warmth of Claire's sweet smile, marred only by the lines of worry on her face which he softly skimmed over with the thumb of his other hand.

If they'd lost their child, the pain would have been unbearable.

But they'd been given their second chance and he would do everything in his power to ease her mind about their future.

The door opened and Mrs. Cleaver and Sunnie stepped out. Sunnie ran to Claire and him and squeezed between them. Blake's insides churned.

Not all was well in his life just yet.

He cleared his uncomfortable, dry throat and looked at Mrs. Cleaver.

Her severe face transformed into a smile when she watched their little family. "I guess there's nothing more for me to do or say. Sunnie is lucky to have found you."

Blake heard Claire's breath hitch, and swallowed hard. "So we get to keep her?"

Mrs. Cleaver nodded. "There will be some steps we have to take. But this will stretch over a period of time. For now. You can take Sunnie home with you."

Blake squeezed his eyes and tipped his head back for a second. Warmth flooded his body.

Now he could take his family home.

For a moment Blake felt overwhelmed, but in a good way, before he reigned in his breath and calmed himself down.

He looked at Claire next to him. Tears were streaming down her face and Blake squeezed her again. "Shh, baby. We're going home now."

Claire bent down, loosened Sunnie's arms, and took three steps toward Mrs. Cleaver, then hugged her.

Mrs. Cleaver looked a little shell-shocked.

Almost uncomfortable.

Not used to this open display of affection.

Claire must've sensed her stiffness because she released her from the hug.

"Thank you, Mrs. Cleaver. Thank you for giving us Sunnie." Claire stepped back a little more and Mrs. Cleaver relaxed visibly.

"Maybe we can meet for coffee sometime soon. There are a few things I want to talk to you about, besides Sunnie."

Mrs. Cleaver raised her eyebrows. Sheriff Travers must not have told her anything about the money.

"Okay?" She worded it more like a question than an answer. "And please, call me Dorothy. Mrs. Cleaver is my mom."

Claire nodded and smiled. "I'm Claire and this is Blake." Claire pointed back at Blake, who waved and grinned.

"I can give you my card." Dorothy rummaged in her purse before Claire stopped her with a hand on her arm, which made Dorothy freeze.

"I don't need it. Sheriff Travers gave one to me yesterday." Claire's smile softened, and she removed her hand when she recognized the distress in Dorothy's eyes.

"I'll call you in a few days. Okay?"

Dorothy nodded, hastily said goodbye, turned, and left them standing there.

Claire and Blake exchanged a puzzled look.

"She's a little socially awkward. Don't sweat it." Sheriff Travers turned to them and patted Blake on the back. "Enjoy your family. And I'll see you around."

Blake and Claire nodded, and Sheriff Travers disappeared the same way Dorothy had.

"Can we go home now?" Claire and Blake looked down at Sunnie, who, with her pink jacket, was all set for the outside.

"Let's take a last glance at the room. See if we've forgotten something, then we can clear out." Blake tousled Sunnie's hair and stepped back into the room.

Sunnie followed him and they both saw Lisa's bear still on the bed. Sunnie ran toward it and grabbed it, while Blake grabbed a bag from the floor.

"Let's go." Claire bounced on her toes, standing in the door.

Blake scanned the room one last time. "Let's go."

Sunnie was at Claire's side and Claire slung an arm around her shoulders and Blake walked behind them.

His girls.

He rubbed his chest, right at the source of warmth that radiated through his body.

Happiness.

This was what happiness felt like.

47

"Shh." Blake closed the connecting door between Claire's room and Sunnie's bedroom. "She's finally asleep," Blake said over his shoulder.

They'd moved Claire's things to one of the family rooms in the Inn, which was comprised of two rooms connected by a door. The small room Claire inhabited before might have worked for Claire and Sunnie, but Blake planned to be here with them as much as he could, so the small room wasn't an option.

Staying at the Inn would work best for their temporary situation.

Sunnie could become more familiar with Lisa and her mother, and Claire could start working again.

Blake frowned.

The fear he'd experienced when he'd thought they would lose the baby and later when Claire was in the hands of her ex's brother—whose drug test came back positive for cocaine and an assorted cocktail of other stimulants—had awoken in him the urge to wrap her in bubble wrap, or better yet make her stay in bed for the rest of the pregnancy.

When he very tentatively had come up with this suggestion, he'd earned a snort and a pat on the shoulder with advice from Claire to get over himself, and quickly.

So bubble wrap was out of the question.

Claire pressed herself against his back and relaxed.

Blake turned around, wrapped his arms around her, and pressed her against the front of his body.

Her belly nestled between them and Blake stared into her beautiful face. "Are you tired? Your eyes look tired."

Claire sighed. "No, I'm not. Just, being in the hospital for so long, not moving a lot, kinda zapped my energies."

Blake laid his hand against the side of her face and Claire closed her eyes and snuggled her cheek into it. "Should we just go to sleep?"

Claire said nothing, but Blake could feel her slow, deep breaths and her limp limbs, which confirmed his notion. "Come on, lovely, let's go to bed."

Instead of turning around, Claire kissed him.

Just a series of short kisses.

She didn't even open her eyes, but she did wrap her arms around his neck which meant she needed to go on tiptoes to reach that far up.

Blake picked her up, careful to not squeeze her belly too much, but Claire's legs wrapped around his torso and, in a heartbeat, those short kisses turned into some serious making out.

Blake's one hand stayed under Claire's sweet behind, to prop her up, and his other hand moved to the back of her neck and pressed her tighter against him.

He could feel a shiver run over her back and stopped for a second to look at her. "Okay?"

Claire opened her eyes and nodded.

Blake looked down at her lips, shiny and red from his kisses, and dove in again.

This was heaven.

They kissed for a good, long time before he sensed her hesitation again. He stopped only a hairsbreadth away from her lips and raised his eyebrow. "What now?"

Blake could feel the small whoosh of air that Claire blew out. "I-I forgot to ask. You know. The doctor. If sex is okay."

Blake smiled softly and laid his hand back on her cheek; he moved toward the bed and sat down, careful to not sit on Claire's legs or anything. "I did."

"You did what?"

"Ask."

Claire's eyebrows shot up before a grin settled on her face. "You did?"

Why did she think this was so funny? He watched her grin slowly grow into a giggle.

Blake loved to see this side of Claire again.

The carefree side.

The side where she enjoyed everything around her.

"Was it awkward?"

Blake nodded.

"So?"

"What?"

"What did the doctor say?"

Blake wet his lips when he recalled the exact words Dr. Michael had said to him. She had looked him up and down first. Gauging him.

"She said sex would be okay—just nothing too extreme."

Claire's eyebrows shot up. "She said that?"

Blake nodded.

"Wow, I'd have died from embarrassment right then and there."

There was a small gap of silence between them.

"Did you have something extreme in mind?" Claire asked, wiggling her eyebrows.

Blake chuckled. "No, I didn't. I like to cuddle."

Claire cocked her head to the side and looked at him. "You like to cuddle afterward. Your sex—you like a little on the rough side, mister."

Blake chuckled but his stomach hardened. He liked a little edge to his sex, and as far as he could tell, Claire did too.

But not that he absolutely needed it every single time.

"I'm fine. We can save all that for after the pregnancy and make it loving and soft and cuddly for now."

He kissed her on the nose, which evoked a smile from her.

"I love you, Sebastian Blake. I really do."

The warmth that exploded in his chest every time Claire said it still amazed Blake. "I love you, too."

They resumed the kissing until a noise stopped them again. Their faces hovered just inches from each other.

"Did you hear that?"

Blake nodded. "Sunnie?"

Claire shrugged.

They waited a few more minutes, but when they heard nothing from the other room, they resumed their kisses.

Blake's hands wandered under Claire's shirt and soon they both lost their shirt and Claire's bra followed.

He loved the softness of Claire's skin and soon he turned with her on his lap and moved to hover over her outstretched body on the bed.

"God, I love your skin." He kissed her slowly, down her throat, her left collarbone, then the right one, and a path down the cleft between her beautiful breasts—they were even bigger than the last time he'd had the pleasure.

He touched them reverently, carefully gauging how sensitive they were already.

After a while he continued his journey to her belly.

Followed the light line that had developed from her navel to her pubic region.

Blake settled in and unceremoniously pushed Claire to her first orgasm in under a minute.

Familiarity and a burning desire to please his woman.

He kept with her while she slowly came down, couldn't wait to lose himself in her when Claire suddenly froze.

He looked up, but Claire's eyes were focused on the door. Then Blake heard the light knock.

How the hell did he miss someone approach their door? Usually he was always aware of all of his surroundings. Claire's eyes met his and Blake got up, handed Claire her T-shirt, donned his own again, and sorted his business.

He waited until Claire was decent and under the covers and his cock had calmed down, then gave her a quick peck on the lips before he opened the door.

"Hey, I'm sorry to disrupt your evening. But I need you to come down for a sec." One look into Lisa's pale face and her haunted eyes was enough to let the hair on his neck stand up.

His muscles tensed.

"What's wrong?" Blake narrowed his eyes.

"I don't know."

Blake could see the pulse hammering on the side of Lisa's neck.

"Julie's downstairs. She's..." She shrugged as if she couldn't find any words.

Blake touched her shoulder and could feel a slight tremor. He darted a glance back to Claire, who returned his look with a shrug. Blake held up one finger and closed the door behind him.

He gently led Lisa toward the staircase and preceded her down the stairs.

Once they reached the kitchen, he zeroed in on Julie,

who sat on a chair in the breakfast nook, with her arms wrapped around herself, white as a sheet.

"Hey." Blake kept his tone soft and his voice deep so as to not agitate Julie any further.

He squatted down in front of her and looked into her overly bright eyes. "What happened?"

Julie blinked rapidly and gulped down a breath before she started stuttering. "I think he followed me home."

Blake frowned. "Who followed you home?"

Julie's lips trembled. "There's this guy. I was his physical therapist for a while. Until..."

"Until what?" Blake clenched his jaw to reign in his impatience.

"Until he got overly friendly. That's when I resigned as his therapist. But he didn't stop. I always made sure to not be in when he had his appointments, but today I had an appointment I couldn't move, so..."

Blake clenched his jaw.

"I can't say for sure, but I think he followed me home. One of my coworkers escorted me to my car, but I got the feeling on the way home that there was someone following me. I didn't know what to do, so I made the turn into Moon Lake. But then I couldn't bring myself to make the turn to my parents' house, so I just drove straight ahead, until..."

"Until you came to the end of the road."

Julie nodded.

"How long's this been going on?"

Blake turned his head to Lisa, who was still standing at the entrance to the kitchen with her arms crossed over her chest. "Call Peter," he mouthed. It wasn't more than a whisper, but Lisa nodded and left the room.

"A few months, maybe. At first, I thought he was just one of those guys, you know. They think, just because I touch them, it's okay to touch me back. But then...I don't know."

When Lisa stepped back into the kitchen, Blake straightened. "Okay, I'll take a quick look outside. See if there's anyone out there. Lisa will stay with you for a sec."

Blake grabbed the cell from Lisa, took his jacket from the hook by the back door, "lock up behind me," he said to Lisa who nodded.

He stepped outside. "Hey, Steel."

"Hey, Blaze, I'm on the way. Shouldn't take long—I was on patrol anyhow."

"I'm outside now. But I don't see any cars. I will proceed toward Julie's parents' house. Meet me there."

Blake slowly went along the cul-de-sac that led to the Inn. It was dark already, and the light of the few street lamps was sparse, the darkness amplified by the trees on one side of the street.

Soon headlights blinded Blake, but he'd already identified Peter's sheriff's cruiser from the sound alone.

He hopped in, and they drove back to the Inn.

"Didn't see anyone. No strange cars parked anywhere, or anything," Peter said.

Blake shrugged his shoulders. "Julie seemed pretty upset. So I don't think she was imagining things."

"I'll talk to her. Get his name and look into it."

They parked right in front of the back door to the kitchen, and Lisa unlocked the door once they moved out of the car.

"I'll go get back to Claire, if you don't need me?"

They grinned at each other.

Once inside the Inn, Peter went to Julie right away, who seemed a lot calmer by now, and Blake left them alone after he was satisfied his buddy could handle the situation.

He took two steps at a time, then opened the door to Claire's and his room and stepped inside. On his side of the bed lay Sunnie, who was fast asleep. Claire looked at him, and they shared a smile.

"She couldn't sleep, so…" Claire said in a soft voice.

Blake just got rid of his jeans in silence and slipped into bed next to Claire, half his body hovering over the edge, but he didn't care.

"It's okay, I heard children cramp your style when it comes to sex." He snuggled himself against Claire, who turned to him and laid her head on his chest.

"Yes, heard that one too," Claire said in hushed tones. "So, what's wrong with Julie?"

Blake shrugged. "Don't know. Seems like she had trouble at work with a customer and he's stalking her or something. Peter is downstairs with her, taking care of things."

Claire raised her head and looked at him. "Is she okay?"

Blake kissed her nose. "Don't know, yet."

He didn't want to think about Julie anymore. And more than that, he didn't want Claire to worry.

Peter would do everything he could from the official perspective, and Blake would stay in the loop about what needed to be done.

He wracked his brain for a change of topic. Something calming, that wouldn't distress Claire. "So, about the wedding?"

"What about it?" Claire positioned her head back on his chest and put her right arm under his shirt and her hand above his heart.

"Are you okay with a small thing? Just us, and Peter and Lisa?"

"What about your family? Don't you think your mother wants to attend? And what about your teammates?"

"Hmmm." He wanted his mother to attend and Jessie too. The team…he didn't think they would get time off soon enough.

And if they did, they wouldn't want to spend their precious free time in Moon Lake attending another wedding. "Maybe you're right. I'll ask Mom, and I'll tell the boys, but I'm pretty sure they don't get to have time off again soon. And I'm not going to wait."

"I didn't know you were in such a hurry to marry me."

"Why wait? I want you to be my wife...the sooner, the better."

Claire grinned at that. "Well"—Claire yawned—"whoever's there, it will be perfect."

Blake felt Claire's yawn against his chest. "That's because you're perfect."

"Yes, that's exactly why." Claire grinned at him, and they shared a soft kiss before they both fell asleep in each other's arms.

48

"God, I love this meadow," Lisa said.

Claire looked from Sunnie, who was playing in the snow, to Lisa, who lay next to her on the nearly finished back porch in a lawn chair.

They were both bundled up into multiple blankets.

Blake had fussed over them so much, making sure they weren't too cold and he even brought them hot tea, to keep them warm.

She agreed with Lisa. The meadow behind Blake's house, their house, was possibly the best playground any child could hope for.

"But I'm still concerned with you living up here and making the drive down to the Inn every day."

Claire wasn't concerned. Now that she made the drive up here daily it became less and less intimidating. "It's the best solution. Blake will handle Sunnie in the morning while I'm preparing breakfast at the Inn. Then they get down there for breakfast."

Claire shrugged. "Once Sunnie is attending school again, it will be easier for her to get to school from the Inn anyway."

Lisa nodded but still wasn't convinced. "And when the little one comes?"

Claire groaned. They'd talked about every possible scenario for weeks now. Their plans were still that—plans. If and how it all would work out, they would see what happened when their plans met reality.

"Your mom takes over breakfast duty for the first few months. After that, we'll reassess. Why are you bringing this up again?"

Lisa shrugged. "I don't know. I just don't want you to stretch yourself too thin or Blake to get too little sleep."

"Trust me, Blake doesn't need much sleep."

They grinned at each other and Claire looked at the nearly finished back porch.

She didn't know how Blake did it, but he worked like a madman to finish the house so that everything would be done before the baby came.

"I hope in spring Blake will fence a small portion off the meadow so I can grow some vegetables in the summer." Claire pointed to a small patch on the right. "Do you see where the snow is all melting? I think that's the best place for it—lots of sun."

Lisa looked in that direction but shook her head. "You're such a nerd."

Claire smiled and sipped her tea. She watched Sunnie build a snowman and slowly shook her head. How could anyone be so happy? Her pregnancy was going on without a hitch. She already felt big as a tent, but Blake told her how beautiful she was every chance he got.

Sunnie was settling in, as well. She still came to sleep in their bed almost every night, but they understood.

She was adapting.

"Hey, how was your visit to the doctor? Did Peter go with you?"

Lisa laughed. "God, it was the funniest thing ever—he stared at the ultrasound wand like it would cast a spell on him any moment."

Blake hadn't been with her to the OB/GYN. But he had promised the next time they'd go together.

How far they'd come in such a short time. Just a month ago Blake looked tortured anytime someone mentioned the words pregnancy, baby, or family.

She'd been ready to call it quits. Give up on him. Give up on her dreams.

And looking at them now.

Now, it was the polar opposite.

"Look at us, sitting here, both pregnant. Who would've imagined that in spring, when we arrived here?" She said.

"Hmm." Lisa stared silently into the woods.

Was she remembering her kidnapping? Claire didn't want to bring up bad memories, but it amazed her what had happened in just half a year's time.

Some of those times had been tough.

Sometimes she still woke up in a sweat, but more often now, she dreamed of Dew wielding a scalpel than Jeff beating her.

But she was getting better, and Blake was almost always right there, ready to take her in his arms and give her a sense of safety she'd never experienced before.

"So, you got your first picture?"

"Yes, I forgot to bring it. I'll show you tomorrow. You're coming to Julie's opening party, aren't you?"

Claire nodded. "Have you talked to her?" She swallowed —she could feel her stomach tense. "Since that night?"

Lisa pursed her lips and shook her head. "Nope, I tried to bring it up, but she kinda pretended it didn't happen." Lisa stopped for a second. "No, that's not right, she tried to downplay it, said she'd overreacted. But I didn't buy it."

They both fell silent.

Claire thought about her ex-husband. How violence had always been a possibility but at least he wasn't stealthy about it.

She looked at Lisa, who stared straight ahead and mechanically sipped her tea.

This situation must have awoken all kinds of memories for her. On the other hand, they hadn't known she had a stalker until he'd abducted her. Similar to her situation— not knowing that Jeff's brother was after her money.

Maybe their's and Julie's situations weren't comparable.

Claire hoped Julie's situation would play out well in the end.

And she had faith Blake and Peter wouldn't let it go.

Julie was in their friend. And keeping their friends and loved ones safe was their highest priority.

"I'm curious how her studio looks, though—she's worked hard. I wonder..." Claire stopped midsentence when the back door opened.

Dorothy Cleaver stepped through the door, with a blanket around her shoulders and a haunted look on her face.

Blake followed her with a cushion for the third lawn chair.

"Dorothy!" Claire had met Dorothy the week before and they'd talked about the money, but also Sunnie.

They'd hit it off immediately, so Claire had invited her to come visit when they talked on the phone earlier.

"I'm sorry for interrupting. I just. I thought..." Dorothy stalled out and Blake took her arm and led her to the third chair.

"Can I get you a cup of tea?"

Dorothy nodded and Blake turned toward Lisa and Claire. "Any refills?"

They both handed him their cups, and he took it, but not without leaning down to Claire and giving her a wet kiss right on the lips.

"Ugh, too sloppy." Claire pinched her lips and Blake grinned.

"Yes, I think I need lots of practice to improve," he said.

Claire rolled her eyes at him and Blake chuckled before he turned to the back door. "Three teas, coming up."

Claire looked into the grinning faces of Lisa and Dorothy. "What?"

"Practice? What a dork," Lisa said and all three of them giggled.

When Claire got a grip again, she leaned forward to look at Dorothy. "Hey, I'm glad you could make it. The road up here is a little rough, but Blake got a used snowplow for his truck, so it's at least drivable.

Dorothy smiled and nodded while she watched Sunnie. "Sunnie looks great."

Claire nodded and exhaled deeply. "She's acclimating well. Well"—Claire hesitated—"besides sleeping. She still sleeps with me every single night. Especially when Blake is working."

Dorothy sat up straight and turned to face Claire. "These are huge changes for Sunnie—be proud that you are the one she seeks for shelter. She could be closed off and quiet. Then it would be hard for you to get through to her. So, it's perfect the way it is. Children who go through much less traumatizing things than Sunnie sleep in their parents' beds. It's perfectly normal."

Claire nodded. Yes, it felt normal.

It felt like they were already a family.

Blake came back out balancing three teacups on a tray. "Look who I found out front. Open house, today."

Peter and Sheriff Travers stepped through the back door onto the porch.

"Sheriff Travers." Claire nodded.

"Claire. What do you think? Could you all ditch the sheriff and call me Richard?"

Claire's brows rose. "Of course...Richard."

Peter leaned down toward Lisa and they shared a beautiful smile before they kissed.

Claire turned her attention to Blake who nudged her forward. "What?"

"Make space."

She leaned forward and Blake settled on the lawn chair right behind her. Claire leaned back and closed her eyes for a second. Heat radiated from Blake even through his jacket and her blankets.

"I love you."

It was just a whisper right by her left ear, but Claire lost awareness of all the surroundings and concentrated fully on the whispered messages from Blake.

How could anyone be so happy? She remembered standing on the pier, after she told him she was pregnant, and watching Blake retreat.

She hadn't understood his motivation, his overreaction then, but now—how lucky they pulled through the dark times, even though it seemed impossible.

Maybe it was destiny or sheer luck.

But now they were precisely where they wanted to be.

Needed to be.

Claire watched Sunnie, who was still rolling the upper part of her snowman around. Either way, she snuggled against Blake.

This here was heaven.

Claire turned her head and watched their guests.

Peter and Lisa settled into their lawn chair in the same

way as she and Blake did, but when she looked over at Dorothy and Sheriff Travers, Claire stiffened.

Sheriff Travers, no, Richard and Dorothy were sitting next to each other on the lawn chair, their legs not quite touching, but there was an invisible connection between them while they talked quietly.

Dorothy squeezed the blanket around her body and appeared to be nervous. Richard on the other hand looked happier than Claire had ever seen him.

Of course, he'd always been on duty when they'd met.

But there was some chemistry between the two that was worth keeping an eye on.

Claire leaned back and stopped listening to the conversation between Blake, Lisa, and Peter; she just enjoyed the vibrations, every time Blake said something, that made her body hum.

After a while, Claire must've fallen asleep because Blake shook her softly.

"They're leaving, babe—let me up." Claire's spine stiffened, and she sat up and turned to Blake who returned her gaze with a small smile. "You fell asleep, didn't you?" Claire nodded and her face heated up.

"Don't worry, nobody noticed." He kissed her on the nose, then got up.

Peter and Richard were standing, ready to leave.

They said goodbye and left the women alone.

"That was strange—I wonder why they came by?" Lisa shook her head and sipped from her teacup.

Claire watched Dorothy closely, who sipped her tea, as well, obviously lost in thought.

"How long do you and Richard know each other, Dorothy?"

Dorothy shrunk into her lawn chair, bit her lip, and avoided eye contact. "Oh, we've known each other forever."

Her tone was light, but her hands were wringing the ends of the blanket. "Went to school together. He actually was my high school sweetheart back then."

Claire's eyebrows rose and Lisa straightened.

"No way, really? What happened?" Claire turned sideways on her chair and leaned forward to get a better look at Dorothy until her belly stopped her.

"Well...we were young...I guess...life happened." Dorothy swallowed. "We had a fallout...he and Kiki...they got pregnant, married. They lost their child, and stayed married. Just normal life."

"And what did you do? Get married, as well?"

Dorothy slumped down even more, as if she wanted to crawl into the chair. "It was all a long time ago."

Claire met Lisa's gaze. There was a story worth investigating. But maybe not now. They had to get to know each other first.

"Hey, how about you come to Julie's opening party tomorrow?" Lisa asked Dorothy.

Dorothy shook her head. "I don't know."

Claire felt Dorothy retreat and chimed in. "No, you should totally come. I'm sure Julie would love to meet you. And you know people all over the county. Maybe you can spread the word about her physical therapy studio in Moon Lake."

Dorothy still didn't look convinced so Claire went on. "Also, you're now our friend and it would be a good opportunity to meet Julie, and Holly, as well. So you could get to know them before we invite you to our next girls' night out." Claire slipped back into a more comfortable position on the lawn chair. "Actually, it will be more of a girls' night in." She moved again, unable to get comfortable.

"Yeah." Lisa leaned closer and stroked Claire's forearm.

"I don't see us doing the Night Life thing in the coming months."

She shared a small smile with her friend.

"Might be better to stay in," Dorothy said. "It would be pretty embarrassing to have Claire fall asleep in the middle of the dance floor."

Claire gaped at Dorothy who grinned at her so broadly and empathetically, she just joined in the laughter that soon had them all in stitches.

"So, Blake lied," Claire said, after they all calmed down.

Lisa and Dorothy nodded and Claire shrugged.

They had all seen her fall asleep in the middle of the afternoon.

On a lawn chair.

Behind the house Blake built for them.

With her friends and family all around her.

In the arms of the man she loved and who protected her.

Even if it was only small stuff, normal, everyday life.

Claire smiled again and looked at Sunnie, who had nearly finished her snowman.

God, how she loved her life.

49

When Blake opened the door to Julie's Moon Lake physical therapy studio, the noises from inside engulfed them immediately.

Claire had been a little nervous to leave Sunnie with Lisa's mother back at the Inn.

But they had to start somehow, and this was probably the best opportunity for getting used to being away from each other—without really being away since they were no more than two minutes down the road.

Didn't matter.

Claire'd made sure Josephine had both their numbers programmed into her cell. And it was a first step.

He helped Claire out of her coat and hung it with his own on the wardrobe in the lobby.

"It's okay, babe. Josephine knows to call if there's anything."

Claire looked up from her phone and gave him a weak smile.

He ignored the prickling of his scalp when he glanced into the room.

It was filled with a hell of a lot of people standing around and he eyed the exit longingly before he entered.

Julie—dressed in a navy-blue jumpsuit—excused herself from a group of people and headed their way.

She hugged first Claire and then Blake. "Hey, I'm so glad you could make it. Where's Sunnie?"

Claire picked at her fingernails and said nothing.

"She's at the Inn—Josephine's taking care of her. First time."

Understanding swept over Julie's face. "Oh honey, you're nervous about leaving her alone, aren't you?"

Claire nodded and relaxed a little.

"Don't be nervous—we all hung around the Inn when we were little—she'll take good care of Sunnie."

Someone tapped Julie on the shoulder, and she excused herself.

Blake steered Claire to the right side of the studio.

The waiter, who was lugging around a tray filled with some sort of frilly purple drink, stopped their progress.

Claire took an orange juice from the back of the tray but Blake declined.

He sure as hell wouldn't drink anything purple.

They progressed to the right side of the room and stopped there, Blake with his back against some stall bars mounted to the wall.

Claire checked her phone again but put it into her pocket with a sigh.

"Come on, babe, try to relax. We're only two minutes away and we won't be long."

Claire's small smile was interrupted by Lisa who embraced her from behind.

"Come on, the girls are standing by the windows in the back." Lisa looked at Blake. "I'll kidnap your woman for a minute—Peter's around somewhere."

Claire and Lisa turned away and Blake looked toward the windows to where they were headed.

He saw Holly, the owner of the café in town, who chatted with Dorothy.

Blake had to look twice to identify Dorothy. She wore a purple little dress and her hair, that was usually a curly halo around her face, was straightened and fell in soft waves down her back.

Blake glanced across the room until his eyes stopped at Richard who apparently had recognized the change in Dorothy's appearance, as well, if his longing looks in her direction were any indicator.

"Hey, buddy, got something for you." Peter handed Blake a bottle of beer and positioned himself next to Blake with his foot on the stall bar, back to the wall.

"Thanks, bud. You seen Travers staring at poor Dorothy?"

They both grinned at each other and Blake took a sip from his bottle.

"She cleans up nice," Peter said and took a sip, as well.

Blake pointed across the room with his bottle, in a movement from the mirrored wall on the right side, to the windows in the back.

There, all the equipment was crammed into a corner, to make space for the people standing around.

"Julie did good—professional equipment too. Now she just needs a few clients to get her business off the ground."

Peter nodded. "Talking about clients, did you have a chance to meet Kevin Reyes? He arrived earlier today."

Blake shook his head. "No, we were at the house all day and then dropped Sunnie off at Josephine's right before coming here."

"He checked into the room under the roof. I think his words were that he needed privacy." Peter narrowed his eyes. "Hope he isn't trouble. You know how those elite athletes are."

Blake nodded.

"Not that we've been angels. But hockey players. They're a rough bunch."

Blake smiled at the memories of their team, wreaking havoc in their early twenties.

But an NHL star, on rehab, and not only the physical type—if the magazines were right, he was unpredictable, to say the least.

"At least he didn't seem like a douche. So we'll see."

Blake watched Julie, who made her rounds around the room. "What about Julie and the other night?"

"Well"—Peter shrugged his shoulders—"she kinda downplayed it. Said she wasn't sure anymore, that maybe she'd imagined being followed."

Blake's face hardened. "Do you believe her?"

Peter scowled. "Nope. She was too scared for it to be a fluke. She just doesn't want to face it."

Blake shuffled his feet. "Shit."

"Uh-huh," Peter agreed.

They both watched Julie for a minute.

She seemed hyped and enthusiastic, but her eyes looked somewhat haunted and repeatedly darted to the door.

Blake could see the black rings under them from his spot on the side of the room.

Was it because of the stress of opening her own business or was it something else?

The door opened again and Paul Brooks, Julie's NHL-playing brother entered.

"That's Kevin Reyes," Peter said.

Blake studied the man who entered behind Paul.

He was big, maybe six-three. But he supported himself

on crutches and, after getting rid of his leather jacket, hopped inside.

Paul's gaze swiped the room, and when he saw them, he immediately moved toward them, Mr. Reyes in his wake.

"Hey, guys."

"Hey, Paul, long time no see," Peter said.

They embraced and patted each other on the back.

"This is my friend Kevin," Paul said.

Then shook hands with Blake, and Kevin took his crutches into his left hand and shook hands with them, as well.

Paul leaned back against the wall. "So, what do you say? Looks like PT to me."

Peter and Blake both nodded. "Your sister did good," Peter said before the return of Claire and Lisa interrupted them.

The ladies hugged Paul and shook hands with Kevin, before Claire snuggled back into Blake's side.

Blake turned his head and kissed her temple.

"Kevin, you haven't met Claire—she's the co-owner of the Inn. If you have any problems or questions, one of us should usually be around." Lisa said.

Kevin nodded and Blake could see he struggled to not look at Claire's belly; she had proudly switched to pregnancy clothes and her bump was clearly visible now.

"So, Kev, ready to enjoy some PT?" Paul joked and Peter and Blake grinned.

Every one of them knew from past experience that physical therapy was no joke.

"And he will be up and running before you even know it." Julie entered their little circle and the conversation and shook hands with Kevin.

The handshake took a little long and Blake watched for

the first time how the myth of love at first sight might have come into being.

Julie's face had an expression of pure shock while Kevin looked like he'd just received a brain-rattling charge of electricity.

It was nearly comical to witness Kevin's expression slip and turn into one of forced indifference, when Paul, oblivious to the moment his sister and teammate just shared, intercepted their handshake, picked Julie up, and swung her around.

"You did good, Sis. I'm real proud of you."

Julie recovered and laughed out loud, before she hit her brother on the shoulder. "Let me down already, you oversized bull."

"Hey, Son." Mr. And Mrs. Brooks approached the scene and demanded Paul's attention.

Paul switched from whirling around his sister to whirling his mother who shrieked but laughed at her exuberant son.

Blake studied Kevin, who witnessed the scene with a quiet detachment, all the while stealthily increasing the gap between him and Julie, who was standing beside him.

This would be a fun dynamic to witness in the coming weeks and months.

The chemistry between those two was palpable, but they both didn't seem inclined to act on it.

Blake's focus was solely on them until Claire hit him in the side with her elbow.

"Ow." Blake stroked his side, and turned his head toward Mr. Brooks, who'd apparently tried to get his attention.

"So, from father to father: start saving, because, believe me, having kids is expensive. Especially girls. Because you will want to give them everything their heart desires."

Mr. Brooks smiled at Julie and Paul, who were bantering again, like only siblings did. "But nothing is as rewarding as seeing them grow up to be their own people."

Blake nodded.

He couldn't wait to see Sunnie all grown up.

He pressed Claire to his side again.

And he couldn't wait for their child to be born.

Claire smiled up at him, and it lighted up his universe. "I love you." He said loud enough for everyone around them to hear.

That made her smile even more. "I love you."

When his mouth descended on hers, everything else fell away.

He didn't care they were standing in a room full of people, didn't care if he looked like a sappy fool.

Because he was.

He didn't know how he deserved all the happiness and peace in his life, all because of this woman in his arms.

But he sure as hell would appreciate her and the family they created every single day for the rest of his life.

Thank you for reading Guarded Blaze. The Moon Lake Protectors Series continues with Julie and Kevin's story in **Fallen King.**

Still hung up on Claire and Blake? Me too! Go to https://links.katbammer.com/ml2-bonus to get the bonus scene and settle in for some sexy times.

DEAR FRIEND,

... this story wasn't at all what I'd expected. Sure I knew from Burning Steel that there's more to Blake and Claire, but this...

... I did not expect this. Their struggle, Claire's traumatic past. Letting fear keep you from going for what you really want. Just heartbreaking to witness.

And Sunnie. As a mother this is my worst nightmare. I once walked my dog just outside our apartment with my then-babies sleeping inside. (Had my baby monitor with me and everything.) Then suddenly a bolt of lightning struck not that far from me. (There wasn't a thunderstorm or anything, just a single lightning that came out of the blue.)

Needless to say, I was scared shitless and the dog and I ran back up to our apartment with my mind running crazy with all the possibilities of what would've happened with the kids if something had happened to me.

I'm still working on overcoming that fear even though my kids are now considerably older and they know exactly what they have to do if something happens.

I'm so glad there's always a happy end in my books, even when the road to get there is a rocky one.

And I have something to prove it to you. A super-duper second epilogue. Download it HERE!

(Or, if you're on a Kindle or reading this on paper, and clicking the link doesn't work (been there, very frustrating) go to https://links.katbammer.com/ml2-bonus to sign up and get the bonus scene.)

Now it's back to the writing cave for me. Julie and Kevin's intense chemistry is so fun and I can't wait to see how their journey will look like.

Keep on reading!

Kat

Made in United States
Orlando, FL
23 October 2023

38160383R00200